'I beg your pardon, my lord.'

The apology was made promptly but there was no meekness in it. She was proud, was Miss Emma Woodhill, too proud for a servant. Who was she? Where had she come from? Why was he so taken with her that he had no heart to dismiss her?

Born in Singapore, **Mary Nichols** came to England when she was three, and has spent most of her life in different parts of East Anglia. She has been a radiographer, school secretary, information officer and industrial editor, as well as a writer. She has three grown-up children, and four grandchildren.

**Recent titles by the same author:**

THE RUBY PENDANT

# DEAR DECEIVER

Mary Nichols

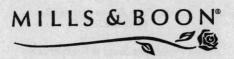

MILLS & BOON®

*First published in Great Britain 1998*
*Harlequin Mills & Boon Limited,*
*Eton House, 18-24 Paradise Road, Richmond, Surrey TW9 1SR*

© Mary Nichols 1998

ISBN 0 263 81036 4

*Set in Times Roman 10½ on 12 pt.*
*04-9807-82025 C1*

*Printed and bound in Great Britain*
*by Caledonian International Book Manufacturing Ltd, Glasgow*

# *Chapter One*

*1816*

Emma stood leaning over the rail of the *Silken Maid* as it made its way up the river estuary, but she could not see the shore for the mist which blanketed everything except the deck at her feet and the grey water immediately around the brig, in which floated the detritus of a large city: lumps of wood, cabbage leaves, even a dead dog. It was every bit as dirty as the Hooghly in Calcutta, though the smells were different, less spicy, more rank.

The mist was enough to soak her cloak and make her auburn hair spring into tight little curls, but it was nothing like the fog of Calcutta, nor the torrential rain of the monsoon they had left behind them; it was simply wet and uncomfortable.

So this was England! This, grey, murky, cold place was the country which the British in India referred to so longingly as home. Even her father, who had lived in India over twenty-five years, had spoken of it with a wistful note in his voice. She and her brother, Teddy, had been born in Calcutta, had left it only in the summer to go to the hills away from the oppressive heat; they had never dreamed they would one day be sailing into London docks on a cargo ship with everything they possessed contained in one tin trunk and two canvas bags.

The mist lifted as they left the flat estuary behind and entered the London docks and she could see the dock basin was filled with ships, flying the flags of all nations and dozens of different shipping lines, but predominantly that of the British East India Company, known to everyone employed by it as The Company.

Dockers were swarming everywhere, moving backwards and forwards from the warehouses which lined the quayside, loading and unloading cargo: sacks, barrels, and great oil-skin wrapped bundles were being winched out on hoists, to the accompaniment of shouting and banter and the noise of squealing chains.

As the brig bumped against the side and the lines were thrown out, her brother joined her. He was tall and well built for his sixteen years, but there was still something of the boy about his features and the expression in his blue eyes. They were still bleak; he had not yet come to terms with the death of the father he idolised. But then, neither had she.

She turned to smile at him. 'It's a little like Calcutta, don't you think? All this shipping and the mist over the river and men at work.' She paused. 'Not Indian, of course.'

'Colder,' he said, pulling up the collar of his coat. 'Mrs Goodwright said it would be pleasantly warm at this time of the year. April is surely springtime in England.'

'Ah, well, you cannot take a great deal of notice of Mrs Goodwright. She thinks Calcutta winters are too hot to be borne.' Mrs Goodwright was the adjutant's wife and had appointed herself their guardian when the news arrived that their father had been killed in action.

Emma could see Captain Greenaway making his way towards them. He had a full, almost white, beard and craggy features which bore evidence of long periods spent on the open deck in all weathers. But the toughness was mitigated by twinkling blue eyes and a jovial smile.

'Well, here we are, ma'am, safe and sound,' he said. 'A welcome sight, don't you think?'

'Yes, indeed,' she said, watching two men coming up the gangplank onto the ship, not sailors or dockers, but officials of some sort.

'I am sorry the weather is not welcoming. April showers they call it. The sun will come out directly and you will see what a pleasant country this is, not too hot, not too cold.'

'Yes, I am sure you are right.'

'You will be wanting to go ashore. As soon as the revenue men and the health inspector have done their work, you will be free to disembark. I will have your trunk taken to the quay.' He held out his hand. 'I shall be busy later, so I will say goodbye now.'

She took the proffered hand. 'Goodbye, Captain. And thank you for everything.'

'It was my pleasure. And may I say, ma'am, you have been a doughty sailor.' He turned to Teddy. 'And you, too, sir. May I wish you luck with your endeavours.'

'Thank you.' Teddy said, shaking him by the hand.

He turned and left them to join the newcomers, greeting them cheerfully and taking them below to his cabin.

It had been a rough voyage, during which a great deal of salt water had found its way into their baggage and Emma had told Teddy she was looking forward to being on dry land again, finding a respectable hotel, repairing the ravages to her wardrobe and washing the salt from her hair. As she watched the crew stowing the sails and clearing the deck ready to open the cargo hatches, however, she felt a strange reluctance to set foot on the land of her ancestors.

What was she letting herself in for? Why had they set out, she and Teddy, on this journey into the unknown? The *frisson* of fear she had felt during the storm at sea was nothing compared to the dread she felt now. What if they had made a terrible mistake? In this strange country she had no one to turn to for advice, no one who cared. She almost wished they had not come, that they could go back...

The rocking of the ship's motion against its mooring ropes, the shouts and laughter of the men on the docks faded and she was on horseback, galloping across the Maidan in Calcutta, the beating of hooves loud in her ears.

The vast open space around the fort had been cleared from the jungle by Robert Clive over fifty years before in order to allow the guns a clear view. The guns had been silent for years; now it was used by the British and the higher castes of Calcutta Society as a place for leisure, somewhere to ride in the early morning, to stroll in the cool of the evening, a quiet place with English lawns and gardens, where cattle grazed and goats were tethered.

It was a place where snake-charmers and jugglers amused the passers-by and where festivals were held, and cricket played, where monkeys climbed the banyan trees. But on that never-to-be-forgotten day there were few people about, it being very early and also the end of the rainy season.

She reined in and sat straight-backed in the saddle to look about her, waiting for her brother to draw up alongside her. The sun was rising and a small trickle of perspiration ran down between her shoulder blades. Later it would rain, as it did every day at this time of year. Then the temperature would drop a few degrees and it would pour down in torrents, which was hardly less uncomfortable than the torrid heat which preceded it.

It would run in rivulets down the hard-baked roads, making puddles in the cart tracks. The trees would drip, the gutters overflow, and the usually sluggish River Hooghly would threaten to burst its banks, as it had done on numerous occasions before.

But Emma and Teddy were used to it; their concerns were not over the weather, which was predictable, but over the prolonged absence of their father, Major Edward Mountforest, on active service against the Gurkhas who were attacking Indian lands from the hills of Nepal.

'It's no place to fight a campaign,' Teddy said, repeating the dissenting views he had picked up from some of his classmates at Fort William College. 'Nothing but rocks and ravines, bare mountains and raging torrents. It's practically impossible to get supplies and artillery through without the problem of knowing there's likely to be a marksman behind every boulder.'

Emma laughed, bringing her green eyes to sparkling life behind the veil of her riding hat. 'It wouldn't do for the Colonel to hear you say that. It's tantamount to treason.'

'He's with Papa, as well you know, so he cannot hear. And Papa thinks the same because I heard him say so before they left and all he got for his pains was a dressing-down and a hint he was lacking in courage. Papa a coward! Why, he's the bravest man I know. He would never duck a fight if he thought the cause was just.'

'I know, Teddy,' Emma said softly, aware that her brother hero-worshipped their father and missed him every bit as much as she did. 'Let's go back; perhaps we shall have news of him today.'

They turned towards the fort where the horses were stabled and handed them over to a *syce* to unsaddle and groom, then walked side by side past Government House to the residential area to the north where their bungalow was situated. Sita, their house servant, would be preparing their breakfast. Teddy, as always, was hungry, but hunger left him as soon as they came within sight of their verandah, for there was an officer standing on it, watching for their return.

'It's Captain Goodwright!' Teddy exclaimed. 'They've come back.' He began to run, followed by Emma, impeded by her lightweight riding skirt, which she gathered up in her hand.

By the time she reached the verandah, Teddy was already bombarding the Captain with questions. 'Where is my father? Did we win a great victory? How long did it take the regiment to get back?'

The Captain turned to greet Emma before attempting to answer. 'Good morning, Miss Mountforest. I come on behalf of Sir David...'

Emma's heart sank into her riding boots; the poor man looked so uncomfortable, his usual cheerful expression so gloomy, she knew at once something was wrong. 'Please come inside where it is cool,' she said, forcing herself to sound calm as she led the way into the house. 'You have news?'

'Yes.' He paused to swallow. 'I am afraid I am the bearer of sad tidings.'

'Papa?' queried Teddy. 'Tell me at once. What is it?'

The Captain overlooked the arrogant tone of the boy's voice because it was laced with anxiety and he was sorry for him, but Emma felt constrained to exclaim, 'Teddy!'

'Sorry, sir.'

'It is I who am sorry, my boy. It is my painful duty to tell you that your father, Major Mountforest, fell in battle.'

'Fell?' Emma queried, clenching her hands into fists to stop them shaking. 'You mean he is…' she gulped '…dead?'

'Yes. I am sorry. They were ambushed, taken by surprise in a narrow pass to the north of Gorakhpur, and all perished, a hundred good men.'

Emma sank into a chair, unaware that Sita had come in and put the tea tray down on a low table or that the *punkah-wallah*, who sat outside on the verandah, had ceased his rhythmic pulling on the cord of the *punkah*—the heavy matting which covered the open window of the bungalow—and the cool breeze the movement created had suddenly stopped.

It was a moment of stillness in which no one spoke, for each was remembering the man who had been a gallant soldier and a beloved father. It did not seem possible that they would never see him again, not even in death, for in the heat of India, interment followed swiftly upon demise; and bringing bodies back for burial was out of the question.

'Are you sure?' Teddy asked, unable to believe the news. 'He might have survived, he could still come home. If he was caught by the rains, the roads might be washed away and the bridges would certainly be down. It might take him months to return.'

'No, that isn't possible,' the officer said. 'A few grasscutters, who had been sent out to gather fodder, rushed back when they heard the gunfire, but too late. There was no one left alive. They were the only survivors.' The Captain turned to Emma. 'Miss Mountforest, if there is anything I can do for you, please ask. My wife will visit you later and discuss what is to be done, but I expect you would like to be alone now.'

'Yes. Thank you, Captain.'

He left, but she was hardly aware of his going. The only sound was her own ragged breathing and Teddy's muffled sobs, smothered because he believed it was unmanly to cry. In another room to the rear of the bungalow, Sita was wailing and another servant was reciting a prayer in Hindi, over and over again. Teddy rose suddenly and fled from the room.

Emma started after him but changed her mind; he would not wish her to witness his tears. She sat, looking with unseeing eyes at the tigerskin rug on the floor at her feet. Her father had shot the man-eater years before when it had been terrorising villages in the interior. He and Chinkara, his Indian servant, had brought it home on the back of a bullock cart, laughing together like a couple of schoolboys. She would never hear their laughter again.

Her own grief suddenly overwhelmed her. And as she wept the day's rain began, a sharp patter which grew in volume to a crescendo, beating against the *punkah*, thumping on to the verandah, swishing like a fast-flowing river, down the road outside. It was as if the very earth was crying with her.

It was a full hour before she roused herself, scrubbed at her eyes with a handkerchief and took the tea tray back to Sita.

Sita, who had long ago been converted to Christianity, always remembered her Hindu origins in times of stress. 'He has gone to his next life,' she said, looking up from kneading chuppatti dough. 'And it will be a better one, for he was a good man, and surely Chinkara is with him there, looking after him still. You must look to Teddy-Sahib. He is the master now.'

'Yes, he is, isn't he?' Emma attempted to smile, for the idea of Teddy, the schoolboy, taking over the management of their lives would have been amusing in other circumstances. There was no doubt in her mind who would have to pick up the reins and make the decisions. And for that, she must remain strong and not give way to the grief which was eating away at her heart and mind, making thinking objectively almost impossible.

But when she forced herself to try, her head was filled with a thousand questions, the most important being: how could they manage without Papa? It was not the housekeeping that troubled her, for she had been doing that for years, but whether they would be allowed to remain in the bungalow which belonged to the East India Company and, if not, where would they go? She imagined her papa had left some money, but was it enough to keep Teddy at college? Was there a pension?

There was also the vexing question of Calcutta Society, which might turn a blind eye to her living alone when her father was simply away campaigning; but when the officers' wives learned he was never coming back, they would be round like flies, giving her gratuitous advice, the gist of which was that she should not live alone with no one for company but her brother and a handful of Indian servants; it was unseemly and she would earn a 'reputation'.

She was twenty-two, well past the age of needing a

chaperon, if she ever had; she dressed as she pleased, went where she pleased within certain practical limits and felt perfectly safe. In her view, her totally loyal servants would be far more help to her in a crisis than any hidebound European woman, concerned only with protocol and etiquette. If they had their way, they would marry her off to one of the newly arrived officers within a month of the poor man's arrival.

Her fears were confirmed when Mrs Goodwright arrived by *ekka* which she drove herself, just as soon as the rain ceased. The temperature had dropped a few degrees, but the little garden steamed, so that the trees, shrubs and outbuildings were seen through a haze with no clear outlines. A palm frond near the door dripped on to the wooden steps of the verandah.

'You must come and stay with us,' she said briskly, removing her gloves and lifting her veil. Emma wondered why she persisted in dressing as if she were still in Europe, which must have made her unbearably hot. 'We will have to find you a husband. I've no doubt there will be several eligibles coming out from home to replace the men we have lost.'

'It is very kind of you, ma'am,' Emma said, wondering if the woman would be quite so cold-blooded if her husband had been among those who had perished, instead of staying behind a desk at headquarters. 'But I am not ready to think of such things yet...'

'Oh, surely you are not still grieving for John, child? That was four years ago—it is foolish to go on mourning.'

It wasn't mourning, it was prudence. She had met John when she was eighteen and he had just arrived from England. He had swept her off her feet and in no time they became engaged. And though she was sure she loved him dearly, she had soon realised he adhered to the widely held view that the British in India were a blessing for which the natives ought to give thanks.

'We are not here as conquerors,' he had said. 'We came to trade, but how can trade be properly carried out if the kings and princes are always warring with each other over who should succeed whom and who pay tribute to whom? It has been necessary to preserve law and order and that means having a military presence. You are a soldier's daughter, you must surely understand that. Besides, the natives are no more than children, needing education and guidance.'

She had hoped that when he had been in India a little longer, he might come to know and love the country and its inhabitants, as she, her father and brother did. Whether he would have done she was never to know, for he had died of sandfly fever during his first summer. When his parents came out from England to visit his grave, they had not bothered to hide their disapproval of her; she was too free and easy and did not behave like a lady, which had made her laugh, in spite of her grief.

She realised she would never have broken down their antagonism. She and John would probably have regretted marrying if he had lived and taken her back to England. She had mourned him sincerely, but she was determined that if she ever fell in love again, she would be careful that it would be with someone who understood her love of all things Indian.

Such a man had not materialised and now, though still slim, exceedingly healthy and independent, she was almost an old maid.

'No,' she said. 'I meant I would not marry for expediency's sake.'

'Then I strongly suggest you go home to England. There is nothing like family when you have a bereavement. I am sure Viscount Mountforest will be delighted to receive you.'

Emma doubted it. There had been bad blood between her father and his older brother and they had never corresponded in all the years Papa had been in India. As far as she was aware, her uncle did not even know of the existence of his niece and nephew.

She had asked her papa once why that was. She remembered it clearly because it was just after her mother died. He had returned from the Poona campaign in 1802 too late to see Mama alive and the effect on him of her untimely death had been distressing to watch. He blamed the climate; he blamed the way they were always being separated by campaigns which he felt were due to British expansionism and nothing to do with defending The Company's people and property which was what he was paid for. But most of all he blamed himself.

'I should have taken her home, no matter what,' he had said, when he came out of his anguish sufficiently to speak of his wife at all. 'The doctor said the climate would kill her...'

Emma, then eight years old and grief-stricken for her beloved mama, had not tried to placate him, she had simply demanded, 'Why didn't you? Take her back to England, I mean.'

He had looked at his little daughter and sighed. 'It is not so easy, sweetheart, I am an exile, your mother understood that. She knew the whole story.'

'What does exile mean?'

'It means I was sent away and cannot go back.'

'Not ever?'

'I do not think so. Not unless certain people are prepared publicly to admit the wrong they did me and I do not think they will ever do that.'

'Why not?'

He had smiled and taken her on to his knee, rubbing his chin across her hair, which had not yet taken on the auburn tones it now had and was a soft light brown. 'Why all the questions? Do you wish to go to England?'

'Not without you, but I think I might like to go on a visit, just to see what it is like.'

'One day, perhaps, you will, when you are grown up and very rich, then it will not matter what the gossips say.'

'What do they say?'

He had said nothing for a whole minute and she had begun to think he did not intend to answer her; when he did, his voice was so low she could hardly hear him. 'They say that I have besmirched the name of a noble family, that I am responsible for a man's death, that I am a coward, that I have no honour.' He paused and then added softly, 'But it was honour which bound me as surely as chains.'

She hadn't understood then, nor even now when she was old enough to comprehend the meaning of the words. Her answer, spoken from the heart of a child, had pleased him. 'Papa, you are the bravest man I know.'

His eyes had taken on a faraway look as if he were in another place at another time. Then he had hugged her and set her down. 'Don't worry, child, it was all for the best. I met and married your mother, here in Calcutta, and not for a single second have I ever regretted that. India has become home and I would have it no other way. I shall die here and no one in England will mourn me.' He had put on a cheerful voice, but she had

detected the note of sadness and knew he would brood
over it until the end of his days.

'Have your servant pack a bag and come with me
now,' Mrs Goodwright said. 'You can stay with us until
you leave.'

'Thank you, ma'am, but I would rather stay here.
There is so much to do, arrangements to make.'

'Of course. But if you change your mind, you know
you are welcome.'

Emma hadn't contemplated leaving Calcutta, not even
then. It had taken another shock to force her to consider
it. She had gone to see Mr Chapman, who looked after
her father's legal and financial affairs. Papa had never
spoken of money to them and, as they had never been
stinted, she imagined they would be comfortable.

She realised how wrong she was before she had been
in his office five minutes. Apart from small bequests to
the servants, her father's will left everything to her and
Teddy equally. This was no surprise, but what took her
aback was the tiny amount involved.

'Your father was always generous and never saw the
need to husband his resources,' Mr Chapman said. 'He
was indifferent to money and never bothered to collect
his debts, though he was always scrupulous in paying
his own.'

'But surely he must have done some trading?' she
queried, knowing that it was common practice for
Company employees and soldiers to supplement their
pay with private trade. Some of them had become very
wealthy by it. 'Everyone does that in India, don't they?
Silks, spices, precious stones, opium, bought and sold
for profit.'

He smiled at her over the top of his spectacles, which
were perched on the end of his nose. 'The days of the

nabob are passed, Miss Mountforest. Company employ-ees, whether civilian or soldier, are no longer allowed to trade privately. Oh, I know it is still done, but if your father was ever engaged in it, I know nothing of it.'

'He was obviously a great deal more scrupulous about such things than his contemporaries,' she said. 'An hon-ourable man.'

'Yes, indeed.'

'I believe he received an allowance from England,' she said. 'Will that continue?'

He looked embarrassed and shuffled the papers on the desk in front of him as if reluctant to speak. 'The allow-ance was paid to Major Mountforest by his father and was conditional on his never returning to England,' he said. 'It ceased when his brother succeeded to the title.'

'My uncle stopped it?' she asked, in disbelief.

'Yes.'

'Then what are we left with, my brother and I?'

'A small pension from The Company. It may be enough to live on if you are frugal. It is certainly not enough to pay school fees.' He paused, then went on in a kindly voice, 'I am so sorry, my dear; perhaps you should write to your uncle. I cannot believe he will hold his brother's sins against you. As soon as he knows your circumstances, I am sure he will send for you to go and live with him.'

'The sins were not my father's but his brother's,' she retorted. 'I would not go to him.'

'Whatever the rights and wrongs of it, you may have to,' he said, as Emma stood up to leave. 'It might be as well to swallow your pride and make the best of it, for what can you do here?'

She returned to the bungalow where Teddy, red of eye and puffy of cheeks, had been going round touching everything—the ornaments, the pictures, the tiger's head—as if by doing so he could convince himself of the enduring nature of things, that if everything around him stayed in exactly the same place, their father might still be alive.

It worried Emma, because he hardly spoke and was certainly in no mood to make plans which would mean altering their way of life. She delayed saying anything, hoping he would come out of his grief and listen to her, though what she was going to tell him, she did not know.

Instead she set about finding work. Everyone was kind to her, though critical of her father who had been so shortsighted as to think he was immortal, and him a soldier too! But it didn't alter the fact that no one had anything to give her to do for which they were prepared to pay her and Mrs Goodwright wanted to know why she had changed her mind about returning to England when it was so obviously the thing to do. She could not, of course, tell her the true story, nor admit that they simply did not have their passage money.

Her prevarication came to an end very suddenly a month later, when, in the middle of the biggest downpour Calcutta had seen for years, she received notice to quit the bungalow.

She took it to Captain Goodwright, whom she found at the fort, hoping he might be able to help her. 'I cannot believe anyone could be so callous,' she said. 'It is only a month since...'

'I know, my dear, but the bungalow is the designated quarters of a major and there is one coming soon to replace Major Mountforest. You do understand, don't you?'

'But where are we to go?'

'England,' he said. 'I really think you should consider

it. The war in Europe is over at last and Napoleon has been sent into exile. There would be no danger.'

Exile: her father's, Napoleon's and now her own, for that was what it seemed like to her. She left him quickly before he could see her tears; the first she had shed since the day she learned of her father's death. And now they had come, she could not stem the flow. People were looking at her with curiosity and she sought shelter among the trunks of a banyan tree on the Maidan, where she allowed herself the luxury of a good sob, watched by a couple of monkeys, who were sitting in its branches.

Later, when her ribs ached and her handkerchief was sodden, she stopped. Feeling sorry for herself would not achieve anything, but letting herself go had done her good. She emerged from her hiding place, straightened her back and walked home, unaware of the horses, carts of produce, fiacres, tongas, *ekkas* and pedestrians that eddied round her, nor the steady drip of water from trees and rooftops, which soaked her bonnet. Her mind was still in tumult, but one decision had been taken from her; she could no longer put off speaking to Teddy.

Her brother was still apathetic, but at least he was coming out of the trance-like state which had so worried her, and he sat down to listen to what she had to say with grave attention. 'We have to leave the bungalow,' she said. 'And I think it best if we go to England. We have relatives there.'

'What relatives?' he demanded. 'I have never heard of any.'

'Viscount Mountforest is our uncle. I am sure he would help us.'

'Why did Papa never mention him?'

'I believe they quarrelled.'

'What about?'

'I do not know. All I know is that Papa was blamed and sent out here to India and told never to return.'

'And you expect us to go cap in hand to him?' he demanded, getting up from floor and pacing the room.

'Then what do you suggest we do?'

'Work. At least, I will and you must find yourself a rich husband with a title.'

She managed to laugh, though it sounded hollow. 'I tried to find work, but no one would give me any. And there are no rich men with titles out in India…not un-married ones, anyway.'

'Then we'll go to England, but not to our uncle. We'll manage without his help. We'll make our own way and when we've done it, we will force him tell the truth. Papa would never do a dishonourable deed. Never.'

His anger was preferable to his misery, she supposed, but she was beginning to wonder what devils she had unleashed in telling him about their father's exile. He had suddenly turned from a grieving boy to a very angry young man. And who could blame him?

'No, of course he wouldn't,' she said, deciding to say no more about their uncle for the present. Later she would try and talk to him again. 'But we cannot go until we've raised the passage money.'

'You've got jewellery, haven't you?'

'A little, yes. Not enough.'

'And there is the furniture and the…' He gulped sud-denly, but he was too angry for sentiment. 'The horses. Prime beasts they are.'

'Teddy, are you sure?'

'Yes.' He kicked at the tigerskin rug. 'This should fetch a few rupees.'

'But Papa shot that.'

'So he did, but what is it good for now, when very soon we will not have a floor to lay it on?'

It had taken time to wind up their father's affairs, to pay off the servants and make sure they had good positions to go to, to sell the horses and every last stick of furniture, though Emma drew the line at parting with the tigerskin. She would take it with her as a memento of her father. Long before their preparations were complete, they were obliged to take Mrs Goodwright up on her offer.

Within a week Emma was thankful that it was only a temporary state of affairs. The good lady, while meaning well, was dictatorial to say the least, and full of advice about what Emma should and should not do in England. She even gave her a little book of etiquette which afforded her guest a great deal of merriment.

'And we must do something about your clothes,' she said. 'I have one or two gowns I no longer need, they are far too warm for this climate. I am sure with a little deft needlework, we can make them fit you.'

'It is very kind of you, ma'am, but—'

'No buts. I shall not miss them, I assure you, and you certainly cannot travel to England in a sari. People will think you are half-Indian.'

Emma did not think that was of any consequence, but the matter of a wardrobe had been giving her some problems. The more she spent, the less there was left to live on and telling herself that beggars can't be choosers, she accepted gratefully and set about her sewing, with the help of a pattern book Mrs Goodwright had had sent out from England.

It was well into the new year before they said goodbye to all their friends, both European and Indian, and paid

a last visit to their mother's grave in the English cemetery. 'We will come back,' Teddy said, hiding his distress behind anger. 'When I have avenged Papa.'

Emma did not remonstrate with him; it would have
done no good and she was too choked with tears to
speak.

Later in the day, they went aboard the *Silken Maid*
for the voyage to England and a new life with a new
name.

Unsure if the scandal attached to their father was still
remembered and not wishing to draw attention to themselves, they decided to change their name. So it was
Miss Emma and Mr Edward Woodhill who sailed up the
Thames to the East India Dock that misty April afternoon.

Emma saw the revenue man and the health inspector
leave and knew it was time to go. She could see her old
black-painted tin trunk sitting on the quay not far from
the gangplank. It looked lonely and isolated, just as she
felt. She sighed; it was no good standing there, waiting
for a miracle. She turned slowly and made her way along
the deck to the gangway but before she could begin the
descent, she became aware of a man starting up towards
her.

He had evidently not seen her for otherwise he would
have stood aside to allow her to come down first, there
being no room to pass. It was difficult to see his face
because at that angle his top hat obscured it, but he was
young and lithe, judging by the way he dashed up the
plank. He was dressed in a brown frockcoat and beige
pantaloons and was certainly not one of the dockers.

He checked himself when his head reached the level
of the deck and he saw her feet, clad in soft black kid.

Looking upwards, past a voluminous burnous, he met the gaze of a pair of amused green eyes. In one bound, he reached the deck and stood to doff his top hat, revealing a shock of fair curls. He was also very tall. 'I beg your pardon, ma'am, I did not see you waiting. Pray, forgive me.'

His voice had a warm quality matched by his brown eyes, eyes that held her in thrall. She stood motionless, unable to turn away. It wasn't like meeting a stranger; it was as if she were being reunited with an old friend, someone she had known forever. She could have told anyone who asked, that he liked his fellow human beings, that he was always gentle with them, that his favourite food was pork and apple pie; that he enjoyed a glass of wine, but was by no means a drinker; that he was chivalrous to women and honourable to men; that he disliked humbug and hated racial prejudice.

She smiled suddenly at her fantasy, realising she had been describing her father, but that didn't alter the fact that she was sure she was right. Pulling herself together, she put her palms together in front of her face in the Indian manner, and bowed towards him. 'Think nothing of it, sir.'

For a moment he was taken aback. She had a graceful carriage which reminded him of pictures he had seen of Indian girls in saris, balancing jugs on their heads. Her complexion was smooth and golden, but her eyes were green and the wisp of hair which had escaped from the hood of her cloak was a warm chestnut brown, almost auburn, and though her voice had a soft lilt, it had no accent. He smiled. 'May I escort you down?'

'No, thank you, my brother is with me.' She looked about for Teddy, but he had disappeared. Trust him to wander off, just when she needed him. 'I expect he has gone to fetch our hand baggage from the cabin.'

He bowed and left her, making for the companionway and she went down the gangplank, setting her foot upon English soil for the first time, wondering who the young man was. The ship's owner, perhaps, then she should have taken the opportunity to speak to him of the poor accommodation.

On the other hand he might be a passenger, intent on the outward journey and in that case they were bound in opposite directions. Or he might simply be a friend of the Captain. She turned to look back but he had gone from sight.

Dominic made his way down to the Captain's day cabin, musing on the encounter and wondering what was beneath that all-enveloping cloak. The girl was not a beauty by accepted standards, nor was she dressed in anything like the latest mode, but there was something about her that made her out of the ordinary. It might have been her grace; that simple movement of her hands had charmed him. But those green eyes! They were speaking eyes, if such a thing existed.

They told of humour, sadness, pride and compassion in equal measure, yet behind them was a mind that was thoughtful and independent. He checked himself suddenly. How could he possibly deduce so much from a few seconds' exchange? He smiled at his own foolishness and knocked on Captain Greenaway's door. There were other things to occupy him. His cargo, for one.

'Lord Besthorpe.' The Captain left his desk to come forward, hand outstretched. 'How good it is to see you.'

Dominic took the proffered hand. 'Not half as good

as it is to see you, Captain. Did you have a good voyage?'

'It was somewhat rough, but we weathered it. I believe the cargo took no harm. I have spices and the finest silks, saltpetre, opium and precious stones. I have kept those here.' And he took a key from the drawer of his desk and unlocked a stout cupboard. 'They are mostly uncut diamonds and rubies, but they should make a tidy profit.' He took a bag from the cupboard and tipped its contents on the desk. 'There! What do you say to those?'

Dominic picked up the largest of the diamonds and smiled to himself. He had proved his critics wrong. They had said trade was demeaning in a peer of the realm who should be above such things, and what had he ever done to make him think he could make a profit from it? Profit was vulgar.

There might have been a time when he might have agreed with them, a time when he was young and his father was alive, a time when he had no idea his inheritance would be a pile of debts with an estate which had been allowed to run down until there was nothing left but the old house and the land itself.

The year before, at the age of twenty-six, he had succeeded his father and had cast about him for a remedy, short of parting with the house and its contents. A small parcel of land had been sold in order to stave off the immediate threat, but he needed more, much more, if he was to restore his home and make the land fruitful.

It was Bertie Cosgrove, a boyhood friend, who had told him about the profits to be made from trade, especially with India, and cited an acquaintance of his lately come home from several years out there, who was as rich as Croesus. It was, so he said, impossible to fail and now the war was over and all danger from Napoleon a thing of the past, trading vessels were moving freely again.

There were many reasons why Dominic could not go to India himself; he had a young sister who was dependent on him, there was the estate which needed his attention and, most of all, there was Sophie.

He had asked her to marry him the year before, somewhat prematurely because he was in mourning for his parents and had only then become aware of the parlous state of his finances. They had gone on a picnic party to Richmond at which there had been a great deal of horseplay among the men and some surreptitious flirting. Although she had always been on the periphery of his acquaintances, he had suddenly become aware of her beauty and easy charm.

She was very popular and was to have her own comeout ball that Season which his mourning precluded him from attending, a source of great regret to him. She had laughingly told him that she expected several offers of marriage on that occasion, which was probably no less than the truth, for she was a viscount's daughter whose dowry was said to be considerable.

He told himself that the dowry had not been a factor; he wanted her for herself. Afraid of losing her, he had proposed at the picnic and been accepted. All London knew of it, though they had postponed the announcement until he should be out of mourning and had brought his finances about. It was a matter of pride, he had told her; he would not have it said he married her for her money.

It was that more than anything which had made him look seriously at the idea of trading with India and Bertie, who had once been a seagoing man, had introduced him to Captain Joseph Greenaway. The Captain had served throughout the war, but was on half-pay, a

state of affairs he had been anxious to remedy. He had
a little prize money saved, and Dominic put in all the
money he could scrape together, to lease a brig with its
crew and pay for a cargo. It had been a gamble, but a
gamble that had turned out well.

That first voyage had made a good profit so he had
handed the bulk of it back for a second trip, and now
here was the *Silken Maid*, home again with yet another
cargo. If they went on like this they would soon be able
to buy the ship. A fleet of ships!

He turned the diamond over in his hand, smiling at
his own fantasy. 'This will make a fine betrothal ring,'
he said, tying the stone in the corner of his handkerchief.
'I'll take it to Rundell and Bridges myself; they'll make
it up for me. You know what to do with the rest.'

'Yes, my lord. While I was in Calcutta I was given a
glimpse of a diamond the size of a pigeon's egg which
might be for sale at a good price. Obtaining that would
set the seal on the venture because I don't doubt it would
make a good profit. The Regent himself would covet it.'

'Maybe, but buying it would depend on the profit we
make on this cargo and what you can make with the
outgoing goods.'

'You have a return cargo?'

'I am in the middle of negotiating one. It will take
another week or two, so take some leave. By the time
you come back, it will be ready and waiting. In the
meantime, will you come and take a celebratory drink
with me?'

'I thank you, my lord, but my family will be expecting
me as soon as news that we have docked reaches them.'

'Of course.' He was on the point of leaving, when he
turned back. 'Who was the young lady I met on deck?
She was wrapped up in a cloak which was certainly not

in the latest mode, but I think she must be a lady by the way she spoke and the way she carried herself. She told me she was travelling with her brother. I did not know we had the facilities to take passengers.'

'That was Miss Woodhill.' The Captain smiled. 'A charming young lady, but I know nothing about her except that she has recently lost her father who was in the employ of the East India Company and she is now the sole guardian of her young brother. It is a great responsibility for one so lacking in years. They were looking for a cheap passage and I thought why not? It's all grist to the mill.

'I turned my cabin over to the lady and slept in here on the settle. The boy went in with the first mate; there is a second bunk in his cabin. They both seemed very content with the arrangement, possibly because I asked little more than their board by way of fare. You do not object, do you?'

'No, though it can hardly have been comfortable. Do they have a family here?'

'That I do not know, my lord. Do you wish me to make enquiries?'

'No, not at all, I asked out of curiosity, no more.'

Which was nothing but the truth, he told himself, as he returned to his carriage and ordered his driver to take him to Bond Street. He would have a few rounds of sparring at Gentleman Jackson's and then go on to Grillons where he had arranged to meet Bertie Cosgrove.

# Chapter Two

'I really think this hotel is too dear for us,' Emma said, looking round the crowded dining-room at the splendidly dressed patrons. 'Everyone seems so top of the trees.'

The men were clad in bright coloured coats and even brighter waistcoats. Their starched cravats sat under collar points which reached their cheeks and their legs were encased in tight-fitting pantaloons. The younger ladies were dressed in gowns of flimsy silk or net over satin which revealed more than they covered, having high waists with low necklines, while the more matronly were in heavier brocades and velvets with padded skirts from which their ankles peeped in brightly coloured stockings.

It was not that she was over-awed or even particularly envious; hadn't she attended Society functions at the British Consulate in Calcutta with her father? And held her own. No, it was simply that, in their straitened circumstances, she felt out of place. Her own gown was one of Mrs Goodwright's, a deep mauve sarcenet which the good lady had said might do in lieu of mourning, and though it had been made to fit Emma's slim waist and was trimmed with white lace, the colour did nothing for her complexion.

'Just look at the gems round that lady's throat,' Emma said, nodding towards a neighbouring table. 'They must be worth a fortune. Why, she even has them in her hair. And her gown must have cost a thousand rupees.'

'You know they don't have rupees in England,' Teddy said, making inroads into the lamb cutlets and vegetables with which his plate was piled. Ladies' fashions did not interest him, though he had thrown an admiring glance at one of the patrons, who had just entered. His double-breasted blue tailcoat fitted across his broad shoulders as if he had been poured into it. His waistcoat was a shining creation of blue and yellow stripes and his white muslin cravat was starched and tied with such precision that Teddy could only stare in admiration.

The man seemed thoroughly at ease and very pleased with himself, chatting animatedly to his companion, a big man with red-gold curls, wearing buckskin breeches and a cord coat.

'Of course I know,' Emma said. 'But it is difficult to think of guineas and half-crowns; it makes my head spin trying to convert it. And you are not above making mistakes. I heard you asking for the *dhobi-wallah* when we were shown to our rooms.'

'I wanted my shirt washed.'

'Now, of course, we are a laughing stock. I wish we had not come here.'

'Don't be a ninny, Em, no one is laughing.' A loud guffaw from the gentleman in the buckskin breeches gave the lie to that statement, though he was not laughing at them but at something his companion had said. 'And what other could we do? I asked the Captain to recommend a good hotel and he said we could not go wrong with Grillons.'

'He did not know how impecunious we are,' she said.

'Though I think he might have guessed, considering we were obliged to travel on a cargo ship with no passenger accommodation. It is too late to go anywhere else to-night, but tomorrow we must find more modest lodgings. And then we must both search for work, if you are still set against going to Mountforest Hall.'

'You know I am,' Teddy said grimly. 'I would rather starve. But we'll not do that, for I intend to go to Leadenhall Street and ask for work at Company head-quarters. I can be a Writer just as well here as in Calcutta.' He stopped suddenly and leaned forward. 'Don't turn round, but there is a dandy at the next table who is looking at you as if he knows you.'

'Don't be foolish, Teddy, how can anyone know us here?' She pretended to drop her napkin and, in bending to retrieve it, took a surreptitious look behind her. Her eyes met the laughing eyes of the young man who had boarded the *Silken Maid* earlier in the day. His hand reached Emma's napkin before hers. He smiled and handed it to her. 'Yours, I believe, Miss Woodhill.'

She sat up, knowing her cheeks were burning. 'Thank you, sir, but how did you know my name?'

'Why, from Captain Greenaway, of course. We do not usually take on passengers and I asked him who you were.'

'We? Oh, you are the owner of the *Silken Maid*?'

'Let us say I have an interest. I trust your voyage was a comfortable one?'

She laughed, revealing even white teeth and a dimple in her cheek which captivated him. 'Hardly that. The weather was bad and the sea very rough. The porthole in the cabin did not fit properly and everything became soaked, which is why I had nothing but this old gown to wear this evening.'

'It is very charming,' he said, looking her up and
down. Why on earth had she and her brother chosen
Grillons? It was way above their touch. He was filled
with admiration for her courage; finding herself in a tight
corner, she had chosen to attack. 'But I am sorry about
the porthole. It will, of course, be repaired before the
ship sails again.'

'Which is not much help to me.' Why was she being
so belligerent? He had been nothing but pleasant and it
sounded as if she were determined to quarrel with him.
It was not a courteous way to behave towards a stranger.
And yet he did not seem like a stranger; once again she
felt as if she had always known him.

'No, but please accept my apologies and allow me to
recompense you for the inconvenience.'

'That is not in the least necessary. The laundry
maid...' She caught sight of Teddy laughing and
frowned at him. 'Everything is being seen to and will
be put to rights by tomorrow. But I thank you for the
offer.' She picked up her reticule which lay on the table
at her side and stood up. If she stayed any longer she
could not trust herself not to ask where she had met him
before and that would be embarrassing for everyone. 'If
you will excuse me, I will retire. It has been a tiring
day.'

'Of course.' He rose and bowed to her. 'Are you staying in London?'

'For the moment.'

'Then I wish you a pleasant stay.'

'Thank you. Come along, Teddy.' With that she swept
from the room followed by her bemused brother.

'What was all that about?' he demanded as they made
their way up the stairs to their room.

'Nothing.'

'It didn't look like nothing to me. Why, you were as red as a turkey cock…'

'I was not.'

'Yes, you were.'

'Then it was because the room was so hot, and perhaps I had drunk too much of the wine.'

'It couldn't be because you took a shine to him, could it?'

'No, of course not. I have hardly spoken half a dozen words to the gentleman. Why, I don't even know his name.'

'Do you want to know it? I will run back and find out if you like.'

'You will do no such thing! Go to bed, we have a great deal to do tomorrow.'

Teddy sighed. 'Pity. I wouldn't have minded making his acquaintance. He's a real Corinthian, don't you think?'

'No, I don't. It's obvious he is a nabob. I think he has shares in the *Silken Maid*'s cargo.'

'So what? Are you become so high in the instep, you can look down on honest trading? He seems to have done well from it, judging by his dress.'

'And if he has, what concern can it possibly be of ours?' She paused outside the door of her room. 'Goodnight, Teddy.'

It took her a long time to go to sleep that night. Her head was filled with the newness of everything, the sights, the smells, the sounds of a strange country. And yet it was the country her father had always called home. She must make it her home. But, oh, how difficult it was going to be! She missed Papa dreadfully. If he had been alive and bringing her to England on a visit, it would have been a wonderful adventure, but as it was she felt lost and, in spite of Teddy who was very dear to her, very lonely.

It was all very well for Mrs Goodwright to give her a book on etiquette, but it didn't go nearly far enough. For instance, in England was it permissible for a lady to speak to a strange man in a public dining-room, if he did one a service? Ought she simply to have thanked him and turned away? But that would have been rude, especially after he had taken the trouble to find out her name and ask about the voyage.

Six months ago, she would not have troubled herself about it; she would have done what came naturally to her, secure in the knowledge of her place in society. She would not have given the rights and wrongs of it a thought, much less spent sleepless hours worrying about it.

Had she really blushed? Oh, how mortifying! Whatever had he thought of her? It was just as well they were moving on tomorrow. She didn't want another uncomfortable encounter with that gentleman.

Two mornings later Emma and Teddy set out from two tiny rooms on the top floor of a lodging house on the north side of Oxford Street to look for work. A slight breeze had blown away the misty rain and the sun was shining, a day for optimism, they decided. It was an optimism which was soon deflated. Emma had a notion that she could look after young children or even teach, but, according to the agency to whom she applied, no one wanted their children taught by someone whose sole experience was giving Indian children the rudiments of English. She was very conscious of her outmodish brown bombazine gown and tanned complexion; English ladies seemed to be uncommonly pale.

If she had not been so concerned about their dwindling resources, she would have enjoyed exploring the city. It was so different from Calcutta and yet there were similarities. Many of the fine buildings had their counterparts in Calcutta, which had been dubbed 'the city of palaces', but the people who thronged the streets and rode in a bewildering array of carriages, were, for the most part, white.

The markets, like markets the world over, were colourful and noisy but the produce they sold was different: hot peas, meat pies, herrings, cabbages and bootlaces instead of chuppattis, samosas, melons, copper ornaments and saris. And though there were English churches in Calcutta, there did not seem to be any mosques and temples in London, shining pink and gold in the sun, no ruins, no fort. St Paul's was impressive and one day she might go inside, but at that moment she was too anxious to reach her next interview. Having given up the idea of teaching, she had decided to try for a position as a lady's maid.

The encounter lasted less than five minutes, which was the time it took to realise she would be nothing but a slave to a cantankerous old lady twenty-four hours a day, and for a pittance. Judging by the tiny fire in the grate and the chill in the house which was mirrored in the lady's demeanour, there would be no warmth there. It was the same in many of the places to which she was sent and on the few occasions when she liked what she saw, she was turned down on the grounds of her inexperience. She returned home in the evening, hoping that Teddy had had better luck.

He had not. 'I didn't get any further than speaking to a supervisor,' he said, disgustedly, as they sat over a frugal meal. 'All he said was, "Go to Haileybury and finish your schooling, then we might be able to use you.'' He said Haileybury College was like Fort William in Calcutta, intended to produce Indian administrators.'

'I wish you could,' Emma said. 'But I'm afraid it's out of the question.'

'I know. I thought of journalism, but when I tried a newspaper office, they laughed at me, said I knew nothing, but I could be the *tea-wallah*, if I liked. I am not that desperate, Em.'

'No, of course not.'

'If I cannot work for The Company, then I would wish to do something with some excitement in it. Do you know there are hundreds of stage coaches in London? They go all over the country every day at a bruising speed, twenty miles an hour some of them. And the coachmen are fine fellows. I wouldn't mind being a coachman or a guard. The guard has a blunderbuss to frighten off highwaymen. Come to think of it, it might be exciting to be a highwayman. Your jewels or your life, and all that.'

Emma laughed. 'Oh, Teddy, you are a goose, but what would I do without you?'

'I can't stay tied to your apron strings forever, Em,' he said, suddenly serious. 'If you are worrying what will happen to me if you are offered a position, please don't. Whether you will have it or not, I am a man now and must find my own way.'

'I haven't been offered anything so it doesn't signify.'

'You had no luck either?'

'No.'

'You'll have to find a husband, like I said before.'

'And just how am I to do that?'

'Cultivate any eligible you meet, instead of rebuffing him, as you always seem to do. There was that gentle-

man last night—he was interested, I could tell. All you
did was complain about the voyage and tell him to mind
his own business…'

'I did not!'

'As good as. If you had accepted his offer of compensation, who knows where it might have led…?'

'Teddy, you sometimes talk the most dreadful nonsense. Of course he wasn't interested in me. He's probably married with half a dozen children. Anyway, I have
no intention of marrying for money…'

'Why not? I am persuaded that is how most marriages
begin.'

'How can you say that, when you know how much
Mama and Papa loved each other?'

'They were an exception.'

'Then I shall be another.' She laughed suddenly. 'And
I could hardly be married within a week and that is how
long our funds are likely to last.' She paused, serious
again. 'I will try again tomorrow. I'll go to a domestic
agency…'

'Emma, you can't be a housemaid, it is as bad as me
being a *tea-wallah*.'

'I think this business of having an uncle who is a
viscount has gone to your head, brother dear. We cannot
afford pride.' Which was only too true, though she la-
mented it as much as Teddy did.

The next day she tried a new agency and her luck
changed, though she did wonder if it was because she
furnished them with a glowing reference from Miss
Emma Mountforest who had employed her as a companion while residing in India. 'Society among the
English community in India is very little different from
that in England,' she told the proprietor, tongue in cheek.

'I shall soon adapt.' Emma did not like the deception, but she was beginning to realise she would get nowhere telling the truth. She was given an introduction to take to the Marquis of Cavenham, who required a companion for his sister, Miss Lucilla Besthorpe.

She returned home to leave a note for Teddy, telling him where she was, before following the directions she had been given to the Marquis's house in Bedford Row. It was a tall mansion, identical to those on either side of it, with rows of sash windows and a heavy oak door with a large brass knocker and flambeaux either side. She took a deep breath and knocked, prepared to lie, if necessary, to obtain the post.

The maid who answered the door took the agency's letter from her and left her waiting in an anteroom for several minutes, which seemed like an hour to Emma, who found that her hands were shaking with nerves. She gave herself a good scolding and managed to calm herself by the time the girl returned.

'Come this way, please.'

She led the way up a curving staircase, covered with Turkey carpet, to a large sunny room on the first floor, where she left her. Emma, looking about her at the upholstered sofas with their faded gilt scrolling, the spindly chairs and satinwood sofa table, the secretaire in the corner, the gilt framed pictures which could have done with cleaning, the spotted mirror and ormolu clock on the mantel, the striped taffeta curtains and worn carpet, came to the conclusion that the room had once seen better days.

She had thought there was no one there, but a slight movement by the window caught her eye and a young lady emerged, from behind the curtains. She was about seventeen, Emma judged, dressed very simply in a morning dress of spotted muslin, with a deep frill at the hem and lace about the neck. Her hair, which was fair, was worn tied back with a blue velvet ribbon with no attempt at fashionable arrangement. And yet she was lovely, mainly due to a cheerful countenance and sparkling blue eyes.

'I thought I would take a look at you before you saw me,' she said, coming forward and seating herself on one of the sofas.

'Oh, and what conclusion have you come to?' Emma asked, deducing that this was the Marquis's sister and would be her charge if she were to be appointed.

'You are not what you seem.'

Emma gasped. Surely she had not been seen through by a schoolmiss? 'Whatever do you mean?'

'At first I thought you rather dull, a little brown sparrow, but then I saw the way you looked about you, as if summing us up, and I realised that there would be no deceiving you.'

'Does anyone need to deceive me?' Emma asked, conscious of the irony of that remark.

'No, but you have already deduced that we are not as plump in the pocket as we would like. Dominic wants to set the place to rights, but it all takes time and he has not been the Marquis for long enough to bring us round…'

'Should you be telling me this, Miss Besthorpe? It is a private matter, surely?'

'But if you become one of the household, you must know what you are falling into.'

'Your brother, the Marquis…?'

'Oh, Dominic is as open and honest as the day is long. Everyone knows our circumstances, but matters are improving. Dominic has just made a huge profit on some investment or other and so I am to have a Season, after all. You do not know how relieved I am, for otherwise I would have been packed off to Aunt Agatha in Yorkshire, and that is not to be borne. She is old and so strict, I might as well be in purdah. Even Dominic does not wish that on me.'

'Miss Besthorpe, I really do not think you should be divulging that.'

'Oh, do call me Lucy, everyone does. If I am to have my come-out this year, I need a maid who will also be a companion and chaperon. I think we should suit very well, don't you?'

Emma felt as though she were being swept along on a tide, but she liked Lucy, who had a refreshing candour and was not in the least conceited. 'Yes, but I have yet to meet the Marquis and he may not agree.'

'Oh, Dominic will like you, I know. And besides, I can bring him round my little finger, if I have a mind to. I have already turned down three applicants—three old dragons breathing fire.'

Emma found herself laughing and it was at that point Dominic entered the room.

He stood watching them from the doorway, realising that when Miss Woodhill laughed, her whole face lit up and she came vibrantly alive. Even in her dowdy brown clothes there was something about her that made her stand out; she had a natural grace, a way of carrying herself, a quiet dignity which, to his way of thinking, reflected good breeding, and yet she seemed totally unaware of it. She had, he supposed, found out who he was and decided to take advantage of his offer of compensation, after all. He was both disappointed that she might have a mercenary streak and delighted to see her again.

He took a further step into the room and Lucy, seeing him, ran to take his arm and drag him forward.

'Dominic, this is…'

He smiled. 'Miss Woodhill, I know.' He bowed to Emma. 'Your servant, ma'am.'

'You know?' Lucy looked from him to Emma, who seemed to have been struck dumb. Her face was flushed and her mouth partly open as if she had been frozen in the middle of a laugh. 'You did not tell me you knew my brother.'

Emma was thunderstruck. Her confused thoughts ranged from how handsome the Marquis was in his blue superfine coat, buff pantaloons and polished hessians, to wondering why fate had decreed they should meet again and so soon, too. Then she remembered what Teddy had said the evening before about the gentleman being interested in her and she felt the colour flood her cheeks. Would he think that she had engineered the meeting? Oh, how dreadful if he did!

'I didn't. I don't.' She managed to speak at last. 'I had no idea…'

'Miss Woodhill and I encountered each other yesterday,' Dominic said, realising that the young lady was as surprised as he was and had not come to dun him. 'Twice.'

'Twice! Then you must tell me all about it.'

'There is nothing to tell,' Emma said, pulling herself together. 'His lordship came on board the ship on which I travelled from India and we met a second time when my brother and I were dining at the hotel. I had no idea he would be there. Nor did I know who he was until now.' She hoped he was convinced.

'Oh, but that is good, don't you see? We are connected already.' Lucy turned to her brother. 'Dominic,

Miss Woodhill is applying for the post of companion. Do say you will agree.'

'Miss Woodhill is a little young, Lucy dear,' he murmured. 'I am surprised the agency sent her. I asked for a mature lady, preferably one with a little experience of guiding young ladies.'

'Dragons!' said Lucy scornfully. 'They would be as bad as Aunt Agatha. I don't want to be hemmed in by dos and don'ts and lectures on etiquette and what is becoming to a young lady. And you know after I turned the last one away, they said they would not send any more.'

He smiled. 'No, they said Miss Besthorpe was obviously spoiled and they would not wish anyone of sensibility on her. Which is not at all the same thing.' He turned to Emma. 'I beg your pardon, Miss Woodhill, I did not mean to imply…'

She had recovered sufficiently to smile. 'That I was lacking in sensibility?'

'Not at all. I was simply pointing out that my sister can be impossibly difficult to please.'

'That's not fair!' Lucy cried. 'If I had someone I liked I would be as biddable as you please. And I like Miss Woodhill.'

Emma smiled. 'Thank you, Miss Besthorpe, but it is of little consequence what the agency thinks of my suitability. The decision is his lordship's.'

*'Touché!'* He laughed in delight. Here was no terrified underling, but a girl of spirit and he liked that. Not that Society would consider her as a suitable duenna for his sister. Lucy needed a strong hand. But their present situation was highly irregular, as everyone had been pointing out, ever since their parents had died within a few weeks of each other just over a year before; he was a

bachelor and it was highly improper for Lucy to continue to live with him, either in town or at their country estate, though it wasn't so important at Cavenham House.

Aunt Agatha had offered to take her, but Lucy had begged not to go and, as usual, Lucy had got her own way. She had not been boasting when she said she could wind him about her little finger.

When their fortunes began to take a turn for the better, he had promised her a Season and for that, they must observe the rules of Society, which meant Lucy must have a companion and chaperon, someone who would observe the proprieties and guide her in the correct behaviour, preferably someone of mature years. Miss Woodhill hardly fitted that description.

He paced the room, while the two girls watched him in silence. He ought to turn her away, letting her down as gently as possible, but it was true that Lucy had been very difficult to please and the agency was losing patience. There was the added complication that, because of Princess Charlotte's wedding, everybody who was anybody would be in London this year, even those who had long ago retired to the country, and good servants would be hard to find.

He stopped pacing and turned towards Emma. 'Please sit down, Miss Woodhill, and allow me continue the interview.' He indicated one of the sofas and, as soon as she had taken her seat, sat opposite her, leaving Lucy to prowl about the room.

'Now,' he said, ignoring his sister. 'Tell me all about yourself. Captain Greenaway told me you have lately become bereaved and I offer my condolences…'

'Thank you, my lord. My father was employed as a Civil Servant.' She had decided not to reveal that her father had been a soldier; it was too easy to verify the names of serving officers. 'He died about seven months ago.'

'I am sorry. Tell me why you decided to come to England.'

She hesitated only momentarily. 'It is not easy for a lady to live alone in India, and I had my brother to think of. We thought it would be easier to find employment here. I had no idea it would be so difficult. There is so much prejudice...'

One well-defined brow lifted. 'Prejudice or caution, Miss Woodhill?'

'Both. Although my parents were English, I was born in India and lived all my life there until now; prospective employers seem to think it means I have lived like a savage. I can assure you, my lord, that British Society in Calcutta is every bit as civilised as that in London.' It was no more than the truth, but she knew she was on shaky ground. It was not that she thought he was prejudiced but if he were to check on her story, he would discover that no one in Calcutta had heard of Miss Woodhill.

She stood up suddenly, unable to continue. 'I am sorry to have taken your time, my lord.'

'Sit down, Miss Woodhill. I have not finished.'

His voice was so authoritarian, she almost fell back into her seat.

'Dominic, don't bully,' Lucy said. 'You frighten Miss Woodhill.'

He smiled at Emma. 'Do I frighten you?'

'Not at all, my lord.' Which was true. It was shame, not fright, which had made her want to run away.

'Then let us continue. You are, how old?'

She stifled the retort that it was ungentlemanly to enquire a lady's age; he had every right to ask and, as far as he was concerned, she was no lady. 'Twenty-two.'

'Twenty-two is very young for a chaperon, Miss Woodhill. Why, you are not above an age for needing one yourself.'

'Oh, come, my lord, you flatter me. I am old enough to be independent and to have had some experience.'

'And what form has that taken?'

This business of deception was more difficult than she had imagined, especially when her interrogator looked at her with such warm friendliness. She had to force herself to meet his gaze. 'I was lady's maid and companion to Miss Emma Mountforest.'

'But that's…' Lucy began but Dominic held up his hand to silence her.

'If you persist in interrupting, Lucy, I shall send you away.' He turned back to Emma. 'You have the same Christian name as Miss Mountforest.'

'Yes, I was named for her.' She and Teddy had decided not to change their given names because they might be uneasy with new ones and forget to answer to them. She opened her reticule and produced the reference she had written herself. 'This is from Miss Mountforest.'

He took it but did not read it immediately, preferring to trust his own judgement about people, but the name of Miss Woodhill's previous employer had astonished him. 'Why did you leave her employ?'

Emma faltered. She had not realised how one untruth led to another and was beginning to wonder where it would end. It would be almost a relief if she were turned away, but then what else could she do? 'Miss Mountforest had lately lost her own father and was going to live with friends. I don't know where, but she said she would no longer be able to employ a personal maid.'

'I see. And so you came to England to seek your fortune.' He smiled suddenly and his whole face was lit with warmth. 'You know, it is usually the other way about. People travel from this country to India to make their fortunes.' He paused, watching her face. Why did he have the impression she was hiding something? It made him curious. 'But perhaps not ladies.'

'No, but I am hardly a lady. I am used to making my own decisions and looking after myself.' She brushed a brown, ringless hand over her skirt and noticed it was shaking. His questions were becoming too probing, too personal, and more and more difficult to answer. She would do better to steer him towards more practical matters. She clasped her hands together in her lap and forced herself to look at him. 'I should, of course, like to know exactly what my duties would be and the hours I should be expected to work. And the remuneration, of course.'

'Naturally. Your duties would simply be to be a companion to Lucy, to help her dress, advise her on such things as etiquette, act as her chaperon. It follows that the hours you work will vary from day to day, but rest assured they would not be onerous. Do you think you could manage that? My sister is very self-willed, you know.'

Emma smiled. 'Miss Besthorpe seems to me to be a delightful young lady and no more self-willed than any other of her age and I envisage no difficulty. I am sure she knows very well how to go on. Age is no criteria for wisdom.'

Lucy clapped her hands with delight. 'There! I knew Miss Woodhill would be a match for you, brother. I don't know why you are quizzing her so hard, when I already know all I need to know.'

'Oh, do not be hard on him,' Emma told her. 'He has only your welfare at heart and he would be a poor guardian if he did not make every endeavour for your safety and comfort.'

'Thank you, Miss Woodhill,' Dominic said solemnly, bowing towards her. But his seriousness was counterbalanced by the twinkle of humour in his brown eyes, to which she responded with a smile which almost overwhelmed him. He found himself wanting to help her. How else could he do it but give her employment?

His doubts about her suitability gave way to a conviction that she would be an asset to any household, not as a servant, but as wife and mother. The thought startled him, for was he not engaged to be married? He forced himself back to the matter in hand and tried to look stern. 'I presume you are unmarried with no emotional entanglements? I ask because you will be required to live in and devote yourself to my sister.'

'I understand that, my lord. The man I was to marry died of fever four years ago. There has been no one since then, but, as you know, I do have a brother.'

'I see. He is not yet suited?'

'Oh, Dominic, do find something for Miss Woodhill's brother,' Lucy put in. 'I do so want her to come to us.'

'Lucy,' he said patiently. 'You know how careful we have to be over—'

'Oh, my lord, I did not mean…' Emma said. 'I was not…' She stopped and began again. 'Teddy has been educated to good degree; he is not looking for domestic work. He has gone to India House and will doubtless be given employment there.'

'Of course. Your father's name will be known to them.'

'Yes,' she said, wishing the ground would swallow her. This was becoming harder and harder, but once started on the deception, there was no way she could stop it without confessing all. And she could not do it. Teddy was relying on her.

'As for wages,' he went on. 'What do you say to fifty pounds a year and all found?'

Emma had no way of knowing that this was more than generous and did a quick conversion to rupees, which was a futile exercise because standards were so different in India. On the other hand, she would be living in and, as pin money, it would do very well. The only trouble was that if Teddy did not find a post where he could live in, she would have to pay for his lodgings. 'I would prefer to be paid monthly, my lord,' she said.

'Very well, monthly it shall be.' He smiled and held out his hand. 'Let us shake hands on the deal and you may start as soon as you wish, then you will have time to become accustomed to your duties before the Season begins in earnest.'

Emma found her hand clasped in a cool, dry grip and found herself thinking what an uncommonly attractive man he was, not only physically, but in temperament. His smile made her feel as though she was of some consequence; he treated her like an equal even when he had no cause to think of her as anything but a servant. She hated herself for deceiving him and didn't know how she was going to survive seeing him every day and living a lie.

Perhaps he would be busy, out and about doing masculine, bachelor things, and she would not need to see much of him. Why did that thought sadden her? 'Thank you, my lord,' she said, retrieving her hand. 'I will start the day after tomorrow, if I may.'

'Oh, I am so pleased,' Lucy exclaimed, as Dominic went over to the secretaire and opened a drawer. 'I shall look forward to seeing you then.'

'You will need this.' Dominic came forward, offering a small bag which Emma realised contained coins.

'My lord?' she queried doubtfully. 'I have earned nothing yet.'

'It is customary, Miss Woodhill, to give a small advance for clothes and suchlike.' He gave Lucy a warning look to stop her contradicting him. 'You know better than I what you need.'

Emma wondered if he were criticising her dress, but she was in no position to be disdainful of an advance. She accepted gratefully and took her leave, hardly noticing the young man who was at that moment approaching the house. She had done it! She had a job and somewhere to live, and she only hoped that his lordship never found out the truth. Somehow she knew he would be more hurt than angry and she never wanted to hurt him. She would have to work hard, learn her job and be a true friend to Miss Besthorpe.

Her reverie was brought to a startling end by a commotion in the street. A chimney boy, black as Satan and carrying a bundle of brushes on his shoulder, had turned suddenly towards one of the houses and his pole had come into contact with the rump of a horse which had been hitched to a tree outside the Marquis's gate. The startled animal bolted, to the accompaniment of screams and shouts from passers-by, which only served to increase its terror. Its owner, who had been taking the steps, two at a time, up to Lord Besthorpe's door, turned to run after it. Emma sprang back out of his way as he

brushed past her, just as someone darted out from nowhere and grabbed the runaway's reins.

In that moment she realised, with a shock, that it was
her brother and he was being dragged along the road,
while everyone in the vicinity stood and stared. But he
clung on manfully and brought the horse to a shuddering
halt. He was standing with his head up against the
horse's, murmuring soothingly to it, when its owner
came up to him. Emma hurried to join them.

'I'm obliged to you, young shaver,' the man was saying and Emma realised it was the man who had been
with Lord Besthorpe at Grillons the evening they arrived
in London. There was no mistaking his red-gold locks.
'That was a spunky thing to do. Nelson could have
caused no end of a furore with the traffic. He might done
untold damage, not to mention injuring himself.'

'He is still very agitated,' Teddy said, patting the stallion's neck. 'It is hardly to be wondered at—such an
out-and-out thoroughbred is bound to be spirited.' The
horse whinnied with pleasure at the fondling and soft
voice of the young man. 'See, he knows, doesn't he? I
wonder you subject him to the city traffic, sir.'

'Impudent young bratling!'

'Teddy, do mind your manners,' Emma put in. She
turned to the horse's owner. 'I am sorry for my brother's
rudeness, sir. I am afraid he was always more outspoken
than was good for him. He meant no criticism.'

'Emma, I do not need you to speak for me, much less
tell what is in my mind,' Teddy said. 'A man who subjects a horse like that to the noise and bustle of city
streets don't deserve to own such a one.'

Emma was horrified, but the man started to laugh and
he kept on laughing, until Teddy's own mouth twitched
and Emma found herself smiling.

'You obviously know your horses, young man. Where did you learn about them?'

'In India. We take care of our horses there.'

'So we do in England.' He smiled. 'I do not customarily ride race horses in town and you were quite right to chide me, but, you see, I have only half an hour ago purchased him at Tattersall's and could not resist the opportunity to ride him home.'

'I beg pardon, sir,' Teddy said. 'I should not have been so quick to criticise without knowing the whole, but…'

'No, you should not.' He took the reins from Teddy's hand and patted the horse. 'But I am obliged to you for stopping him.' He felt in his pocket for a coin with which to reward the boy.

'I've seen you before,' Teddy said, reluctant to let the beautiful animal go and ignoring the proffered half-crown. 'You were at Grillons the other night with…' He stopped suddenly confused, when he saw the man he had referred to as a Corinthian striding towards them.

'I heard the commotion,' he said. 'Bertie, what's amiss?'

'I was on my way to see you, wanted to show off my latest purchase, tied him to a tree. Trouble was he was spooked by a chimney boy and this young shaver, not only stopped him, but afforded me a lecture on how I should look after him.'

Dominic smiled. 'And you disliked that, I do not doubt.' He walked slowly round the animal, now standing patiently at the side of the road. 'He's a beauty, isn't he?'

'Top of the trees. I bought him for stud, but I think I might give him a race or two. You should have seen him gallop down the road. Scattered everyone, except the lad.'

Dominic turned towards Teddy. 'Mr Woodhill, I am happy to make your acquaintance.'

'Oh, I am sorry,' Emma put in, suddenly remembering her manners. 'Lord Besthorpe, allow me to present my brother, Edward. Teddy, this is the Marquis of Cavenham.'

'Marquis?' Teddy's expression was almost comical. 'I say, Em, that's a turn-up, ain't it?'

'What is?' demanded the owner of the horse.

'Why, that we should have bumped into his lordship three times in less than a se'ennight,' Teddy said. 'First on board the ship from India, then at Grillons. And I said to Em…' A look from Emma silenced him, for she was sure he was going to say something indiscreet.

'Teddy, his lordship has been kind enough to give me a position in his household.'

'Has he? Oh, that's capital!'

'Are you looking for work, young man?' The query came from the man Dominic had addressed at Bertie.

'Yes, sir.'

'Are you as good with horses as you say you are?'

'Course I am. Ask my sister.'

'Then I'll give you a trial in my stables.'

'A stable lad!' said Teddy in tones of contempt. 'I ain't so sure…'

'Teddy, don't be so ungrateful!' Emma remonstrated.

'Mr Cosgrove doesn't have your ordinary kind of stable,' Dominic put in. 'He's one of the country's foremost racehorse owners and breeders.'

'There's more like this one?' Teddy queried, patting Nelson's shining black neck.

'Yes, several,' Bertie said. 'You'd have to come down

to Newmarket and live in with the other lads. If you come up to the mark, you'd be able to exercise the horses of a morning.'

'That's no problem at all,' Emma put in before Teddy should be foolish enough to turn down the offer. 'He really is exceptionally good with horses. Why, I've known him break the most skittish pony and had him trotting around as docile as you please in no time at all.'

'Let us go back indoors to discuss it over a glass of something,' Dominic suggested. 'We can hardly do business on the road.'

So they all went back inside and the details were arranged to everyone's satisfaction over claret wine for the men and ratafia for the ladies, as Lucy soon joined them. By the time they left, Emma and Teddy felt as if they had known the Marquis and his friend, Mr Cosgrove, all their lives.

'There's a turn-up and no mistake,' Teddy said, as they made their way home, having been persuaded to take nuncheon at Bedford Row. 'It's fate, that's what it is.'

'What is?'

'Why, meeting Lord Besthorpe again. I knew he was top of the trees when I first set eyes on him at Grillons. And to think you saw him before that and never said a word.'

'Why should I? We simply passed each other when I was disembarking and he was coming on board.'

'But he took the trouble to discover your name, didn't he? It must have been more than that.'

'Well, it wasn't,' she said, thoroughly annoyed with him. 'Now, if you please, we will not say another word about the gentleman.'

'I think he's a real out-and-outer,' he continued, ignoring her plea to drop the subject. 'Now you are likely to see him every day, he cannot help but notice you.'

'Teddy, if you do not hold your tongue this very minute, I shall never speak to you again.'

He laughed and skipped out of the way of her upraised hand. Not that she would have struck him; it was a meaningless threat. 'Had you forgot I am going to Newmarket tomorrow?' he said. 'You will not be able to speak to me for a long time.'

It was perfectly true and the reminder saddened her. Because their father had frequently been away from home, they had fallen on each other's company more than most siblings, which perhaps accounted for Emma's ability in what might be considered masculine pursuits like shooting, fishing and riding hard. Only when Teddy was at school had they been parted. But he was right to say that he was no longer a child and must make his own way. She must learn not to mind.

'I am going to spend the rest of the afternoon shopping,' she said. 'Do you need anything?'

'No, thank you. Nor do I wish to be dragged round town looking at fripperies. I am going to Bullock's Museum to see Napoleon's coach. I believe there are other memorabilia from the Waterloo battlefield. Very gory, some of it. I shall see you this evening.' And with that he sauntered off, leaving her to make her own way to Pantheon's Bazaar.

A visit to that establishment had been suggested to her by Lucy when she had ventured to ask where she could buy ready-to wear clothes at a reasonable price. The name made her think of India, but the emporium, when she found it, was nothing like an Indian market, for it was a large store.

She spent some time wandering through its departments bewildered by the array of garments and accessories for sale and carefully enquiring the price of everything. The Marquis's advance had been generous but she was determined not to spend it all at once. One good day gown and something for evenings should suffice, together with a pelisse, a good pair of half-boots, and a bonnet and gloves. These, together with the clothes she had brought from India would, she decided, make up an adequate wardrobe. After all, she would not be going on the town herself. When it came to choosing style and colour, she found herself wondering what Lord Besthorpe would prefer, which was very silly and did not help her make up her mind.

In the end she chose a round gown for day in a green and cream striped jaconet with a cream lace pelerine collar and puffed sleeves. The evening gown was more difficult; there was a bewildering display of materials: silk, satin, net, gauze, some of it almost transparent and in every colour imaginable, trimmed with beads, pearls, ribbons and feathers. The temptation to buy one of these gorgeous creations would have been almost impossible to resist if they had not been above her means.

She was not a giddy schoolgirl going to her first ball, she told herself, she was a mature woman who was expected to watch over the morals and well-being of her young charge. She must blend into the background. On the other hand, she must not be a dowd for that would reflect badly on the Marquis. She must be a credit to him.

She had been excessively cross with Teddy for his teasing, but that did not alter the fact that his lordship's good opinion was very important to her. He had believed every fib she told him, and that made her feel distinctly unworthy. It behoved her to prove to his and her own satisfaction that she deserved the chance he was giving her.

The shop assistant was looking at her with a degree of impatience and there were others jostling behind her, clamouring for attention. She seized upon an open gown of amber crepe over a pale lemon satin slip. It had short puff sleeves and was decorated under the bosom with a cluster of silk primroses and floating velvet ribbons.

After that, buying accessories was a simple matter and having given instructions for her purchases to be delivered to Bedford Row, she made her way back to her lodgings for a last meal with Teddy. Tomorrow was the beginning of a new life. Whether it would be difficult or easy, happy or sad, she had no way of knowing, but whatever it was, she was determined to meet its challenge with good humour and fortitude.

## Chapter Three

Emma had expected to find her accommodation a little spartan, probably at the top of the house where the other servants lived, but that was not so. Lucy insisted on having her close to hand and Emma was given a room on the second floor, just along the corridor from Lucy's suite of bedroom and sitting-room. It was large and well-furnished though, like the rest of the house, a little shabby. She didn't mind that; it made it all the more cosy.

She also discovered she was not to eat in the kitchen but with the family, as well as to go out and about everywhere with her charge, even when his lordship himself was to be in attendance, which he was during the first few days. It did nothing for her peace of mind to have him in such close proximity but she supposed it was only natural that he would wish to satisfy himself that his beloved sister was in good hands and that he need have no qualms about his new employee.

He was always elegantly, though not extravagantly dressed, always courteous and good-natured, but he never gave the impression of weakness. Physically he was a powerful man with a temperament to match; he knew what he wanted and was determined to have it, while remaining fair to everyone from his sister down to the potboy in the kitchen. Emma did not need to be told that his servants respected and loved him; it showed itself in their cheerful willingness to do the work allotted to them.

He could also be implacable and she made up her mind she would do her utmost not to put him to the test. So she studied her book of etiquette and borrowed others from the library, learned how to dress her charge for every given occasion, to mend her clothes and arrange her hair, so that he would have no cause for complaint.

If he ever found out the reference she had given him was a forgery...no, not a forgery exactly but written to deceive, she would be bundled out of the house in minutes, and without a character. She had not been long at Bedford Row before she discovered exactly what that unpleasant phrase meant, when she learned that one of the kitchen maids had recently been turned off for impertinence to a guest.

'I'm sure I don't blame her,' Lucy told Emma. They were eating *en famille* and Lucy had been beguiling her with tales of recent happenings. 'Lady Clarence is insufferably top-lofty and to complain the soup was cold when she had let it sit in front of her a full ten minutes while she bored everyone with the tale of how her bran-faced daughter had engaged the attention of the Prince Regent, which I, for one, do not credit, was too much. I had as lief sent her off without her dinner as punish poor Rose.'

'Rudeness is something I will not tolerate,' Dominic put in mildly. 'Not even when it appears justified. If I had not acted at once, it would have been the talk of the *ton* that I am unable to control my servants. And from that it would be a short step to saying the whole household is dissolute. What do you suppose that would do for your come-out and your chances of marriage?'

Lucy conceded that he might be right, but the unfairness rankled. 'I should hope you will wait until the fuss has died down and re-engage her,' she said, to which Dominic laughed and said she must leave justice to him, an enigmatic answer which convinced Emma more than ever that he must not find out that she had lied to him. The very thought of it made her go hot with shame.

A dozen times a day she had to tell herself that her deception was a necessary evil which would end as soon as the unfairness of her father's exile was proved, though how that was to be done, she had no idea. Teddy had said that being given employment in Newmarket, close to the Mountforest family home, had been the hand of fate. He would soon uncover the truth and clear their father's name. Once that was done their uncle would have to acknowledge them and provide them with whatever legacy had been due to their father.

When that happened, she would be able to tell Lord Besthorpe the truth. It was important to her that he should understand and forgive. Very important. She needed his good opinion of her. Already he occupied a tight little corner in her heart, though she would never have admitted it to anyone but her own secret self. At the moment she was content just to be in his house, seeing him, talking to him, looking after his sister.

Lucy herself was a delight. Although anxious to please, she was far from a milksop, having very decided views on a great many subjects and often so determined to have her own way, she came head to head with her brother. It was never acrimonious and very soon one or the other would give way or a compromise would be reached which satisfied them both.

Emma stayed on the sidelines during these exchanges, watching with amusement and marvelling at the way each thought they were manipulating the other, saying nothing unless appealed to and then choosing her words with care.

'Oh, he can be so pompous when he chooses,' Lucy said one day when the two young ladies were sitting over some crewel work in Lucy's sitting-room. 'I did so want to go to Madame Tussaud's today. And I want to show you the town.'

'But his lordship is otherwise engaged, Lucy, and we have no escort.'

'Pooh to that. We can escort each other. What harm can we come to? There will be plenty of people about. And if Dominic would only allow us to take the carriage, we would have Nobbs to protect us.'

'That is not the same thing and you know it.'

Lucy put her sewing down in exasperation. 'What did your previous employer do when she wanted to go out? I'll lay a guinea to a groat she took you for company and didn't wait for her brother to accompany her.'

Emma laughed, though she had a twinge of conscience every time her past was mentioned. 'No, her brother was a schoolboy. And it was different in India.'

'How? Were there no villains?'

'There were as many there as in England, I do not doubt, but that is nothing to the point. His lordship has taken the carriage, as well you know, and he has made his wishes very clear. I am afraid, this time, you must own yourself defeated, unless you want him to call me to account for allowing you to disobey him. He would very likely dismiss me.'

'Oh, no, dear Emma, I could not bear that,' Lucy said. 'But I am tired of sewing and it is such a lovely day.'

This was perfectly true. Emma was beginning to revise her first impressions of England as a cold, dismal place. The sky was a pale blue laced with fleecy white clouds; the atmosphere, while not warm, was balmy and the trees, no longer soot-laden, were bursting forth in a delicate pale green. Lucy was right; it was a day for being out of doors.

'Then let us walk in the park instead,' she said. 'I can see no harm in that.'

Fifteen minutes later they were entering Hyde Park by the Stanhope Gate. Lucy was becomingly clad in a lilac sarcenet walking dress with a matching pelisse in a darker tone of the same colour. Her chip bonnet was trimmed with violets and tied beneath one ear with velvet ribbon. She was charmingly attractive and openly enjoyed the looks of admiration she received while not being in the least conceited.

Beneath her green pelisse Emma wore the green and cream striped round gown she had purchased at the Pantheon and which she had been saving for just such an occasion. Her cottager hat, bought because it would be easy to change its decoration and even its shape to make it look different every time she wore it, was on this occasion trimmed with coloured ribbons in shades of green, cream and buff. It was neat and tidy rather than elegant and she tried very hard not to be envious of her companion; if it were not for Lucy she might be in very much worse straits. That her antecedents were as high as Lucy's must not be allowed to count.

Arm in arm, they proceeded down the path, with Lucy

smiling and greeting every other person they met, including the redoubtable Lady Clarence who was bowling by in a barouche, clad in a purple satin outfit and a matching turban covered in sweeping green feathers. Seeing the two girls, she called out to her driver to stop the carriage. When it had come to a halt, her ladyship lifted her quizzing glass to peer at them both, as if wanting to make quite sure her eyes were not deceiving her.

Lucy curtsied. 'Good afternoon, Lady Clarence,' she said. 'May I present Miss Emma Woodhill who has lately come to stay with us. Emma, this is Lady Clarence.'

Emma was subjected to a minute scrutiny, during which she felt as transparent as glass, but she would not be intimidated. 'Good afternoon, my lady,' she said, affording her ladyship a token bending of the knee. 'It is a beautiful day for an outing, is it not?'

The lady was affronted enough at having to suffer an introduction to someone who was so obviously not Quality, but to be addressed directly by that person was the outside of enough. Addressing her remarks to Lucy, she admitted that yes, it was a fine day, but she found the wind rather chilly, especially now she had stopped. Without further conversation she ordered her coachman to proceed.

'Phew, I thought she was about to quiz us about where we were going,' Lucy said, totally unaware of her *faux pas*. 'I would not put it beyond her to think we had an assignation, though what it has to do with her, I do not know. And why did she stare at you so particularly, I should like to know. You do not have two heads.'

'Perhaps I am a curiosity,' Emma said, very conscious of her tanned complexion, though it was beginning to fade. 'Like the exhibits at Bullock's.'

'Fustian! Let us forget all about her. Look, they are playing cricket over there. Shall we go and watch?'

The match, they discovered on drawing nearer, was one between a team from the Prince of Wales's Own Regiment, two of whom were batting, and another made up of naval officers. Lucy laughed and clapped with everyone else, calling out, 'Oh, bravo!' when a particularly good stroke was made.

Emma began to feel a little uneasy. 'Lucy, dear, do not speak so loudly,' she whispered. 'People are staring at us.'

Before Lucy could reply, there was a shout of 'Look out!' and the spectators suddenly parted in front of them. Emma caught a glimpse of a young man running backwards to catch a well-struck ball and the next moment he had collided with Lucy and sent her sprawling on the grass.

The ball, indeed the game, was forgotten as he scrambled to his feet and put out his hand to help the young lady to rise. 'My apologies, ma'am. I did not mean... Are you hurt?'

'No, no,' she said, setting her bonnet straight and brushing down her skirt. 'Think nothing of it.'

'Oh, but I do. I cannot tell you how sorry I am. Captain Fergus O'Connor, ma'am, your servant.' He executed a perfect leg, though he was not wearing a coat and his shirt sleeves were rolled up to reveal muscular arms.

'I think you had better retrieve the ball and return to the game,' Lucy said, giving him one of her enchanting smiles. 'They are all waiting for you.'

'Then they may wait until I discover who you are.'

'Lucy...' Emma warned.

'Lucy,' he said, grinning at Emma for inadvertently

telling him what he wanted to know. 'That's a peach of a name to match a peach of a girl.'

'Sir, you are impertinent,' Emma retorted.

'So I may be,' he said, laughing. 'But I don't see the little lady objecting.'

Emma took Lucy's arm. 'Come, my dear, we really must be going. Your brother, the Marquis, will be looking for us.' And with that she eased her charge away.

'I shall find you again, never fear,' the Captain called after them, as he rejoined his fellows.

'Why did you say that?' Lucy demanded, looking over her shoulder to watch him return to his place on the field. 'Dominic will not be looking for us.'

'He will if we are not home soon,' Emma said. 'And I have a feeling he might be very displeased if he knew. Don't you know a lady should never speak to a strange man without an introduction?'

'It was not my fault the Captain bowled me over…'

'Emma laughed. 'In more ways than one.'

'Don't be silly. I am not such a goose as to be taken in by empty flattery.'

'I am glad to hear it.'

'He was handsome though, wasn't he?'

'Do you think so? I can think of handsomer.'

'Who? Do tell.'

'No, I will not,' she said, thinking of Lord Besthorpe. Now, there was a handsome man and the lady who married him might think herself very fortunate indeed. The more she saw of him, the more she admired him. And the more she admired him the more she regretted deceiving him. She would so much have preferred to be open and truthful. She was honestly beginning to doubt they would ever be able to discover anything about their father's exile. It had happened so long ago. Oh, if only…

She brought herself up short and her voice, when she spoke, was brisk. 'I do think we should hurry, Lisa will be bringing in the tea tray before we get home.'

Having decided to say nothing to his lordship about the walk in the park, the girls were both disconcerted when, two days later, Lady Clarence paid a call and brought up the subject herself. It would not have been so bad if Dominic had not decided to stay and take tea with them, but as it was they were obliged to listen in growing mortification as she lectured him on the evils of allowing unmarried young ladies out alone.

'Not a soul with them,' she said, with the feathers on her hat nodding in time with her many chins. 'Not even a footman. My dear Cavenham, I cannot think that you would have consented to it. Why, half the *ton* was there and witnessed it, and not a scrap of shame between them, bowing and smiling to all and sundry. Why, your sister even exchanged a nod with that rakeshame, Brummell. Everyone knows he is in disgrace with the Regent.'

Emma was desperately worried and longed to offer a defence, but she was wise enough to know that answering back would make matters worse. She looked at Lucy, but that young lady was studying the toes of her kid slippers.

'Lady Clarence, I thank you for bringing your concerns to my attention,' Dominic said solemnly. 'But I think you worry unduly. My sister and her companion had only got down from the carriage for a short walk; our coachman was not very far away, I do assure you.'

'I saw no coach.'

'Perhaps not, but it was there and Nobbs was watching over them.'

Emma was horrified to think that he felt obliged to lie

to cover their indiscretion, something she was sure he would not do unless there was no other way. It did not bode well for her once Lady Clarence had taken her leave and his lordship would be free to give rein to his undoubted displeasure. She was sure her dismissal was only moments away.

'Then I say no more,' her ladyship said, rising and picking up her gloves and reticule ready to depart. 'But your sister needs a proper duenna to watch over her, if she ain't to make a cake of herself and you too, and I ain't afraid to say it to your face, Cavenham. Your dear mama was my friend and she would wish me to point out where you are going wrong.'

Emma saw Dominic's brown eyes harden and his jaw tighten and she knew the good lady had gone too far, though he was far too polite to tell her so. She exchanged glances with Lucy, who had realised, as she had, that the brunt of his annoyance would land on their heads. He rose as the footman came in answer to his summons to show the lady to the front door.

'Thank you, my lady,' he said, polite as always. 'But Lucy has a very able companion in Miss Woodhill, and I have every faith in her.'

Her ladyship favoured Emma with a look which clearly revealed what she thought of that arrangement. It made Emma throw up her head and meet her gaze with clear green eyes. She could not be subservient to such a one, not even to please Lord Besthorpe.

As soon as Lady Clarence had taken her leave, his lordship sat down again and looked from his sister to Emma. 'I do dislike gabble grinders telling me how I should go on,' he said, in a voice that had lost the silky charm of a moment, before. 'But can you tell me why I should not instantly dismiss you?'

Lucy jumped to her feet, stricken. 'Dominic, you can't do that. It wasn't Emma's fault and we were not doing any harm…'

'You were harming my good name and your reputation,' he said repressively. 'Please go to your room. I wish to speak to Miss Woodhill alone.'

Lucy hesitated. 'Please don't turn her off, Dominic. I will be good, I promise.'

'Do as I say, Lucilla.'

Lucy knew that when he used her full name he was very cross indeed, and decided there was nothing for it but to obey. Arguing would only make him more obdurate. 'Very well.' She put a hand on Emma's shoulder as she passed her on the way to the door. 'Don't let him bully you, Emma. You did nothing wrong.' With that she left the room, closing the door with a sharp snap that was almost a bang.

Emma turned from watching her go, to see a smile twitching at the corners of his lordship's mouth. It was gone in an instant. 'Do you think Lady Clarence was right?' he asked her.

'That Lucy was making a cake of herself, my lord? I am afraid I am not familiar with the term.'

Unable to repress it, he gave way to laughter. 'Oh, dear, I am supposed to be reprimanding you. How can I do that when you look at me with those incredible eyes, pretending innocence? I am perfectly sure you know exactly what was meant.'

She relaxed and allowed herself a little smile. 'If I do, then I deny the accusation. The only person to make a fool of herself is Lady Clarence.'

'Now, I think you go too far. Kindly remember that you are employed as a servant.'

For a moment she had forgotten it. 'I beg your pardon, my lord.'

The apology was made promptly but there was no meekness in it. She was proud, was Miss Emma Woodhill, too proud for a servant. Who was she? Where had she come from? Why was he so taken with her that he had no heart to dismiss her?

'Was her ladyship right?' he repeated. 'Should my sister have a proper duenna?'

'My lord, it is not for me to comment on Lady Clarence's opinion of me.' She stopped. Just why had he asked that question? A moment ago he had been laughing, making her think all would be well and now he looked serious again. 'As for her reference to a *proper* duenna, how can she know whether I am proper or not? I can see no harm in Miss Besthorpe taking a stroll in the park with me in attendance. No harm could have come to her, there were hundreds of people about...'

'Quite.'

Emma was suddenly reminded of Mrs Goodwright's book of etiquette. It had been published many years before, but its truisms were as relevant now as they had been then. One was meant to stick by the rules.

'I am sorry, my lord,' she said, really penitent now. 'I did not think we were doing anything wrong, or I would never have suggested it.'

'Not so much wrong as ill-advised,' he said. 'You must have known you needed an escort for such an outing.'

'No, my lord.'

'Surely Miss Mountforest did not go about Calcutta without a male escort?'

Emma could not help the ghost of a smile which flitted across her face, but she instantly stifled it. 'I am afraid she did, my lord, though there were Indian servants if she felt she had need of one.' She stopped, feeling she was treading on quicksand. 'And, of course, I was there.'

'Then things are done very differently in India, don't you think?' He was speaking softly and she was not deceived into thinking he was going to be easy on her, but neither had he sent her packing immediately as he had done the unfortunate Rose.

'They must be,' she said. 'I am sorry, my lord. I would not, for the world, lead Miss Besthorpe astray or embarrass you with your friends.'

He was laughing again, puzzling her even more. 'Lucy does not need anyone to tell her how to fall into a bumblebath, she has been doing that all her life, and neither do I class Lady Clarence as a friend, but the truth is that she is an inveterate gossip and she does have a deal of influence. A bad word from her and Lucy could be ostracised…'

'Oh, my lord, I am so sorry.' Emma could stand no more of this gentle prodding and rose to her feet. 'I will leave at once.'

'Sit down, Miss Woodhill. I said nothing of leaving. Lucy would never let me hear the last of it.'

'But…' She subsided into her chair again.

'Tell me about Miss Mountforest,' he asked, taking the opportunity he had been waiting for ever since she had first mentioned the lady's name.

Emma felt decidedly uncomfortable. 'What do you wish to know?'

'Was she a mature lady, old perhaps? That would account for her being so independent.'

'No, she was the same age as me.'

'And you have the same Christian names.'

'Yes, I was named for her.'

'You were more friend than servant, then?'

'I suppose you could say that.' She paused and then decided to plough on. 'That is perhaps why I am such a poor companion to Miss Besthorpe, my lord. I thought I should go on in the way I had in India. I was obviously mistaken.'

'Now you have told me that, of course, I understand, but I am still curious about Miss Mountforest. Do you know where she is now?'

Oh, surely he was not intending to write to her? She wished she had realised, when she penned that letter, the trouble it would cause, that she would be tangled in a web of her own making. If only she could go back in time, she would never have tried such a ploy. She had chosen to steer a course as near to the truth as she could, thinking it would be easier to deal with questions about life in India if she could answer with something approaching veracity.

How was she to know she would fall in love with the Lord Besthorpe? She *had* fallen in love with him, there was no doubt of that in her mind. How could she have foreseen that every untruth she told would build a barrier between them which would become more and more insurmountable with every day that passed? The guilt of it lay heavily on her heart; it was almost a physical pain. He was looking at her now with those intelligent brown eyes, waiting for an answer.

'I am afraid she left Calcutta when I did, my lord,' she said, choosing her words with care, so as not to add to her lies. But it was still deception and only increased her burden.

Her evasive reply served only to convince him that

there was something smoky going on. Either she was not who she said she was, or she had never known Miss Mountforest. It was not unknown for servants to forge references, but why choose that name? And why did he think, in spite of all the evidence, that she was not a natural deceiver? If he probed long enough he was sure he would elicit the truth, but he was reluctant to pursue that path. The result would give him no alternative but to dismiss her, which he did not want to do.

Lucy had really taken to her and he knew that she could influence his sister for the better, if only she could be prevented from making any more mistakes in protocol. He had to admit she was a pleasure to have about the house. In the space of a few days she had made herself agreeable to everyone, servants included, for she was always cheerful and never grumbled. Her ready smile brightened his day and he knew he would miss her if she left. Besides, he was still curious.

'It is of no consequence,' he said, noticing how his words made her suddenly relax and let out her breath, as if she had been holding it in apprehension. He smiled. 'I am sure you are intelligent enough to learn what is right and proper, given a little instruction, so in future when you are in any doubt, come to me. If I am not available, err on the side of caution.'

'You mean I may stay?'

'Yes, you may stay. Now, go and find my sister. She will be impatient to know the verdict.'

Emma rose and bobbed a curtsey, something she had trained herself not to mind doing. 'Thank you, my lord.'

She hurried away, glad of the reprieve, even though she did not expect it to last. He was suspicious of something, though she was not sure exactly what had alerted him. Should she leave before it all became impossible to bear? But the thought of tramping the streets looking for work again and having nowhere to live in the meantime, deterred her.

What was more, the prospect of never seeing him again made her miserable; he had become the focal point of her existence.

Perhaps she ought to tell him the truth, confess to her deception, beg his pardon. He was a forgiving kind of man, he had proved that. Although she had deceived him over her name and her experience as a companion, none of it had been directed at him personally.

If she told him the truth, would he understand? Would he allow her to stay, keep her secret? He might even be able to tell her something about Viscount Mountforest. It was not unlikely they were known to each other. In spite of being a different generation, were they perhaps friends? That might make it difficult; his lordship was too loyal to listen to anything said against a friend. But, oh, how she needed to unburden herself, make a clean start.

She could leave, creep away like a thief in the night, which would be an even more despicable thing to do. Where would she find a position as congenial as this? Her working conditions were extremely pleasant and she had become very fond of Lucy. There was also the practical problem of repaying the advance she had been given, which she had not yet earned.

Until she found a suitable opportunity to tell his lordship the truth, or until something happened to make it impossible for her to stay, she would remain, learn to earn her wage and her keep. Love, she told herself sternly, did not come into it.

Lucy was in her sitting-room, pretending to read, but

as soon as she heard Emma's step outside the door, she ran to open it and pulled her into the room.

'Oh, Emma, did he give you a dreadful set-down? I know what he is like when he is on his high ropes, worse than Papa ever was. If he upset you, I shall not forgive him. As for letting you go…'

Emma laughed. 'I am not to be dismissed.'

'Oh, thank goodness. I had a horrible vision of being packed off to Yorkshire and no come-out. I would do anything rather than that. Besides, you are my friend.'

'Then as your friend, it behoves me to make sure you behave properly,' Emma said, allowing herself to be pulled down on to the edge of the bed beside the girl. 'From now on, we follow the rules.'

'Rules! What are rules for if not to be broken?' She paused. 'But you were with him a long time. Whatever were you talking about?'

'Miss Mountforest, for the most part.'

'Sophie?' Lucy queried in surprise. 'What has Sophie to do with it?'

'Sophie? You are mistaken, dear. Miss Mountforest's name is Emma, the same as mine. She was my employer and friend in, India. Surely you remember my saying so that first day?'

'Yes, and I wanted to ask you about her, but Dominic would not let me speak. Heaven knows why, he has nothing to hide.'

Emma was mystified. 'I do not understand.'

'Why, Miss Sophie Mountforest is Dominic's intended. She is the only daughter of Viscount Mountforest. They have been unofficially engaged for ages, but they wouldn't publish it on account of us being in mourning for Papa. We are out of mourning now and

I believe they intend to make the announcement very soon.'

Emma was so shocked she could not speak. No wonder he had been so curious about Miss Emma Mountforest! If he did not know she had been deceiving him, he very soon would, and the knowledge that the object of his desire was her own cousin greatly added to her distress. She had tempted fate and lost, lost her good name, lost her self-respect, lost any chance of happiness.

Why had she imagined he was free? His interest in her had been his natural kindness and consideration, not the early blossoming of something deeper. Oh, what a fool she had been! She would have stood up and rushed from the room if she could have been sure her legs would support her.

'Mountforest is such an unusual name, they must be related,' Lucy went on, all unknowing. 'Did your Miss Mountforest ever speak of kin in England?'

'What? Oh, no, not that I remember.'

'Oh, what a hum!' Lucy began to laugh. 'I wonder what Sophie will say when she hears of it. She has not yet come to town, for you know, we arrived early, but she will be here tomorrow and you will doubtless meet her.' She paused. 'Why, Emma, is anything amiss? You look pale as alabaster. Are you ill?'

'No, a little faint, that is all. I am perfectly recovered now.'

'You poor dear! I am not surprised, I know what Dominic can be like when he is angry and it was not at all your fault.'

'Oh, he was not angry at all,' she said, glad to change the subject. 'In fact, he was very understanding and agreeable…'

Lucy peered into her face. 'Oh, Emma, you haven't developed a *tendre* for him, have you?'

'No, of course not! Good heavens, Lucy, he is engaged elsewhere.'

'Yes, but you did not know it until I told you, did you?' When Emma did not answer she went on, 'You told him the name of your previous employer and yet he said nothing. I wonder what is going on in his head.'

Emma wondered that too. He had questioned her about Miss Emma Mountforest, but he hadn't said a word about his own connection with the Mountforest family. Why? Why had he kept silent? One thing was now certain; any idea she might have had for confessing had been well and truly knocked out of her.

For the first and only time, she wished her father had been a little more thoughtful for the future and made proper provision for her and Teddy; she found it hard to believe he had been so imprudent as to ignore the possibility of his untimely death. He was, after all, a serving soldier. A small income and somewhere to live was all that she asked and instead she had found problem heaped upon problem.

He had left her to look after her young brother, who had so idolised his father that any hint of condemnation must, in Teddy's eyes, be immediately redressed. And who could blame him for that? She should be thinking of her brother, not worrying about her own concerns. Hadn't she and Teddy sworn to clear their father's name and how better to do it than being on the inside, so to speak? Running away was not the answer. She had to play this charade out to the bitter end.

Could she do it? And when she was confronted with

her deception, which was inevitable, could she face her
cousin and, more to the point, her uncle, the Viscount?
What would Dominic say, Dominic whose good opinion
she valued above all other? She dare not think of that.

## Chapter Four

If Emma thought that a good night's sleep might bring the answer to her problem over the imminent arrival of her cousin, she was to be disappointed. It was hours before sleep claimed her, and then she woke at dawn to find all the bedcovers on the floor and nothing resolved. Rest had not been the answer; perhaps physical activity might help drive the demons away.

Dominic kept one or two riding horses along with the carriage horses in the mews and a gallop might clear her head. There would be grooms who would saddle one for her and she did not think his lordship would object. She rose, washed quickly and donned her old dark green taffeta riding habit over a pair of cotton breeches.

She was creeping past Lucy's door towards the back stairs when it was opened and Lucy herself appeared in her nightgown. 'Emma, where are you going so early?' she whispered.

'I couldn't sleep.' Emma, too, was anxious not to wake the household and her voice was low. 'I thought I would go for a ride in the park. His lordship would not mind if I borrowed a mount, would he?'

'Of course not. I'll come too. Come and help me dress.'

'Lucy, I do not think that would be wise, not after the trouble we got into over that walk in the park.'

'Oh, that was nothing. Besides, it's too early for Lady Clarence to be up and about, isn't it? It's too early for anyone of note to be out.'

'I promised your brother I would abide by the rules…'

'What rules? Show me the one that says I may not ride out.'

Emma was reminded of Mrs Goodwright's book of etiquette and, in spite of everything, she smiled. That book had been addressed to ladies, it did not cover the duties of a companion and what to do about a young lady too used to having her own way.

'Why are you smiling?'

'I was thinking about rules.'

'Which are too silly, most of them, and made to be broken,' Lucy said promptly. 'Oh, Emma, let me come. I am wide awake and longing for a ride. Where's the harm?'

'Please go back to bed, Lucy.'

'No, you are up and about, why should I not be? If you don't let me come, I shall simply dress myself and follow you.'

Emma was too overwrought to argue and it was better to have Lucy riding beside her, than let her carry out her threat. She turned into the girl's room and helped her to dress in a becoming dark blue habit with a high-crowned hat with long feathers curling about its brim.

'I didn't know you could ride,' Lucy whispered, as they made their way down the stairs and out of a side door which led down the lane to the mews. 'I should have suggested it before.'

'Everyone rides in India,' Emma said. 'My brother and I were used to going every morning before the sun came up and made it too hot.'

They reached the stables and found Martin, the head groom, who looked at them both and scratched his head in perplexity when asked to saddle two horses. 'But, Miss Lucy, there is only one side saddle,' he said. 'You bein' the only lady in the household…'

'Oh, dear, I had quite forgotten that,' Lucy said.

'It doesn't matter in the least,' Emma put in, with a laugh. 'I have always ridden astride. I'm not at all sure I should know how to go on with a side saddle anyhow.'

'Astride?' queried the astonished Lucy, looking down at Emma's habit. 'How can you do that?'

'If you ask the groom to saddle a horse for me, I will show you,' she said.

Martin went away to do Lucy's bidding, muttering as he did so that he didn't know what his lordship would say to such goings on. And before the streets were even aired! Why, it couldn't be above seven o'clock. Respectable young ladies should be in their beds, not pestering him. Not that he would have dreamed of disobeying Miss Lucy, who was a great favourite of his.

In no time at all, he had saddled both Lucy's mare and a young bay stallion, wondering as he did so if the animal might be a little too strong for the young lady who was not above pint-sized.

He bent to offer Miss Lucy his hand to mount and she was soon in the saddle, then he turned to Emma, wondering a little what he should do. That she would show a great deal of petticoat and leg while mounting he did not doubt and where to put his eyes he did not know. He need not have worried. Emma put her booted foot in his hand and the next minute she was astride the horse, having revealed nothing more than a well-constructed pair of breeches!

As soon as they had trotted out of the yard, he saddled a cob to ride after them. His lordship would give him the bag, for sure, if he let them go alone.

It was a fresh morning and the dew was still on the grass, but it promised to be a fair day, and the two girls were content to trot side by side, enjoying the air. It was too early for most riders and they had the Row to themselves. It was too much of a temptation for Emma, who set her horse to a canter and then a gallop, with Lucy manfully trying to keep up. At the end of the Row, she stopped and waited for Lucy to come up to her.

'My!' Lucy said breathlessly. 'You certainly can ride. Brutus is not exactly easy with a lady on. I tried him once and he didn't like it above half.'

'Perhaps he doesn't like a side saddle,' Emma said. 'It doesn't distribute the weight evenly, you know, and you cannot guide him with both thighs, can you?'

'I never thought of that. Is it comfortable?'

'Very.'

'Do let me try.'

'I am not sure I should allow it,' Emma said dubiously. 'After yesterday, I dare not upset his lordship again. And you are not wearing breeches.'

'What is that to the point when there is no one about to see me? And as for Dominic, how will he get to know? You would not be so foolish as to tell him, would you?'

'No, but...'

'Just a little way, Emma,' she wheedled. 'I won't gallop, I promise.'

Emma relented and, dismounting, helped Lucy mount

Brutus, carefully arranging her full skirt over her legs. 'There! How does that feel?'

'A bit strange, but comfortable.' She dug in her heels, clicked her tongue and Brutus went forward at a walk. 'It's marvellous!' she cried. 'I cannot think why I have never tried it before. Do mount Bessie and come along.'

Emma, who could spring astride most horses without help, found mounting side saddle quite difficult and it was a moment or two before she was seated by which time Lucy had cantered some little way ahead. She was laughing and in great spirits and Emma became concerned that she might not keep her promise not to gallop. She spurred the mare to catch her.

Before she could do so, Brutus had bolted. She had no time to wonder what had caused it, as she set off after her, knowing she had no chance on the gentle mare of stopping the runaway horse. She could hear Lucy crying out and called out to her to hold on.

Other sounds beside the galloping hooves of the mare and her own heavy breathing impinged themselves on her consciousness. Someone was calling out a long way behind her and then, from a path to the side another rider appeared. He passed her in a flash of dark blue jacket and white breeches and was very soon alongside the runaway horse. Reaching out he took the reins from the petrified Lucy and slowly brought the animal to a standstill.

Both horses and riders were blowing hard and Emma had ridden up beside them before either could speak. It was then that Emma, breathless herself, realised that Lucy's rescuer was Captain Fergus O'Connor, and he was grinning with delight. He jumped down and held out his arms to help Lucy down. She fell into them and remained there, even when her feet were safely on the ground, for she was very shaken and her legs would not support her.

'Well, if it isn't my peach,' he said. 'I said I would find you again, but I had no idea it would be so soon.'

'Oh, sir, I am so thankful you came along,' Lucy replied, turning her face up to his. 'You saved my life.'

'And sure, wasn't it well worth the doing,' he said, showing no sign of wanting to release her. 'It was my pleasure.'

'I must add my gratitude,' Emma said, taking Lucy's arm to disengage her from the Captain's embrace. 'I had no idea the horse would bolt like that…'

'Funny creatures, horses,' he mused, as he reluctantly relinquished the beauty. 'They know when someone is nervous and not their master, and if they are the least skittish they play on it. I wonder, ma'am, you allowed it.'

'Oh, do not blame Emma,' Lucy cried. 'I begged to be allowed to ride astride. I had not done it before.'

'I should think not! But stouthearted you were, there's no denying. Allow me to escort you home.'

'There is no need for that, Captain,' Emma said. Now that the incident was over and no one harmed, she was beginning to wonder what her employer would say about the escapade if he learned of it; allowing the Captain to escort them home would lead to questions with uncomfortable answers and that would surely seal her fate. Walking in the park alone was nothing to what had happened here. 'We need not detain you. I should not wish you to be late.'

'Oh, you are not detaining me, ma'am. I had arranged to meet a friend for a ride, but he must have mistaken the time or the date, for there is no sign of him. I have all the time in the world.'

'The Captain could perhaps ride with us as far as the gate,' Lucy suggested, knowing exactly what Emma was thinking. 'No one could object to that surely? I am still feeling a little shaken.'

'To be sure,' he agreed. 'I will see you safely to the highway.' He seized the mare's bridle and brought it round to Lucy. 'This, I think, is your mount, Miss...'

'Besthorpe,' she provided.

'Oh, then the brother you spoke of the other day is the Marquis of Cavenham?'

'Indeed,' she said, putting her small foot in his big hand. He lifted her easily into the saddle, then turned to help her companion only to find that Emma, having already mounted, was sitting easily astride the stallion. He grinned appreciatively and swung into his own saddle, turning his horse to ride between them.

'Captain, I should be obliged if you said nothing of this little episode to anyone,' Emma requested.

'I'm not so sure,' he said. 'After all, if Miss Besthorpe's safety is in your hands, then his lordship should know what a bungle you are making of it.'

'Captain, you are not to say that!' Lucy cried. 'Miss Woodhill is my friend and I will not have her scolded. I asked to come with her when she had no intention of bringing me and I implored her to let me ride astride Brutus. She made it look so easy and I thought I could do it too...'

'Your loyalty does you credit,' he said. 'But if I had not come along...'

'I know and I am truly grateful, but if you tell Dominic any of this I shall never speak to you again.'

He turned towards her, grinning. 'And you will speak to me again, if I remain silent?'

The implication was obvious and Lucy hesitated.

'Why, Captain,' she said, 'if we should meet again by
accident, I could hardly refuse to acknowledge the man
who had saved my life, could I?'

All of which filled Emma with alarm. There was a
great deal more to the business of being a chaperon than
she had realised. It was especially difficult if you were
inexperienced and you had been given charge of a young
lady who was as spirited as she was enchanting.

'Then, of course, I would not dream of saying a word,
you may depend on it.'

'Thank you,' Emma said, knowing that Lucy might
receive a scolding but the punishment awaiting her
would be much, much worse. After yesterday's reprimand she did not think she could bear it. 'Here is the
gate. We must leave you now, Captain.'

'Yes, I am afraid it must be so,' Lucy regretted, her
eyes shining with mischief. 'But I am sure we shall meet
again. I go to Hookham's Library every Wednesday afternoon and for a carriage ride on Thursdays.'

'Then it is no more than *au revoir*,' he said, touching
his three-cornered hat to her.

As soon as he had gone, Emma turned to Lucy. 'Lucy,
dear, I do not think you should have encouraged him.
I'll wager he will be at Hookham's on Wednesday looking for you.'

'I hope he may. He is so very handsome, don't you
think? And those dark eyes of his, were so…so bright
with humour. And don't you think he had the most
shapely legs in those breeches?'

'Lucy!' Emma exclaimed, but the conversation was
suddenly cut short as they became aware that someone
was riding very close behind them. They turned in uni-
son to see the groom on the cob, who had mysteriously
appeared to see them home.

'Martin, where did you spring from?' Lucy demanded.

'I couldn't let you go out alone, Miss Lucy. His lordship would have had my...' he paused to look for an alternative to the word he had been going to use. '...my stuffing, if I had.'

'How long have you been behind us?'

'If you mean, miss, did I see you being carried away by the stallion and me not able to do a thing about it, being so far behind, then yes I did, and I wish I had not, to be sure. What his lordship will say of it, I dare not think.'

'Dominic is not to know, Martin, do you hear? He might scold me and ring a peal over you, but poor Emma would be given her marching orders. I forbid you to say a word, not one word, not about me riding astride, nor being bolted with, nor...'

'Your rescuer, miss? I understand. But if he should ask...'

'Now, why should he? We have been out for a gentle hack and there's nothing more to it.'

He sighed heavily as they turned down the lane to the mews at a sedate walk. He was very fond of the Marquis's young sister and, like so many others, he could not refuse her. 'Very well, Miss Lucy. I will keep silent, though what will come of it, I do not know.'

Emma did not know either. If she had not been so concerned with her own problems, she might have remembered Dominic's stricture to err on the side of caution and been more forceful with Lucy; if that were unsuccessful, she should have given up the idea of riding herself. Once again she had failed her charge; instead of finding a way out of her dilemma she had only deepened it.

She devoutly hoped that Lord Besthorpe would never

hear of the escapade because there would be no second
reprieve. And then her disquiet over the ride was totally
eclipsed by the arrival of her cousin that same afternoon.

Dominic clattered down the companionway to Captain
Greenaway's cabin, feeling rather pleased with himself.
The cargo of the *Silken Maid* had made an exceptionally
good profit and the Captain was due to set sail again on
the next tide with both a full load and funds enough to
fill the hold for the return journey.

They greeted each other cordially and spent a few
minutes discussing the manifest, while the cargo of tin,
tapestries and furniture was being loaded. The silver bul-
lion, its most valuable cargo, had already been stowed
under strict security. The brig would return with cotton,
silks, spices, tobacco and indigo dye, besides precious
gems.

'Buy more diamonds like that big one, if you can,'
Dominic instructed the Captain, who also acted as his
agent. 'It was of excellent quality and the jeweller made
a very fine job of cutting and setting it.'

'The young lady, was no doubt, pleased with it?'

'She isn't in town, so she hasn't seen it yet, but she
will be here soon and then I shall find a suitable occasion
to give it to her.'

The captain smiled. 'May I offer my felicitations?'

'Indeed, you may, and I thank you.' He paused.
'There is something else I would like you to do when
you reach Calcutta. I should like you to make enquiries
about a Miss Emma Mountforest. She may still be living
in India or she may not, but I should like to know her
whereabouts. And while you are at it, ask about Miss
Woodhill too.'

'Miss Woodhill?' the Captain queried in surprise.

'You mean the young lady who travelled as a passenger with us?'

'Yes. Not a word to anyone, mind. This is personal business and I do not want it noised abroad.'

'I understand.'

Dominic held out his hand. 'Bon voyage, my friend.'

He could rely on Greenaway and he might be able to shed some light on the mystery which had been plaguing him ever since he had first spoken to Miss Woodhill. It would be some time before the Captain returned with the answers; in the meantime, he would try and learn a little more from the lady herself, that is, if he could prevail upon her to stay under his roof. He had an uncomfortable feeling she might flee at any moment after the dressing down he had been obliged to give her. She had accepted it, though whether out of necessity he did not know.

She had reminded him of a fawn, bright-eyed, wary, ready to bolt, and yet there had been pride and humour in her eyes rather than fear. She had been brought up not to be afraid, not to be cowed by a reprimand either.

He was convinced of her courage later that evening when he entered the portals of White's, intending to meet Bertie there and have a hand or two of cards. The first person he saw was Lord Clarence.

The man was almost as portly as the Regent but not half as agreeable. Most of the time Dominic avoided him, but this evening he thought it prudent to listen to what he had to say. He did not want him going back to his wife with more tales of the unacceptable behaviour of the Besthorpes.

'Clarence! How do you do?'

'I am well, as you see.' He looked about him for seats.

Most had been taken by players and those still vacant were on tables where the cards were already being shuffled. 'Can we adjourn for a spell? Want to speak to you.'

'Of course,' Dominic said amiably, realising that his lordship was about to reinforce the unsolicited advice his wife had offered and he would have to appear grateful all over again. He led the way into another room, which the members used for smoking and reading newspapers. He indicated an armchair in a corner and sat himself in another. 'What can I do for you?'

'I'm not one to beat about the bush, Cavenham, as you well know,' he said, pulling a snuff box from his pocket and taking a pinch. 'Thing is, wouldn't want you to find yourself in a coil for want of a word in your ear.' He put the snuff to his nostril, took a deep sniff and immediately set to sneezing so hard, Dominic pulled away out of reach.

'Very good of you, to be sure,' he murmured, wondering what was coming.

'Thing is,' the older man continued. 'Was out early the other morning. Saw you sister and that article she seems always to have with her these days…'

'Miss Woodhill is Lucy's companion, my lord, not an article.'

'Female, is it? I could have sworn she was the other gender, at least before I got close enough to realise my mistake. Riding astride she was. In breeches.'

'She was dressed as a man?' Even the usually placid Dominic was taken aback by this.

'No, course not. Skirts on top. But she was astride, no doubt of it, and a bruising rider she is too. Galloped the whole length of the Row and before you say the horse had bolted with her, it had not, for she brought it up as easy as you please.'

Dominic suppressed a smile; he would have liked to witness that, but he wondered how many others had seen it. 'There is only one side saddle in the stables, my lord,' he said, thinking quickly. 'I had been meaning to purchase another for Miss Woodhill, but I have no doubt the young ladies were too impatient to wait. It can have done no harm.'

'On the contrary, it could have done a great deal of harm. I was astonished to see the two of them change horses. Your sister, sir, is evidently not used to a man's saddle. The horse bolted with her.'

Dominic, who had been sitting back in his chair perfectly relaxed, sat forward sharply. 'What happened?'

'You may ask, sir. The companion went after her but I could not see anything but a tragedy about to happen, and set off myself, but I was a long way off and before I reached them, the young lady was saved by the intervention of a naval officer, who had seen all.'

'Do you know him?'

'No, the city is full of officers on half pay. But if you wish, I could make enquiries.'

'No, thank you,' Dominic said. 'I am much obliged to you, but I shall find him to thank him myself.'

'It's that gel you should be thinking about. Not a suitable companion for a well-brought-up young lady. Not suitable at all. Can't think why you took her on.'

Dominic did not know the answer to that either, but he had no intention of admitting it. 'Miss Woodhill is a distant relative—her father and mine were cousins,' he said. 'I promised her papa before he died that I would look out for her. Couldn't go back on my word, even if I wanted to, which I don't. She has a home with us for as long as she wants one.'

'Your generosity will be your undoing, man. If you

want your sister to take well, you had best be advised
to dispense with the services of Miss Woodhill and find
someone who will not lead her into scrapes.'

'Oh, there is not the least need for you to trouble
yourself,' Dominic said, doing his best to remain pleasant, though if the other man had been his own age and
not fat and fifty, he would undoubtedly have given him
a facer. He had no intention of dismissing Miss Woodhill
on the say-so of an old rake like Clarence, whose presence in the park at that hour was questionable. He'd
wager the man was on the way home from a night spent
with his mistress.

'I am perfectly able to conduct the affairs of my own
household. What happened in the park was an unfortunate occurrence to be sure, but no harm was done. A
new side saddle will be procured this very day.' With
that he bade him good evening and left him.

Why he had invented that story about Miss Woodhill
being his relative, Dominic had no idea; it had slipped
out so smoothly he had astonished himself. But what
else could he have done? He had to protect Lucy and
himself, too, for if Sophie heard of it, she would be sure
to have something cutting to say on the matter. It was
not that so much as the overwhelming desire to defend
Miss Woodhill, which had motivated him. And, coupled
with that, was the problem of what to do about her. Now
he had told that hum about her being a relative, he had
made it impossible to dismiss her.

Neither did he want to. He wanted her to stay and it
wasn't just curiosity. He did not really care who she was
or where she had come from. If Greenaway came back
with information which discredited her, he would not
want to hear it. Deep inside him, so deep he refused to

acknowledge it, there was a feeling of unease about the future he had mapped out for himself.

'Why so solemn?' Bertie's voice broke in on his thoughts. 'You look as though you had lost a fortune and found a groat.'

Dominic looked up. 'Oh, it's you, Bertie. Do you mind if we don't play tonight? My mind's not on it.'

Bertie grinned. 'Petticoat problems, eh? Better tell me all about it.'

So Dominic did—at least, he outlined the facts. He did not tell his friend what his feelings were because he did not understand them himself, nor could he put them into words.

'I am intrigued and exasperated,' he said, making an effort to sound rational. 'And what with Clarence and his beastly fat wife making innuendos and offering unwanted advice, I am at a stand. Even if I had been thinking of sending Miss Woodhill away, I wouldn't now. They would be bound to think it was on account of their prompting.'

'Then she will just have to stay, Dominic, old fellow. It don't cost you above pony a year for her wages and board, does it?'

'No, but she is making such a coil of looking after Lucy. It's not that she means any harm; she simply does not understand that what was permissible in India is frowned on here.'

'Sounds as if she'd been gulling you, my friend. In more ways than one.'

'What do you mean by that?' Dominic asked sharply.

'Well, she's a pretty little thing, ain't she?'

'Oh, don't be such a fool, Bertie. Such a thing never entered my head. I am betrothed to Sophie, as you well know. And Miss Woodhill is a lady of breeding.'

'Lady? How do you know?'

'I don't for sure, but I do know there's something smoky about her. I've asked Greenaway to make enquiries in Calcutta. That's if she ever lived there at all.'

'Oh, I do not doubt she did,' Bertie said. 'That brother of hers drops Indian words into his conversation like raindrops on the window. Dashed hard to understand him, half the time.'

'Is he a problem too?'

'No, long way off it. I can't fault his work with the horses and he's a crack rider. My head groom took me up to the gallops to watch him ride Nelson the last time I was home and I put the watch on him. It's a winning combination, no doubt of it. I'm going to put him up at the July meeting and as both horse and jockey will be unknown, the odds will be good. Put some on him, Dominic.'

'Perhaps I will, but it won't solve my problem, will it?'

'Can't see that you've got a problem, old man,' Bertie said cheerfully. 'Sophie's coming to town soon, ain't she? She'll take charge of both girls. Tell you all about the Indian side of her family, too.'

'Yes, but she never told me there was an Indian side and if it is something she would rather not talk about, I would as lief not mention it.'

'Don't be a numbskull, man, it ain't a secret. Her father had a younger brother went out to India over some scandal or other; killed someone. It was years ago, before either of us was out of leading reins, but I remember my parents talking about it. All forgotten now, I expect, which is why Sophie didn't tell you. She may not even know of it.'

Although the Mountforests were aristocracy and the

Cosgroves mere yeomanry, they were near neighbours and had always been friends; Bertie had known Sophie since both were toddlers. It was Bertie who had introduced Sophie to Dominic during a college vacation when she had been staying at his home and they had ridden over to Cavenham. He had stood by with a half-amused, half-wry expression when it had become apparent that Dominic had fallen head over heels in love. It was a match that had been encouraged by their respective parents, especially Viscount Mountforest, who deplored his daughter seeing so much of the impecunious Bertie and needed to separate them.

'Then I shall certainly not say anything,' Dominic said. 'But you are right about one thing. Sophie will take both girls in hand.'

Emma and Lucy were sitting in the drawing room, making out the invitations to Lucy's come-out ball which was to be held in two weeks' time, at the beginning of the Season proper. As they wrote the cards in their best italic script, Lucy gave Emma a pertinent, often amusing, resumé of each of the proposed guests.

'Lord and Lady Clarence,' she said. 'You have met her ladyship, so I need not describe her. Her husband is a bumble bee, busy, striped and with a sting in the tail. He's always bustling about over nothing at all and he wears striped yellow and black waistcoats, perhaps because, in spite of being old, he fancies himself as a member of the Hellfire Club and that's their uniform.'

Emma was laughing and about to ask for an explanation of what the Hellfire Club was, when a footman announced Lady Mountforest and Miss Mountforest. Her laughter died on her lips.

Although she had been half expecting it, Emma was

so startled she dropped the cards she was holding and they scattered all over the carpet. She was on her hands and knees trying to retrieve them, when the ladies entered.

'Lady Mountforest! Sophie!' Lucy rose to greet the visitors. 'We have been expecting you, but not knowing exactly when I am afraid Dominic is not at home to greet you.'

By the end of this speech her ladyship and her daughter had advanced into the room and Emma, having retrieved the cards, was rising to her feet in front of them, acutely conscious of her old brown bombazine and its rather limp lace collar. Her ladyship was very tall and angular, made taller by the vertical green and mauve stripes of her taffeta gown complemented by a green satin turban embellished with several bronze-painted ostrich plumes. She seemed to be looking down at Emma from a great height.

'My lady,' Lucy said, making a neat little curtsy. 'Please allow me to present Miss Emma Woodhill. She has lately come from India to be my maid and companion.'

'From India?' This from Sophie, who had done no more than glance at Emma before turning back to Lucy. 'Why does everything seem to come from India these days?'

'Does it? I did not know that.' Emma, who had just completed a curtsy to Lady Mountforest, turned to her cousin who was almost as tall as her mother and several inches taller than Emma. Her hair beneath a fetching straw bonnet trimmed with rosebuds was fair, though there was a gleam of deeper gold here and there which might, in a darker person, have been auburn, as Emma's was. Her eyes were lighter than Emma's, being a pale blue; her mouth was well-defined and her teeth perfect. Her figure was willowy beneath the pelisse she wore. Its open skirt of white muslin fell straight from the ruched bust and revealed a blue satin slip.

Emma was forced to admit that she was beautiful, but was thankful that there seemed to be no family resemblance. She knew she ought to bob a curtsy but she could not bring herself to do it. Instead she busied herself returning the invitation cards to the sofa-table.

'Oh, Sophie is only bamming,' Lucy explained. 'It is because Dominic trades with India and she does not at all approve.' She smiled at Emma. 'This, as I am sure you have guessed, is Miss Sophie Mountforest.'

'Lucilla, dear, I am sure you must know that it is not done to introduce *servants*,' Sophie said, looking down at Emma with an air of disdain which set her hackles rising.

Emma did not wait for Lucy's usual protest that Miss Woodhill was her friend, but excused herself and left the room. If she had stayed another minute she would have burst. She stood for a moment in the hall, leaning against the door, breathing heavily. So that was her cousin!

She had been telling herself, ever since she had heard about her, that Sophie could not be blamed for the sins of her father; believing she must be a warm, agreeable sort of person if Lord Besthorpe loved her, she would do her best to like her. But she did not. She could not. That sneer of superiority and the put-down she had given poor Lucy were enough to convince Emma that she was far from agreeable and warm. She was a cold fish. How could Dominic, who was gentle and caring, love such a one?

'Lucilla, wherever did Dominic find that dowd?' Sophie's voice came clearly through the closed door. 'I

never saw such a little brown mouse. India, you say. I
suppose she must be Eurasian with that dark skin. She
will have to go. We cannot have you chaperoned about
town by such a one. We shall be the laughing stock of
the *ton*.'

'She is my companion, not yours,' Lucy retorted val-
iantly. 'And if Dominic finds her suitable, it is not for
you to disparage her.'

'We shall see. I shall speak to Dominic as soon as he
decides to put in an appearance.'

'Lucilla, have you forgot your manners?' This from
her ladyship. 'Are you not going to offer us refreshment?'

'Oh, I am so sorry. Of course.'

Emma heard the bell jangling and decided to make
her escape before she was discovered and heard any
more unpleasant comments. She went up to her bedroom
and sat on the bed to think.

How frequently would Sophie and her mama come
calling? The Mountforests' town house was in Park
Lane, which was not so very far away and no doubt there
would be a great deal of to-ing and fro-ing, with a wedding to arrange. Could she possibly avoid coming face
to face with them again?

Would his lordship take any notice of Sophie? He had
certainly disliked Lady Clarence's advice; she had seen
the set of his jaw and the glint in his eye which told her
that he would not be pushed, but his bride's wishes
might carry more weight. What about Lucy's wishes?
Poor man, it would put him in a dreadful quandary.
Perhaps she ought to make it easy for him and disappear.

Heaving a huge sigh of regret, she stood up, fetched
her portmanteau out of the cupboard and began stuffing
her clothes into it, though where to go she did not know.

She left the garments she had bought with the advance on her wages; they did not belong to her. The trunk containing a few precious possessions she had brought with her from India, including the tiger skin, would have to be sent for later.

She had almost finished and was picking up her burnous to throw over her shoulders, wondering how she could creep from the house without being seen when Lucy stormed into her room and flung herself on Emma's bed.

'Sophie's Turkish treatment of you is the outside of enough, Emma. Oh, I know she is to marry Dominic, but I truly cannot think it will make him happy. She is so domineering. I do hope I find a husband before the Season is finished, for I declare I could never live with them.' Suddenly becoming aware of Emma's bulging portmanteau, she stopped. 'Emma, whatever are you doing?'

'Leaving. It is clear I am an embarrassment to you and to his lordship. I do not want to be the cause of dissent.'

'Fustian! I will not let you go. I need you. I… Oh, Emma, never have I had a friend before, not a proper friend, not one who is all my own. If you leave me, I shall be at the mercy of that termagant.'

'Do not be silly, Lucy. She can't be that bad.'

'Oh, she is! I do not know what Dominic sees in her, except, of course, she is all sweetness and light when he is about. I am sure that they won't have been married five minutes before he sees her in her true colours.'

'Oh, I do so hope you are wrong. I should hate to think he was made unhappy.' Which was nothing less than the truth, though she wished she had not spoken;

Lucy would only repeat her assertion that she had developed a *tendre* for her brother.

Strangely, she did not find anything out of the ordinary in, Emma's remark. 'I am not wrong. She is downstairs now, scolding him for not being here to greet her and wheedling him into a good humour at the same time. It is sickening.'

'You have had your brother to yourself for so long,' Emma said, realising his lordship must have returned while she had been packing and she would not now be able to leave without confronting him. It was going to be a very painful interview, made worse by her very strong desire to stay. 'Do you not think you might be just a twinge jealous?'

'No, for if he were going to marry you, I should be as pleased as ninepence.'

'You flatter me, Lucy, but it is nothing to the point.'

'He won't let you go. I know him. Once he digs in his heels, nothing will shift him.'

'I rather fancy it is a family trait,' she said, with a weary smile.

'There you are, then! Now unpack that bag and change your dress for dinner. Dominic has invited the ladies to dine with us and though they have gone home to change, they will be back directly. I shall need your support.'

'Oh, Lucy, it will only cause more trouble…'

'I had not thought you such a pudding heart, Emma. Where's your pride?'

Where was it indeed? Was running away the answer? She was Sophie Mountforest's equal, wasn't she? She had a sudden vision of her papa, pulling her on to his lap and telling her the tale of the injustice done to him and her childhood anger suddenly reasserted itself. She laughed. 'Do you know, I had almost forgotten I had any. You have made me remember it.'

Dinner was an uncomfortable meal, during which Sophie and her mother conversed almost exclusively with Dominic, addressed a polite word or two to Lucy, but ignored Emma as if she did not exist. Emma, who had put on her new amber crepe and allowed Lucy to dress her hair, was content with that arrangement. She did not feel like joining in and it gave her ample opportunity to observe.

The ladies were lavishly dressed in shimmering gauze over silk, her ladyship's a vibrant red, Sophie's pale aquamarine, while Lucy's was white muslin, as befitted a young lady not yet come out. Dominic was splendid in an evening coat of dark mulberry velvet, matching pantaloon trousers, a pink brocade, waistcoat draped with a watchchain, a fob and a quizzing glass, and a starched cravat which must have taken his man hours to tie.

They were going to the theatre after the meal, all except Emma, whose presence would not be required, there being ample people to chaperon Lucy. Emma would have liked to have gone. She had never been to the theatre in London, though she had enjoyed going to theatrical entertainments in India, which were usually of Indian origin, ancient mythical stories told in dance. She had never seen a Shakespearean play in her life.

She sat, picking at her food, allowing the conversation to ebb and flow around her, dreaming of being taken to a play by Lord Besthorpe. Both would be lavishly dressed in the latest mode, they would have a box almost on top of the stage, and he would be attentive, entertaining and knowledgeable. He would take her hand and gaze into her eyes with so much love…

She was jolted out of her fantasy by the sound of her name, being uttered by the man of her dreams. 'Miss Woodhill, you are very quiet and a trifle pale. Are you well?'

'Perfectly, my lord.'

'Would you care for some of this Rhenish cream? It has a very delicate flavour.' Rose, who had been reinstated, had just served him and hovered with the dish. 'Serve Miss Woodhill, Rose.'

'Thank you.'

She didn't look well, or happy, he decided. What was making her so sad? What had clouded those lovely eyes? Guilt, perhaps? If it were, she had shown no signs of it before. She had always sparkled, defending herself vigorously when censured and offering firmly held opinions on a great many subjects when they had dinner table discussions. Tonight she was silent. Was it Sophie's presence?

He looked from one to the other. Sophie knew nothing of the letter of reference Emma had given him. He had intended to show it to her, ask her about Miss Emma Mountforest, but when she and her mother arrived this afternoon, she had no sooner greeted him, than she began complaining about Lucy's companion. Highly unsuitable, she had said, half-Indian, no doubt. He must have been off his head.

She had softened it by saying he was a man only lately come to his inheritance and was not used to taking on female staff. He must leave it all to her.

It was the first time they had quarrelled and though they had made it up, he had decided to say nothing of that letter. Sophie had no liking for India or anything Indian and she would not be fair to Miss Woodhill.

On the other hand, Miss Woodhill must realise it was likely that there was a connection between his bride-to-be and her previous employer. If she had been telling him the truth, she would surely have remarked on it. But if she had been lying, it would account for her looking so melancholy; she knew she was about to be exposed. Why, then, did he feel this surge of compassion for her?

'It must be hard for you to accustom yourself to life in England,' Sophie said, addressing Emma for the first time. 'I am persuaded it is not at all what you are used to.'

'No, for the climate is very different.'

'Oh, I meant other than the climate. We all know that India is very uncomfortable and dangerous to one's health. I would not for the world risk going there. I was speaking of Society.'

'British Society is the same the world over,' Emma said, recovering some of her poise. 'Wherever English people gather, they make a little England for themselves. It is a great shame they are so insular because they miss learning about other cultures. India is full of interest. Its people are by no means uncivilised, you know.'

Sophie laughed. 'Well, you would say that, wouldn't you, being one of them.'

'Sophie!' Dominic exclaimed.

'It is all right, my lord,' Emma put in quietly. 'If I were half-Indian, Miss Mountforest, I would not be ashamed to admit it. Some of my best friends are Indian. In fact, my maternal grandfather's second wife was a Bengali. I loved her.'

'Then I wonder you made the journey if you found them so much more congenial.'

'I had my reasons,' she said softly. 'But they are private.' She stopped, realising she had given the young lady a set-down, which was a very unwise thing to have done. She looked at Dominic, wondering what his reaction might be, and was surprised to see a twinkle in his eyes and twitch of amusement on his lips. For some reason she could not fathom it made her angry.

He sensed the danger and quickly interposed. 'I think if we are not to miss the curtain going up, we ought to go. I will order round the carriage while you ladies fetch your cloaks. Miss Woodhill, you need not wait up for Lucy, I am sure she can manage.'

'I should hope so!' Lucy said, rising. 'If we are going to supper afterwards, we shall be very late. Come, Emma, you can help me on with my cloak.' She left the room with Emma on her heels. Behind them, Emma could hear Dominic remonstrating with Sophie and it gave her a *frisson* of impish pleasure.

By the time they reached Lucy's room, that young lady was convulsed with giggles. 'Oh, Emma! Did you see Sophie's face! She was furious.'

'I am sorry I spoke in that fashion,' Emma said, fetching Lucy's velvet cloak from the wardrobe. 'I did not wish to embarrass you or his lordship.'

'I wasn't embarrassed and neither was Dominic. And it just goes to show, you are not without courage. I don't think I could have stood up to her like that.'

'I wish I hadn't. It was very stupid of me.'

'Was your grandmother really Indian?'

'She wasn't really my grandmother. Grandpa married her after his first wife died. He was lonely, you see...'

'One day, you must tell us all about her and the rest of your family. And India. The proper India, I mean, not the British Society. Now, I must go. I wish you were coming with us. Will you be bored on your own?'

'No, for I intend to answer my brother's letter, and do some mending. Now, off you go, I can hear the carriage coming to the door.'

Teddy's letter had arrived the previous day and filled her with a great longing to see him again, to drop this dreadful pretence just for a few hours and be herself. She wondered if he felt the same, but he had given no indication that he did. His letter was full of his new life: stories of the horses, which he enthused were prime beasts, and of Mr Cosgrove's offer to let him ride Nelson in a race at Newmarket, which was only five miles away.

Being a jockey was not at all like being a humble *syce*, he told her; you were looked up to and praised and, if you won a race, you were given a percentage of the prize money. He had made friends with some of the other lads and she was not to worry about him. It was not until the end that he mentioned what he chose to call 'their crusade'.

'I have discovered that the Mountforest country seat is a dozen miles away and that Mr Cosgrove's father and the Viscount were great friends, though I have not yet seen him. Is it not a small world?'

It was smaller than he realised, she thought, as she sat down to reply. Mountforests, Cosgroves and Besthorpes, all connected, all friends. Exposing Viscount Mountforest would have repercussions all round and suddenly she was not sure if she wanted to do it, even if they could. The last thing she wanted to do was make enemies of Lord Besthorpe and his delightful sister.

The visit to the theatre had been a great success, Lucy told, her the following morning. The play was a farce and the audience had been every bit as entertaining as the players. 'And would you believe it,' she said, 'Captain O'Connor was there with some friends.'

'You spoke to him?'

'Oh, no, he was in the stalls, but he looked up and saw me and winked.'

'Good gracious, did his lordship see him?'

'No, Dominic was too busy trying to placate Sophie.'

'What about?'

'I don't know, they were whispering. He was probably still giving her a jobation over the way she spoke to you.'

'Oh, no, surely not. I'm not worth quarrelling over.'

'You'd best let him be the judge of that. He hates injustice and rudeness, even to a servant. Why, you saw how he brought Rose back. He will not let you go on Sophie's say-so.'

Oh, what had she done? She should have kept her mouth firmly closed and refused to rise to the bait. She had always managed to do it in the past when people had shown their ignorance. Why not now, when it was doubly important to remember who she was supposed to be?

'I don't want to talk about them,' Lucy went on. 'I have been thinking about my come-out ball. I mean to invite Captain O'Connor. I want Dominic to make his acquaintance without knowing how things stand.'

'And how do they stand?' Emma asked sharply.

'Oh, you know,' she said vaguely. 'I would like to know him better and how am I to do that, if we move in different circles? The ball will be just the opportunity.'

'But Lucy, you have not been properly introduced. Dominic would never allow it.' It was the first time she had used his lordship's Christian name. It had slipped out so easily, as if it were the most natural thing in the world, and now she was blushing to the roots of her hair. Strangely Lucy did not even notice.

'I shall tell him the Captain is your friend.'

'Mine? How will that serve? I shall not be there.'

'Of course you will. It is not fair that you should miss all the fun. I want you to come, and not as my chaperon either…'

'Your brother would never agree to that. Goodness, I am already a source of annoyance to him. I am sure he wishes he had never hired me.'

'That I know is not the case. And we needn't tell him. It is to be a costume ball with everyone in masks, so we will disguise you.'

'No, Lucy, it is out of the question. You know chaperons are not supposed to dance.'

'But you would enjoy it, wouldn't you?'

'Oh, yes, but I have made so many mistakes over protocol, I wonder why I am still here. There was that walk in the park and I am truly thankful Lady Clarence did not see us at the cricket match or she would have made it impossible for me to stay. And I allowed you to ride astride and nearly had you killed.'

'Dominic doesn't know about that.'

'I hope you are right. And then last night I made matters a hundred times worse by putting Miss Mountforest to the blush. I wonder he has not given me notice long ago.'

'He likes you, that's why.'

Emma looked up startled. 'How do you know?'

'He said you were brave and spirited and independent and he'd be dashed if he was going to let a gaggle of gabble grinders tell him how to run his household.' She

paused, smiling mischievously. 'And I'll tell you something else…'

'I am sure you should not,' Emma murmured, even
though she was longing to know.

'He told Sophie you were a distant relative, cousin of
a cousin, or something like that, and he had promised
your late father he would take care of you and he meant
to do just that.'

'He said that?' Emma was astonished. 'I cannot think
why.'

'To protect you, of course, and silence the gossips.
But don't you see? Even if he does see you and recognise you at the ball, he will not say anything, not if
everyone thinks we are cousins.'

'Twice removed,' Emma said, with a wry smile.

'Oh, that was because most people know our near relatives and anything closer would not have served. Now,
are you going to come?'

'No, of course not,' she said, but she had to admit she
was sorely tempted. She would like nothing better than
to throw off her role as chaperon and go as herself, to
be part of the social scene, to be welcomed as a guest,
even to make a grand entrance, to dance with Dominic.
Oh, especially to dance with Dominic!

'Then I shall plead unwell and not go myself.'

'Lucy, that's nonsense and you know it. You cannot
stay away from your own ball.'

'Oh, yes I can. You do not know how determined I
can be, when I choose. Besides, I do not need a come-
out, I know the man I wish to marry.'

'You do?' Emma was momentarily diverted from the
discussion of whether she should go or not.

'Captain O'Connor.'

'Lucy, you have only met the man on two occasions and that very briefly.'

'Four. You forget the theatre last night and I saw him at Hookham's last week. You were so busy choosing your own books, you did not even see him.'

'Which just proves what a hopeless chaperon I make.'

Lucy giggled. 'Yes, you do, don't you? Much better to be my cousin and my friend. Why, if you come to the ball, you may find a husband for yourself.'

'I am nearly twenty-three, Lucy, well and truly on the shelf.'

'Fustian! You will come and no more argument. The thing is, what shall you wear? I'll have to ask Dominic for some more pin money to buy the material, but he won't trouble himself about what I want it for.'

Emma thought he very well might; he had already scolded Lucy about her extravagance. 'There's no need to go to your brother,' she said, deciding it was better to humour Lucy than have her beg from his lordship on her behalf. 'I have an Indian sari.'

'You have! Oh, show it to me, do.'

Nothing else would serve but they should go to Emma's room at once and view the costume.

'Oh, it is the most beautiful thing in the world,' Lucy, exclaimed when Emma had pulled out her tin trunk and the material emerged from the tissue in which it was wrapped.

There were yards and yards of gossamer silk in a deep gold, green and blue, the colours merging and shimmering in the sunlight from the window, edged with bands of blue, green and black. Yet it was so fine it could be run through the hand like a slender thread. 'How do you wear it? Do put it on and show me.'

Emma laughed and in no time had discarded her west-

ern clothes and put on the short-sleeved blouse and slim
cambric petticoat which went under the garment. Then,
in deft movements which were a mystery to Lucy, she
laid it about her waist in pleats, tucked one end into her
waist and draped the other end round her and back over
her shoulder. She laughed at Lucy's astonished expression. 'Will it do?'

'Do? Why, it is perfect. It makes you… Oh, I cannot
put it into words. You are beautiful, exquisite, and I
never realised it before. Oh, you will knock them all
over. You must not think of staying away. I can't wait
to see Sophie's face. And Dominic's too.'

'But I must be incognito,' Emma said, throwing herself into the spirit of the fantasy, for fantasy it surely
was. 'I must have a new identity.'

'We shall think of something,' Lucy said, full of confidence. 'I know! Captain O'Connor has been to India,
he told me so. He met you out there. You are the daughter of a nabob, very rich, and able to indulge your taste
for Indian dress. You came to England at his invitation.'

'But I would only do that if I were going to marry
him, surely?'

'Well, we can say you are. It will divert everyone
from connecting me with him.'

'And how are you to contrive his invitation?' Emma
was smiling because she did not think, for one minute,
that Lucy was serious.

'Why, he is known to Sir Richard Godfrey, who was
one of his party at the theatre last night, and Sir Richard
is a friend of Dominic's and a perfectly acceptable guest.
They may come together.'

'No, Lucy, that is the outside of enough. It is all very
well to jest with me, but to talk of involving someone

from outside is not to be thought of. Your brother would hear of it and the last thing I want to do is to anger him.'

'He won't find out and if he does, he will think it is all a glorious hoax. He was up to all sorts of pranks when he was a boy. Why, he pretended to be an Indian prince one day and presented himself at Almack's with a blackened face and dressed in magnificent satin trousers and a huge turban. His coat was straight and long and wrapped round with a wide satin belt. He had one of those great curved swords stuck into it.

'Lady Jersey was in such a taking about receiving him, fussing round, not knowing whether to curtsy or give him his right about because he was not in breeches, which is obligatory at Almack's, you know.'

'What happened?' Emma asked, intrigued. That Dominic had a sense of fun she had never doubted. 'Did she let him in?'

'No, he gave himself away by laughing. Everyone took it well, when he said he had done it for a wager. Papa gave him a set-down the next day, but that was all. If he cuts up rough, I shall remind him of that.'

'It's not the same for an adventurous young man, is it?'

'Why should the men have all the adventures?' She paused and took Emma's hand. 'Dear, dear Emma, please do not fail me. I do so want you to be there and Captain O'Connor too. It is very important to me.'

'And how am I to arrive? I can hardly come down from my room.'

'No, silly. I shall contrive to introduce you to Lady Godfrey next time we go for a ride in the park. She is there most afternoons in a hideous yellow barouche. You shall come together as a foursome. It will be easy because Dominic will understand if Miss Woodhill does not wish to attend; after all, being a chaperon at a ball must be the most boring of occupations and there is not the least need with him being there with Sophie and her parents to keep an eye on me. As soon as we go to put on our costumes, you will slip out and meet Fergus who will take you to Lady Godfrey's. That way you will arrive in their carriage.'

It was such an outlandish plan that Emma never thought for one minute that it would work. On the other hand, it made her shiver with excitement just thinking about it. The mysterious woman from India, the beauty who set all the tongues wagging, wondering where she had sprung from, making all the men dance attendance because there is nothing they like so much as an enigma, and it would make all the other ladies jealous. Oh, what a commotion she could cause!

And when she disappeared on the stroke of midnight, just like Cinderella, the conversation would buzz about who she was, where she had gone and they would set about finding her, but without success, for the Godfreys would not have been told the whole truth and who would expect to find her under their host's own roof? It would quite take the wind out of Sophie Mountforest's sails. The trouble was that fantasies rarely happen in real life and she was thankful that Lucy would never get the Godfreys to agree.

However, it seemed that Captain Fergus O'Connor was every bit as persuasive as Lucy when it came to having his own way. Sir Richard, a young man with a fine sense of mischief, fell readily into the plan when Fergus outlined it to him, and his wife, overcome by curiosity, consented to play the vital role of chaperon to the chaperon. It was all arranged one day when Emma stayed indoors nursing a severe headache and Lucy went to the library with no other escort but a footman, who was bidden to wait outside for her.

'There!' she said, after ascertaining that Emma's headache was better and regaling her with her success. 'Was it not clever of me?'

'I would rather say it was mischievous, Lucy. I was not really serious about going, you know.'

'But you must!' Lucy wailed. 'Oh, you will break my heart if you do not. I shall elope. You will be in even worse trouble if I do that.'

'Lucy, you wouldn't.'

'Then just you wait and see.'

Emma was appalled. How, in heaven's name, was she going to get out of it? Or should she simply give in? She was in so much trouble already, that she might as well be hung for a sheep as a lamb. She laughed suddenly. She would go out with a bang, not a whimper.

## Chapter Five

Emma had been caught up in the preparations for the ball, so the setting for it was no surprise to her. The large first floor drawing-room was converted into a ballroom. All the furniture except a few chairs was removed, the carpet was taken up and a small dais for the musicians was set up at one end. The floor was polished until it was as slippery as ice, the crystal chandeliers were taken down, washed and rehung, flowers by the barrowload had been imported and by the afternoon of the great day, were being arranged in enormous vases around the room.

The dining-room which was next door to it was rarely used except on grand occasions, there being a more intimate and convenient room on the ground floor which was normally used for dining *en famille* or when there were only a few guests. Tonight the immense dining table and both sideboards were groaning under the weight of food set upon them. Extra cooks had been called in to help in its preparation and there were additional waiters and footmen galore.

Lord Besthorpe supervised everything himself, dashing from the kitchens to the ballroom, overseeing the staff, stripping off his coat and helping to move the furniture himself. Nothing was too good or too much trouble for his dear sister and he knew that this ball, coming early in the Season, would set the standard for all that followed.

He met Emma coming out of the library, her mauve sarcenet dress covered with a large white apron and the auburn coils of her hair hidden under a starched cap. The gentleman were to leave their cloaks and hats in there and she had just fetched two oil lamps for cleaning, gentlemen being as vain as ladies and needing a good light to adjust their cravats. 'My dear girl, there is no need for you to be doing that,' he said, in surprise. 'There are servants in plenty…'

She smiled. 'Yes, but you have your sleeves rolled up and smuts on your nose, so why not me?'

'Have I?' He grinned, rubbing his nose. 'I am enjoying myself.'

'Then so am I. I want everything to be perfect for Miss Besthorpe. An evening to remember.' To herself she added, 'For me too, because I fancy it will be my last under this roof.' The thought made tears spring to her eyes. She could not go through with this charade. She just could not.

'Why, Miss Woodhill, what is the matter?' He took the lamps from her hands, set them down on the floor and took her elbow to lead her back into the library. 'Now tell me, what is troubling you?'

'Nothing, my lord. Nothing at all.'

'You are homesick and Miss Mountforest doesn't help, does she?'

She looked up at him, startled. 'Miss Mountforest?' Her voice was a whisper of fear and he had to hold himself severely in check otherwise he would have taken her in his arms to comfort her. 'I meant Sophie with her unkind remarks about India. Try to forgive her, she doesn't understand…'

'But you do?'

'I certainly try.' He put his finger under her chin and lifted her face so that she was obliged to look into his eyes. The threatening tears were being manfully withheld but the lovely green eyes were soft with moisture. 'If I have said or done anything to upset you, I ask pardon.'

She blinked hard, hardly daring to meet his gaze. 'You have done nothing, my lord.'

'Then why the tears?'

'There are no tears, my lord. I must have a smut from one of the lamps in my eye.'

'Then let me see.' He took his handkerchief from his pocket and gently inspected her eyes. 'No smuts there.'

She blinked rapidly. 'Thank you, my lord.'

'Oh, what a noddicock I have been! I should have known you would not take it for granted.'

'Take what for granted, my lord?'

'That you would be invited to the ball. You must have been thinking you had been left out…'

'No, my lord, such a thing did not occur to me.'

'Of course you must come. And not as a chaperon. Lucy does not need one tonight. Be our guest.'

Emma was startled. Just how much did he know of Lucy's scheme? He was a deep one and saw more, understood more, than he seemed to and was calling her bluff. Or was he simply being his usual considerate self? How could she accept? How could she refuse? Oh, how she wished Lucy had never met Captain O'Connor. More than that she wished she had never come to this house, never seen the Marquis of Cavenham, then she would not have fallen so frantically, so foolishly, so hopelessly in love. She pulled herself away from him. 'No, my lord, I thank you, but…'

'You have nothing to wear? I am sure Lucy can find something, you are of a size.'

'Oh, my lord, please do not be so kind to me. I do not deserve it.'

'How so? Am I to learn of more *faux pas*?' It was said with such gentleness, that she was undone. She made a vain attempt to stem her tears. Silently he gave her his handkerchief. 'I cannot tell you,' she said, mopping at her face. 'I beg of you, let me take the lamps to the kitchen. The potboy is waiting to clean them.'

'No.' He would have to be stern, softness was not going to work. 'You will sit there and you will not budge until you have told me all.' He indicated a sofa which stood in the window alcove.

She sat down and looked up at him but her vision was blurred and she did not see the tenderness in his gaze. 'What have you done?' he went on. 'Am I about to endure another visit from Lady Clarence?'

She attempted a smile. 'Is she not coming to the ball?'

'You know very well she is, since you helped to write the invitations. Now stop hedging and tell me everything. I need to know what I am going to be faced with.'

'You will be faced with nothing, my lord, because I shall not go through with it.'

'By that I perceive you mean your charade.' He paused, waiting for her to go on, wanting her to confess her deception, to tell him why she had come to England pretending to be a lady's maid, when anyone with half an eye could see by her bearing and manner she was nothing of the sort.

'Yes, I told Lucy it would not work and it was wrong to hoax you…'

'Lucy? What has she to do with this?' He spoke sharply out of surprise, not anger, but she was too distressed to see that.

'Oh, my lord, do not be angry with her. It started as a joke when I showed her my sari. I did not mean to let it go so far.'

He sat down beside her and found himself possessed of her hand, a warm brown hand, devoid of jewellery. 'Go on.'

She took a deep breath and told him all about Lucy's scheme to have her admitted to the ball, though she was careful not to mention Captain O'Connor's part in it and all the while she was aware of her hand lying in his, like a trapped bird. 'I was to creep out when you went to dress, my lord, and come back with Sir Richard Godfrey and his wife. They are bringing a friend with them who was to be my escort.'

He let go of her hand suddenly and leaned back in the seat, convulsed by laughter. 'Oh, this has Lucy's stamp on it and no mistake.'

'My lord, no. It was my idea, I wanted to show off the sari. Please do not be angry with Lucy. I know I am an unmitigated failure as a mentor for your sister. I will leave at once.'

'You will do no such thing. You may not be the best chaperon in the world, but you are very good for Lucy. And I know you would always take care of her and I can trust you never to do anything to hurt her…'

Oh, it was becoming worse and worse. She had dug herself into a pit from which she could not escape. 'Naturally, you may, my lord. I am very fond of your sister. Who would not be?'

'Then you will attend the ball as our cousin, lately come to stay, but I forbid you to do it in the havey-cavey fashion you planned. I shall send a message to Sir Richard not to expect you.'

'Oh, my lord!'

'Now take those lamps to the kitchen and then go and find Lucy. Tell her I wish to see her.'

She scrambled to her feet. 'Thank you, my lord.'

'And please stop addressing me as ''my lord'' all the time. Cousins do not carry on like that; you will make everyone suspicious. I am Dominic.'

She fled before he could see the colour flaring in her face and while she still had enough strength in her legs to carry her.

Emma was still in Dominic's mind when he set out for the Mountforest's Park Lane house later in the day. In spite of her obvious duplicity, in spite of her refusal to tell him what was troubling her, he was convinced deception was not part of her nature and she must have been forced into it. But by what or whom? And why was Sophie so incensed over her? Did she know something he did not? He would ask her, but not today.

Today he was calling on her to give her the engagement ring and he did not want anything to distract her from that. He had intended to slip it on her finger just before they left for the theatre two weeks before, but she was in such a dreadful mood over Emma's spirited defence of herself, he had decided to wait until a more propitious time, and concluded the ball would be an ideal occasion.

He had changed his mind because it was, as Emma had only today reminded him, Lucy's come-out ball and he wanted everything to be perfect for her. He should

not detract from that with his own affairs. If he gave
Sophie the ring then, she would make a great to-do about
it and poor Lucy would be put in the shade.

'Dominic, how nice!' she greeted him, as an upper
footman showed him into the drawing-room, where she
was sitting with her mother. She was dressed in an afternoon gown of deep pink grosgrain which emphasised
her delicate colouring and he was struck again by how
lovely she was. 'I had thought you would be too much
occupied with the preparations for the ball to visit us
today.'

He made his bow to Lady Mountforest and asked how
she did, before answering, 'Are you not pleased to see
me?'

'Of course I am, silly.' She motioned him to sit beside
her on the sofa.

Her ladyship rose, smiling. 'I will leave you to each
other,' she said with an arch smile. 'I see no necessity
to chaperon you. After all, you are an engaged couple.'

'Is everything ready for the ball?' Sophie asked, after
her mother had left.

'No doubt there will be a last-minute panic, but at the
moment everything is going smoothly. I left Lucy and
Miss Woodhill seeing to the flowers and very excited
they were.'

'I see no reason why Miss Woodhill should be excited. Lucy will not need a companion tonight.'

'No, which is why I have asked Miss Woodhill to
come as a guest. She has so few pleasures and I know
it will please Lucy.'

'Dominic, I cannot believe you have done that, not
after the way she treated me the other night. You have
given her far too much freedom to speak her mind and
as a result she is impertinent.'

'Oh, Sophie, must we quarrel over her?' He smiled, trying to lighten the atmosphere. 'I didn't come here today to talk about Miss Woodhill, you know.'

'Then get rid of her. She is obviously out to make trouble between us.'

'Sophie, that is nonsense,' he said, but it left him wondering if there was any truth in it. After all, there was that Mountforest connection, however tenuous. But having publicly stated that he was looking after Miss Woodhill on a promise to a dying man, he could not send her away, not even to please his betrothed; it had become a matter of honour. He smiled with wry amusement at his own folly.

'I am afraid that is not possible,' he said. 'I made a solemn undertaking…'

'Then you must make sure she stays in the background and is not in a position to put me to the blush again.'

'I don't think she will push herself forward tonight, Sophie. She knows it is Lucy's night and, besides, she won't have a costume. And what I have seen of her wardrobe, it is hardly the latest mode. Please let us put her from our minds.'

Her air of grievance suddenly left her and she smiled. 'You are right, we should not be quarrelling over that little brown mouse. There are far more interesting topics of conversation. Have you received an invitation to Princess Charlotte's wedding?'

He did not like Emma being referred to as a little brown mouse and was on the point of saying so, but thought better of it. Having won Sophie round to a better frame of mind, he ought not to spoil it. He smiled. 'Yes, though I fancy I shall be left kicking my heels in an anteroom; Carlton House is hardly big enough to accommodate all the aristocracy in England and I am hardly one of the Regent's favourites.'

He paused to take a small box from his pocket. 'But what of our own nuptials? Shall we set the date and put the notice in the *Gazette*?'

He opened the box and took out the ring, smiling at her gasp of astonishment as he picked up her left hand and slipped it on her third finger.

'Oh, Dominic, it is beautiful and so big!' She held out her hand, twisting it this way and that, admiring the many facets of the jewel as it sparkled, white, blue, pink and mauve. 'Oh, you are the most generous of men!' She turned and threw herself into his arms and kissed him. 'Oh, my friends will be green with envy.'

He kissed her back, smiling. 'And the date?'

'The day after Christmas.'

'Christmas?' he queried. 'Why then?'

'Oh, I have a fancy for a winter wedding in the country. It will be a grand affair, with the whole of the *haute monde* coming from all over the country to be there. All the fuss about Princess Charlotte will be forgotten and all those empty-headed debutantes of the Season who tried emulating her will be green with envy because, of course, they could be nothing but pale shadows of the real thing. I mean to be different.'

Dominic did not doubt it and he was glad the enormous expense would fall to Viscount Mountforest who, having only one offspring to indulge, would not begrudge it.

He remained long enough to be congratulated by her parents and share a glass of claret with her father, then took his leave. He should have been feeling on top of the world, but he didn't.

For some reason he could not fathom, he felt decidedly flat, almost as if he had performed an unpleasant duty instead of mapping out a golden future. His friends would call him a lucky dog and he supposed he was; Sophie was undoubtedly a catch, but something was not quite as it should be. She had sparkled, just as he had expected her to; the problem was inside himself, a kind of unease, almost a premonition.

He laughed at his own fancies and set off for Bond Street and Gentleman Jackson's boxing emporium where he had arranged to spar a few rounds with Bertie. That would knock the nonsense out of him and set him up for the evening to come.

Dominic was standing at the head of the first flight of stairs to greet his guests that evening when he caught sight of Emma coming down from the floor above. He felt as if someone had dealt him a blow to the heart and winded him. If asked, he would have said she was an attractive young lady, but not one to take the breath away, but now he hurriedly revised his opinion. She was dazzlingly beautiful.

Her hair had been parted in the middle and pulled back to a knot at the back of her head, but the severe style served to emphasise the perfect proportions of her face: the high cheekbones, the well-shaped brows, the straight nose, the perfect mouth, neither too full nor too thin—a mouth for kissing, a thought which shocked him to the core.

The material of the sari was almost iridescent and fell in soft folds about a figure that was nothing less than perfect. She glided, rather than walked. Her expression, as she approached, was perfectly composed but the eyes, behind the green velvet mask, gave away a little of the excitement she was feeling. She was no longer the timid

companion, the little brown mouse; she was, for tonight
at least, an aristocrat, one of the *ton*.

He was dressed in the Indian prince's costume with
Lucy on one side of him, dressed as Venus in a diaph-
anous white crêpe gown which fell from her slender
shoulders in soft folds, and Sophie on the other as Queen
Elizabeth. Both girls were beautiful, but beside Emma
they appeared commonplace. When she reached the little
group, she stood and put her palms together before her
face and bowed her head in the way she had done when
she had first set eyes on him. Dressed as he was, the
only appropriate thing to do was return the greeting in
like manner. He did not speak; for once in his life he
had been rendered speechless.

Lucy laughed lightly, breaking the spell. 'Oh, Emma,
you look wonderful. And isn't it strange that Dominic
should also decide on an Indian costume?'

'Yes, indeed.' Emma had seen the look of astonishment on his lordship's face and was gratified by it. She,
Emma Mountforest, could compete with Sophie if she
wanted to, even if it was Sophie who wore that osten-
tatious diamond ring. Tonight she would shine, tonight
she would be rash and careless. Tomorrow... Oh, she
would not think of tomorrow.

'Will you save me a dance?' Dominic said, watching
that lovely face and the sparkling green eyes. Something
in him stirred and quickened, made him feel reckless.
'In fact, I had better put my name down now, before
they are all taken.' With that he took her card and the
little pencil that was attached to it, writing his name
against a quadrille and a waltz, hardly taking his eyes
from her.

Sophie looked from the slender figure of Emma in the
sari to that of Dominic in his wide satin trousers as they

stood gazing into each other's eyes and her brow clouded with anger.

'Dominic, how could you?' she hissed, as soon as Emma had passed into the ballroom. 'You have made me look a fool.'

'Why should that be, my love?' he queried mildly. 'I must dance with my guests, you know.'

'I did not mean that, though you did not have to undertake to waltz with her. I meant the costume.'

'Oh, that. I have had mine for some time and I did not see the necessity of going to the expense of hiring another.'

'Then she chose hers on purpose, the little schemer.'

'No one knew what my costume was to be, my dear, not even you. It is pure coincidence. And as for Emma, do you not think the sari entirely suitable?'

She gave a harsh laugh. 'Yes, for nothing will persuade me she is not half-Indian; the colour of her skin gives her away. Is there a skeleton in your family cupboard, Dominic?'

'Oh, I should think there are skeletons in every family's cupboard, don't you think?' he responded mildly.

'Sophie, I think you are being very unkind to Emma,' Lucy said. 'The colour of her complexion is due to the strong sunlight in India. It is fading already.' Then her attention was taken by the latest arrivals, among whom she recognised Captain Fergus O'Connor, even though he was masked and dressed as a cavalier in a plumed hat with a very large brim. She smiled conspiratorially at him and held out her hand.

He took it and raised it to his lips, winking at her over it. 'Your obedient servant, Miss Besthorpe.'

She blushed. 'How good of you to come, sir. You will

find Emma already in the ballroom. She is dressed in Indian costume.'

'Then I will go at once and find her, but may I beg a dance or two from you, before I go?'

She handed him her card and he started to write his name all the way down it. She snatched it back before Dominic could see what he was doing. He laughed and left her.

'I think that is everyone,' Dominic said, holding out his elbows for the two ladies. 'Let us join our guests.'

The ballroom was noisy with laughter and bright with light from the many chandeliers. Everyone seemed to have entered into the spirit of the costume. There were kings and princes, matched by queens and princesses, churchmen and beggars, pirates and highwaymen, milkmaids and nymphs, their faces hidden behind masks, though many were easily recognisable.

Emma spotted Lady Clarence and a portly man in a yellow and brown striped waistcoat, who could only have been her husband. And there was Mr Cosgrove and Captain O'Connor who was bearing down upon her as the musicians struck up for the first dance.

He bowed before her. 'Miss Besthorpe has commanded me to find you. Will you stand up with me for this *Chaîne Anglaise*?'

Emma put her fingertips on his proffered arm and allowed him to lead her into a set.

'What happened to our little plan?' he demanded as they promenaded down the line of dancers. 'I received a message from Sir Richard not to meet you after all. I was worried that our plot had been exposed and I would no longer be welcome.'

'It was discovered, though not your part in it, so you may rest easy. His lordship said I might come—he had never intended that I should not—but not with Sir Richard. I am glad, for I hate deceiving him.'

When the dance finished he led her back to her place and claimed the next dance from Lucy. Emma noticed Dominic looking at them with close attention as they whirled away in a gavotte and wondered just how much he knew of Lucy's *tendre* for the young captain. He turned away and bowed before Sophie who was standing beside Lady Mountforest and a gentleman who could have been no other than the Viscount. Although far stouter, Viscount Mountforest was so like her father that Emma was taken aback. She had not expected him to be like him at all, simply on account of the differences in their characters. She must have been staring for she became aware that he was looking closely at her. Embarrassed, she turned her head away to watch Dominic and Sophie, who were smiling at each other like any engaged couple. But she could not help noticing the steely glint in Sophie's eyes and the firm set of Dominic's jaw. Surely they had not had another tiff?

She lost sight of them as her next partner bowed before her and blocked her view. She smiled and accepted his hand, determined to forget all her problems and enjoy herself. Her card had been filled from the moment she entered the room and she knew everyone was wondering who she was and where she had come from and it amused her to keep them guessing.

Lucy was in the height of good spirits. She danced and flirted, and speculated upon the identity of her partners, which was not too difficult for most of them had been known to her for years, though Emma had the greatest difficulty in dissuading her from dancing with Captain O'Connor for a third time even before the supper dance, which was halfway through the programme.

To his chagrin, she gave in gracefully and Emma gave a sigh of relief, as Dominic appeared at her side to claim his waltz.

From that moment the evening took on the quality of a dream. She became acutely aware of his hand about her waist and the nearness of his body, the light of affectionate amusement in his eyes as he looked down at her. He waltzed supremely well, which did not surprise her; he had the carriage, the litheness of movement, the rhythm found in every good dancer. She followed his lead without the least difficulty.

He did not speak and she made no attempt to force a conversation; it was enough to be in his arms. Emma knew, as surely as life and death, that she had not imagined she loved him. She loved him with all her heart. The exquisite joy and the fearful pain of it made her feel as though her heart would burst. The other dancers, the sounds of conversation and laughter, the brilliant lights, faded into nothing; she was alone in a twilight room with him and the music that guided their feet came from a heavenly choir.

'Emma.' His voice, uttering her Christian name seemed to come from a long way off. 'Emma.' That was all.

She looked up at him and discovered the laughter had gone from his eyes and been replaced by a look of such sadness, it hurt her to see it.

'Yes, my lord?'

He smiled suddenly, shrugging off his mood. 'Dominic, remember? You dance uncommonly well. Who taught you?'

She forced a laugh. 'Believe it or not, my brother; he was taught at school. It was considered a necessary accomplishment for Indian administrators. I did sometimes go to one or two dances held in the cantonment.'

'With Miss Emma Mountforest?'

She wished he had not mentioned that name. 'Yes.'

'It is strange that I should be engaged to marry Miss Sophie Mountforest, don't you think?'

'Very strange.' She paused, then plunged headlong into the mire, as if wishing to punish herself for her wayward emotions. 'Do you think they are related? I mean, has Miss Sophie said so?'

'No, I have not spoken to her of it.'

'Why not?'

He did not know why not. It might have been because any mention of Miss Woodhill seemed to make Sophie prickly as a hedgehog, or it might have been that he did not want to stir still waters and bring back a past that was better left where it was—in the past. Or it might have been a wish to protect Miss Woodhill from her own folly. Looking at her now, so softly beautiful, stirring into wakefulness a yearning which had been asleep inside him for years without number, he could not bring himself to believe there was any wrong in her.

'Do you think there is?'

He had been silent so long that she had forgotten what she said and his counter-question startled her. 'Is what, my lord?'

'Any connection between the Misses Mountforest?'

'It is possible. But I never heard Miss Emma Mountforest speak of relations in England.'

'Nor have I heard Sophie talk of relatives in India. In fact, she seems to have a particular dislike of the sub-continent.'

'That is a great shame. There is so much to see and learn and admire there. You would like it.'

'Perhaps one day I will go on a visit.'

She smiled up at him, though inside she was quaking with her newly acknowledged love and a terrible fear of being found out. But as usual, her remedy was to confront her anxieties head on. 'On your honeymoon, perhaps.'

'Perhaps,' he said softly, as the dance ended and he bowed towards her, palms together, fingers almost touching his nose.

She reciprocated and then laid her fingers on his arm ready to be escorted back to her place. The dream-like quality of the evening was still with her, which was why she did not, for a moment, recognise the face that seemed to loom up from nowhere and stare at them.

Slowly her eyes focused on a dumpy little woman in a padded costume of fifty years before, which made her seem as wide as she was high, especially as she was wearing a wig which was dressed and pomaded at least a foot above her head. She wore white maquillage and a red spot on her cheek. She was weaving her way towards them through the throng in a very determined fashion and was only a few feet from them, when Emma remembered her.

Her mind flew back to the Park Street cemetery in Calcutta, to one particular spot: John's grave. She was standing beside it, looking down with a kind of sadness which was not exactly mourning, not the dreadful sense of loss she had felt when her mother died, nor the grief on learning of her father's death. It was more regret for what might have been. She had brought John's parents to visit the grave and they stood beside her, Mr Morton, dour, unsmiling but not visibly affected, Mrs Morton, weeping and bemoaning the fact that her beloved son had died so far from home and she would never see his last resting place again after that day.

Now that same Mrs Morton was wending her way towards her, putting her quizzing glass to her eyes, as if to make sure they had not deceived her. Emma, terrified, excused herself and fled.

Dominic took a step to follow her, but Mrs Morton barred his way. 'Dear Lord Besthorpe,' she said, dropping the quizzing glass on its ribbon about her neck. 'It is you, is it not?'

'Indeed, ma'am.'

'It is so difficult to tell when everyone is masked.'

'Yes, it is.' His mind was still on Emma and her sudden flight. What had startled her? Had he said something which touched a raw nerve? Was he coming closer to the answer to the puzzle? He did not want to know the answer if it meant he must think less of her. He wanted his illusions to remain intact.

'The young lady who was here a moment ago, dressed in an Indian sari,' she said. 'Who is she?'

'Miss Emma Woodhill, ma'am, a distant cousin. She is staying with us as my sister's companion.'

'Miss Woodhill. I thought…'

'What did you think?'

'Oh, no matter. Doubtless I was mistaken. It was the costume, I suppose. I went to India four years ago to visit my son's grave, he died out there, you know, and… No matter, it was a grieving woman's fancy, no more. Think nothing of it.'

She departed, leaving him standing with a puzzled frown on his face. When Sophie appeared at his side and reminded him he had promised her the next dance, he excused himself. 'I'm sorry, Sophie, something's come

up. Bertie will dance with you, he's kicking his heels by
the door. There is something I must attend to.'

He hurried from the room and did not hear the invec-
tive she directed after him before she glided over to
Bertie. 'Dominic is the outside of enough, Bertie. He
has gone dashing off and left me standing. Do dance this
cotillion with me, before everyone starts chewing over
it, there's a dear.'

'Delighted, my dear Sophie,' he said, executing a leg.


Dominic could not find Emma in any of the first-floor
rooms. He climbed the stairs and made his way towards
her bedchamber, determined to stop prevaricating and
demand the truth. Mrs Morton had recognised her, he
was sure of it.

The door of her room was wide open and she stood
just inside with her back to him, staring down at a tigerskin rug which he had never seen before, but which
he supposed she had brought with her from India. She
did not appear to hear him approach.

'Emma.' Her name again, softly spoken, full of hurt.

She had run to her room, fighting back tears, and been
brought to a halt by the sight of that rug. It brought back
memories of her dear father, reminded her most force-
fully of why she and Teddy had come to England.
Dominic's voice immediately behind her startled her.
She whirled round. 'Oh, it's you, my lord.'

'Who else would it be? Unless you expected an ad-
mirer.'

'I did not!' she cried angrily. 'How could you think
that I would do such a thing…?'

'Then why did you leave so hurriedly? Are you ill?'

'No, I am not ill. Please go away.' She tried to push
him out of the room and close the door on him, but he

would not be moved. Instead he grasped both her hands in his.

'Not until you tell me why you fled from the ball-room.'

'I didn't flee. I was overcome by the heat, that is all.'

'Forgive me if I do not believe you. There is something troubling you and I want to know what it is.'

'Please, my lord…' She pulled her hands from his and hid them in the folds of the sari. 'You must go back to your guests.'

'They won't miss me. I want to know the reason for your hurried departure. What are you afraid of? Was it Mrs Morton?'

'Mrs Morton? Who is she?' She remembered just in time that she was not supposed to know the lady. Why had she not noticed the name when she and Lucy were writing out the invitations? They were doing them the day of Sophie's arrival and she had left the room before the task was completed—Mrs Morton's name must have been towards the end of the list. Lucy had finished them herself.

'The lady who approached us at the end of our dance. She seemed to know you.'

'She was mistaken. Unless, of course, we have met at a soirée or a tea-party where I have gone with Lucy. I have no recollection of it.'

'India, she said.'

Emma gave a cracked laugh. 'Oh, that was the sari, I expect.'

'Yes, perhaps so,' he agreed, though he was far from convinced. 'Then why take flight?'

'I didn't take flight, my lord. Why would I? I was tired. I am tired. I want to rest.' If only he would go away. Sir Walter Scott's lines came unbidden to her mind: 'O, what a tangled web we weave. When first we practise to deceive!' How right he was! She was caught in a web of her own making and the only way out was to compound her sins with more.

'I have been working you too hard. Oh, how inconsiderate of me!'

'No, no, it isn't that.'

'Then tell me.' He put his hand on her shoulder and felt her flinch beneath it. Whatever the trouble was, it went a great deal deeper than he had thought, so deep that she was petrified. His annoyance at her reluctance to confide in him turned to sympathy. 'Don't be afraid I'll be angry. I want to help you.'

'There is nothing wrong,' she lied. 'Please go, my lord.' Once again, she tried to eject him. 'If anyone should come...'

He knew she was right, but he could not bring himself to leave her. 'Then come into Lucy's sitting-room and we'll talk.' He grasped her hand very firmly and, brooking no argument, led her along the short stretch of corridor to his sister's rooms. He kicked the door shut behind them and made her sit on the *chaise longue*.

'Emma, do not be afraid,' he said, sitting down beside her, holding both her hands, watching her face, the green eyes, softened by weeping, the brilliant tears standing on her lashes, the pallor of her complexion. 'I would never let anyone or anything hurt you.'

She could stand no more and burst into tears. He took her in his arms and held her. 'It's all right, Emma dear, please, don't cry. Whatever it is, it doesn't matter. It really doesn't matter at all. I can't bear to see you so unhappy.'

He knew then what he had been too blind to see before, that he loved her. It was a revelation both joyful and exquisitely painful. He forgot Mrs Morton, who had only been invited to the function because she was a close friend of his Aunt Agatha; he forgot that he meant to quiz Captain O'Connor because he had a shrewd idea he was the officer who had stopped the runaway Brutus; he even forgot Sophie, abandoned on the dance floor. He forgot it all in the pleasure of holding a slip of a girl in his arms and trying to comfort her.

'Can't you tell me what it is that is troubling you?' he asked softly. 'Am I such an ogre?'

'No, of course not.' Her tears had subsided and she was making a valiant effort to regain control of her emotions. 'Why are you being so kind to me?'

'Why not?' he queried. 'You are brave and beautiful and far too independent for your own good. I have the greatest admiration for you. I...' He stopped suddenly, unable to go on, to say what had been on the tip of his tongue. But he did, didn't he? He did love her. Oh, what a fool he had been! He was not free to speak of it and they both knew it.

She pulled away and looked at him sharply, her surprise etched on her face and he realised he had almost given himself away. 'I should never have come here,' she said.

'To England? To my house? Or to this room?'

'None of them. All,' she said. 'Oh, you confuse me.'

'Do I?' The shock was subsiding a little and he forced himself to speak lightly. 'Now, I would have said you are not easily confused. Most of the time you carry yourself with great poise.' He smiled crookedly. 'When you are not giving a good imitation of a watering-pot, that is.'

'Oh, you make me angry,' she said suddenly. 'Can't

I have a little weep without you making a drama of it?
Perhaps I am a little homesick.'

'Are you? We have tried to make you feel at home,
Lucy and I, but I can see that you would sometimes
think of what you left behind.'

'Oh, you have been kindness itself, my lord, but I
cannot stay.'

'Cannot stay? Oh, I am not having that, not without
good reason. We are cousins, remember? You are my
kin and my responsibility.'

'But that is not true, you know it is not. I cannot think
why you fabricated such a Banbury tale.'

'Neither can I, except that you are so unsuitable as a
companion for Lucy I had to think of something, or be
known as a gull-catcher.' He had smiled a little wearily.
'The things we do to save our pride!'

That was all it was. Pride. His pride. Hers. She
straightened her back. 'Do you think, if I had any choice
at all, I would be here, earning my living as a lady's
maid?'

It was the nearest she had ever come to a confession
and his pulse quickened. 'Not a lady's maid?' he queried.

She realised her mistake at once and for a second she
was tempted to tell all. How could she? If he had not
been engaged to marry her cousin, she might have done.
But no one would believe she had not known of the
engagement and had insinuated her way into his home
with the express purpose of destroying his happiness.
'No, I meant not in England.'

He felt disappointed, hurt, a little angry. 'I am sorry
you do not care for us,' he said gruffly.

'Oh, my lord, naturally I did not mean you or Lucy.
I am grateful to you both…'

'But not grateful enough to confide in us, it seems.'

'There is nothing to confide.'

'Very well.' He sighed heavily. 'But you must promise me something. Promise me you will not think of leaving until we have talked again. I must satisfy myself you know what you are doing and you have somewhere to go. I can't turn you out on the streets to fend for yourself, however resourceful you may think you are. Besides, Lucy would never allow it.' He smiled at her. 'So do I have your promise?'

He would not leave until she gave it, she knew. And he was right, where would she go? She nodded almost imperceptibly.

'Good.' He could see she was near to tears again and he did not want to distress her further, but he would not rest until he had found out what it was she was hiding. There was no thought in his mind of punishing her; he wanted desperately to help her. Impulsively he gave way to temptation and, taking her face in his cupped hands, bent and lightly kissed her lips. 'Now, we will have no more talk of leaving.'

It took all her self-control not to burst into tears again; the kiss had been so bitter-sweet, so much a taste of what might have been but could never be. She must not cry again. She must not. Instead she gave a cracked laugh. 'Kissing cousins, my lord?'

Her spirited response surprised him and made him smile. 'Kissing cousins,' he agreed. 'Now, do you wish to return to the ball? I cannot neglect my guests any longer.'

'No,' she said. She was exhausted, physically and mentally, by all that had happened and she could not face anyone, not Lucy, Sophie or Mrs Morton. Besides, she knew her eyes were puffy and red from weeping and how could she explain that away to Lucy? 'I would rather go to bed, if you don't mind.'

'Would you like me to send Lucy up to bear you company?'

'No, you must not drag her away, she is enjoying herself so much and it is her come-out. Please don't say anything to her.'

'Very well.' He stood up and relinquished her hand. 'I'll leave you now, but if you ever feel the need for someone to talk to,' he said, as gently as he could so as not to frighten her, 'you must come to me. Some burdens are too heavy to be borne by one person and sharing them halves them, you know.'

It was not until the door had closed behind him that she burst into tears again.

Dominic returned to the ballroom, where the music and gaiety were in full swing. The supper dance, which he had undertaken to dance with Sophie, had just begun. He looked about for her and discovered her dancing with Bertie, laughing up into his face, eyes a-sparkle. He wondered whether to go and claim her, but decided against it; she was not above giving him a jobation for neglecting her and she would not care who heard her. He turned in search of Lucy. But she was nowhere to be seen. Neither was Captain O'Connor, whom he had every intention of quizzing about the ride in the park. Did he know Emma's secret? Did everyone know it except him?

He wandered into the dining-room to make sure everything was ready for his guests for the supper interval. It was quiet in there, and cool. He picked up a pasty and went to the window, biting into it, as he looked out on the garden.

It was raining slightly, pattering on the window and running down the pane. He could see nothing of the garden, no moon, no stars, nothing but his own mirrored image in that ridiculous Indian costume. Emma. Oh, Emma, why have I found you too late?

'There you are, Dominic. I have been looking for you everywhere.'

Sophie's shrill voice shattered the soft memory of Emma's lips on his. He sighed and turned to face her, just as everyone followed her into the room and began piling plates with food, chattering noisily, shattering the quiet of the room.

'I am sorry, Sophie. I had something to attend to.'

'I hope it was important. I was never so mortified as when you rushed off and left me standing.'

'I am sorry, my dear. But I noticed you soon remedied the situation.'

'Goodness, you are jealous of Bertie!' She went into peals of laughter.

'Not at all,' he said stiffly. 'I was merely pointing out that you were not alone above a minute and I doubt anyone else noticed, so saying you were mortified, is an exaggeration, surely?'

'How can you stand there and scold me, when it is I who have been wronged?'

Why had he ever thought he loved her? Beside Emma she was shallow and cruel. 'I did not mean to scold, my dear, please forgive me.'

'Yes, but you must be extra attentive for the rest of the evening to make up for your neglect.'

'Of course, my dear.' He forced himself to smile and take her arm. 'Let me help you to some of this chicken in aspic.'

The rest of the evening was a blur of lights, conversation in which he must have taken part, though he did not remember it, forced laughter and dancing. It was four in the morning before he tumbled into bed.

He was tired enough but he could not sleep and spent the hours until dawn going over and over in his mind the conversation he had had with Emma, the words they had said, and more importantly the words left unsaid; the feel of her hands in his; the look in those expressive green eyes, paler when they were filled with tears; the softness of her mouth against his. He must never let it happen again.

He was engaged to Sophie; the wedding was being planned. Her parents approved and had settled a generous dowry on her. Oh, how could he think of weddings and dowries when his happiness, the whole nub of his existence, lay in two small brown hands? It was too late. He was not free and there was an end to it.

He fell asleep as the cock crew and did not stir until mid-day when his valet brought his shaving water and a pot of coffee. His head was thick, as if he had drunk too much the night before, but as the host he had been particularly abstemious. He rose and went to the window.

The sun was shining and the street was busy with traffic and street vendors, calling their wares. The chestnut trees in the garden were just beginning to come into bud. In a week they would be in full flower, filling the air with heady scent. He had to pull himself together and go on with his life as if nothing momentous had happened. But it had. Oh, it most certainly had!

# Chapter Six

Although Lucy behaved towards her exactly the same as she always had, Emma found she was excluded more and more from the outings and entertainments the young lady attended. It was explained to her that as Dominic and Sophie were almost always present at the same functions, they were able to act as chaperons. Emma's services were only required to help Lucy dress and when she was going out alone, and that meant daytime calls on her friends, visits to the library and milliners, and an occasional hack in the park with Martin in attendance and both girls riding side saddle, which Emma found decidedly uncomfortable.

In some ways she was glad of the curtailment of her duties because being in the same room as Dominic was torture to her. Every look, every smile, turned her heart over; every touch, however accidental, set her limbs on fire. She felt naked, her every nerve end exposed for all to see.

But no one behaved any differently towards her, no one accused her. And Dominic himself, on the rare occasions when she saw him, was as considerate as always, apparently oblivious of the tumult which heaved and rolled inside her. He must never know; she must concentrate on her duties, on being a friend and companion to Lucy and stamp out all errant thoughts.

It was very difficult, almost impossible. Seeing him with Sophie hanging on his arm, made her throat constrict so that she found breathing difficult and ordinary conversation impossible. Adding to her misery was the thought that Sophie had everything, a place in society, great wealth and, most of all, Dominic's devotion.

If her father had not been banished, he would have been his brother's heir, and it followed that, as the present Viscount had no sons, Teddy would become the next Viscount Mountforest. Instead of inheriting the Mountforest fortune, Sophie would have been dependent on Teddy's generosity. The thought made her smile to herself, but the smile was short-lived.

Teddy would soon work things out for himself, if he had not already done so, and he might be foolish enough to make his claim public. After all, they had come to England to clear their father's name. To do that, they had to declare themselves and have their true identity accepted. Not only that, they must find proof in the shape of witnesses to what had really happened all those years ago and ones who were prepared to speak up.

Teddy would take great pleasure in doing that, as she would have done a few months before, but now the thought of what it would do to Dominic filled her with alarm. She was not such a ninny as to be unaware that he needed Sophie's dowry; Emma had heard her making plans for the refurbishment of both his town house and his country mansion.

Sophie would fight tooth and nail to keep what she had and she would be aided and abetted by her fiancé. Dominic, whom Emma loved with an intensity which was almost a physical thing—manifested in shaking limbs, a wildly beating heart and a tendency to jump out of her skin whenever he addressed her—would come to hate her.

Neither could she deny her brother the satisfaction of claiming his inheritance. She could not win either way. It was like living on a knife edge, made worse by unrequited love and the knowledge that Mrs Morton could denounce her whenever she chose. She was lucky that the lady did not seem to be part of the Besthorpes' close circle of friends; Emma had not seen her since the night of the ball.

What she would have liked to have done was discuss it all with Teddy, but Teddy was miles away in Suffolk. There was only one other person she could trust and that was Lucy. She would tell her the whole story and ask her what she ought to do just as soon as she returned to the house.

Lucy and Dominic, resplendent in court clothes, had gone in the carriage to Carlton House to witness Princess Charlotte's wedding, leaving Emma and several of the servants to make their way on foot to a vantage point on the corner of The Mall and Horseguards. Here they hoped to catch a glimpse of the bridegroom arriving and, after the ceremony, the newlyweds leaving for their honeymoon.

The crowds were wildly excited, pushing and shoving and craning their necks to get the best possible view. Some had even managed to climb on to roofs and lamp standards. Hanging on to each other's hands so as not to be separated, Emma, Rose and Lisa, allowed themselves to be pushed along by the seething mass; there was no way they could force themselves against the tide.

As Prince Leopold's carriage and its outriders passed through the gates of Carlton House, the crowds cheered, waved and shouted 'Good Luck!' They loved the princess a great deal more than they did her father, whom they preferred to ridicule, and she had defied him to marry the man she loved.

Emma found herself comparing the sight of the guests' carriages with the lavish ceremonies she had witnessed in India, ceremonies with highly ornamented elephants plodding in the dusty heat, bearing princes and princesses in the curtained howdahs on their backs, followed by a retinue of armed horsemen, carts carrying goodness knows what regal paraphernalia and servants on foot, stretching for miles behind them. She sighed. There was nothing to see here after all and the crowds were thinning out. 'Let's go home,' she said to the other two. 'I don't think we shall see any more.'

The sooner she spoke to Lucy, the better.

The wedding ceremony had been magnificent, Lucy told her that evening. The princess had been radiant in a silver tinsel gown with diamond roses in her hair. She had walked between the ranks of dukes, duchesses, bishops, ambassadors and high-ranking army and navy officers on the arm of her father to where her bridegroom stood waiting for her at the altar in skin-tight white pantaloons and dove-grey coat, rainbow-hued with medals and orders, his dress sword hanging at his side in its jewelled scabbard.

'He was so handsome,' Lucy said, with a sigh. 'You had only to see the way they looked at each other and smiled, to know they are truly in love. And the tears were pouring down the Regent's face, especially when the princess dropped a deep curtsy to him after the ceremony and he raised her up and took her into his arms. Oh, it was so romantic.'

Emma was helping Lucy dress ready for a ball being given by the Mountforests. Ostensibly it was to celebrate the wedding of the princess, but Sophie had made no secret of the fact that later in the evening her father would make the official announcement of her engagement to Dominic. It did not really need announcing, everyone knew of it, but Sophie, who had been deprived of her opportunity to shine at Lucy's come-out ball, wanted to make a glittering occasion of it to show off that diamond. None of her friends had been given a ring anything like as valuable.

Emma was glad she had not been invited; it would have broken her heart to watch them, and the felicitations, which she would be obliged to offer, would have stuck in her throat.

Lucy was sitting on a stool before the mirror in a white satin gown trimmed with silk rosebuds over which she had fastened a cotton cape which protected it while Emma brushed her hair. The brushing slowed as Emma considered how to begin her tale and the more she thought about it, the more difficult it became.

Lucy was too young to be able to advise her and it was not fair to put such a burden upon her. She would only say 'Tell Dominic.' But how could she speak to his lordship? How could she intrude on his happiness and admit she had lied to him and then expect him to get her out of the fix she was in? He would not do it, especially when he discovered she intended to discredit his future father-in-law. If he had been engaged to anyone but Sophie…

'What are you dreaming about, Emma?' Lucy asked

as the brushing stopped. 'Do you wish you could come with us?'

Emma resumed her brushing, more strenuously than she intended which drew a cry of 'Ouch!' from Lucy.

'I am sorry, dear, I did not mean to hurt you. Now, how do you wish me to dress this? *À la grecque*, don't you think?'

'You haven't answered my question. Shall I ask Dominic if you may come?'

'Don't you dare!'

Lucy swivelled round on the stool to peer into Emma's face. 'Whatever is the matter?' When she received no answer, she added, 'Why, Emma, I do believe you are wearing the willow for my brother...'

'No, no. You must not say things like that. If he hears it, he will think you are serious. And...'

'But you are serious, aren't you?'

'Don't be silly, Lucy.' She spoke sharply. 'All this talk of weddings and engagements has gone to your head. I simply meant that I am employed here as your maid and companion and you do not need either at the ball tonight. I have already displeased his lordship more than enough...'

'He is not displeased with you. I certainly hope he is not, because I want you to do something for me.'

'Oh, no, Lucy, not more mischief! I really cannot indulge it, truly I cannot.'

'No, it is not mischief. You know Lord Billings has offered for me?'

'Lord Billings!' Emma was shocked. 'But he's old and fat and he smells. And isn't he a widower with a young family? Oh, Lucy, surely you are not considering him?'

'No, I am not. But after my ball, he spoke to Dominic and…'

'Dominic would never make you…'

Lucy laughed suddenly. 'Oh, so it is Dominic!'

His Christian name had slipped out so easily and now Emma felt as though her face were on fire. She grabbed a handful of Lucy's hair and began twisting a string of beads into it. 'Don't be a goose, Lucy. And we were talking of you, not me. What does your brother say you should do?'

'He said it is only courteous to listen to that bumbling old fool…'

'That rich, bumbling old fool…'

'What is that to the point? He says I must allow him to offer for me and then if I want to turn him down— which he sincerely hoped I would—I must let him down lightly. He was Papa's friend, you see, and Dominic, who is too soft-hearted by far, does not want to hurt his feelings. The trouble is, I know I shall not be able to stop myself laughing.'

'Lucy, you must not do that. It would be so unkind. How would you feel, if it were you being turned down?'

'You know, you are so exactly like Dominic and not a bit like Sophie, who would have me consent…'

'Oh, I am sure she would not.' She secured Lucy's hair into a topknot with combs and began teasing out a few curls to fall over her ears, glad to have something to do with her hands.

'She would, then she would have Dominic all to herself and do what she likes with him.'

'I am persuaded she does that already.' Emma put down the brush, took off the cape and stood to appraise her handiwork, trying to keep her voice light, but finding it almost impossible.

'Oh no, he may seem as easygoing as you please, but he would never allow himself to be under the cat's paw. When he makes up his mind to something, nothing will move him. She will find that out before long, if she has not already done so.'

'Then what are you in the suds about?'

'Fergus.'

'What about Captain O'Connor? And should you make so free with his given name?'

'You used Dominic's.'

'A slip of the tongue. And that does not answer my question. What about the Captain?'

'I want to marry him.'

'But you hardly know him.'

'I know him well enough. He says you don't have to know someone a lifetime or even be properly introduced to fall in love…'

'He has spoken to you of it?'

'Of course. At my ball. We went into the garden. It was raining a little and we went into the gazebo.'

'Oh, no! I did not see you go.'

'No, but you were dancing with Dominic and had eyes for no one else. Oh, don't look so bothered, I only noticed because I know you so well, I am sure no one else was aware of it.'

'I wish you would not keep prosing on about me, when it is you we are discussing,' Emma said sharply. 'Did anyone see you go?'

'No I don't think so. We were very careful.'

'Oh, Lucy, you know that was very wrong of you. Did Captain O'Connor…?' She stopped, not knowing how to put her fear into words.

'Fergus was a perfect gentleman,' Lucy put in, aggrieved. 'We only went there to talk.'

Emma knew Lucy would not lie to her, but she was still very worried. 'You said you wanted me to do something for you. If you are planning to run off with Captain O'Connor, I shall refuse point blank to help you and not only that, I shall feel obliged to tell his lordship.'

Lucy laughed. 'I am not planning any such thing. At least, not unless all else fails. I want you to speak to Dominic on Fergus's behalf. He has nothing but his captain's pay and a small allowance from his father, who has an estate in Ireland, but that won't come to him because he is a second son.'

'I am sure your brother will think him totally unsuitable, Lucy, and you must know that. I am very sorry, indeed, that I was instrumental in bringing you together.'

'Oh, no, that was a cricket ball.'

'And a runaway horse. That was most decidedly my fault. His lordship is unlikely to listen to me, even if I were to agree to do it, which I will not. Captain O'Connor is an adventurer.'

'He is not! He is a darling man and he loves me very much.' She was in tears now. 'I am not asking to marry him tomorrow; he would not have it anyway. He wants to prove himself first. I want you to ask Dominic to help him to find employment. You need not even mention me. Say he is your brother's friend.'

'I can't do that, Teddy has never met him.'

'Dominic does not know that and your brother is not here to refute it. We were going to do that at my ball if Dominic had not found out, so what is different now?'

'He will find out again, just as he did before, and I am already in enough trouble with him without adding to it. No, Lucy, I cannot do it.'

'Then we will elope.' She stood up, picked up her

mantle, fan and reticule and turned to Emma. 'It is not
an idle threat, you know. I mean it.'

Emma was appalled. She looked across the few feet
of carpet which divided them, trying to assess how serious Lucy was and decided she was very serious indeed.
Even if the runaways were tracked down and brought
back, Lucy's reputation would be ruined and so would
Dominic's good name. She could not let it happen. 'Oh,
very well, I will speak to him, but in my own time.'

Lucy flung her arms around her. 'Oh, Emma, you are
a darling. I don't know how to thank you.'

'I haven't done anything yet. But I want a promise
from you in return.'

'Anything.'

'You will not see Captain O'Connor again until your
brother says you may.'

Lucy pouted. 'Please do not ask that of me. I could
not bear it. Please, Emma.'

But Emma was adamant. 'If Captain O'Connor is half
the man you say he is, he will contain himself in patience
until the time is right for you to meet in the proper way.
If his love cannot survive a short parting, then it is not
worth having.' The despair on Lucy's face tugged at her
heart and she relented a little. 'You may write him a
short note explaining this and I will see that he has it,
but that is the last time I shall perform such a service
and God help me if Lord Besthorpe ever gets to hear of
it.'

They heard a step on the landing outside the door,
followed by a sharp rap at the door. 'Lucy, what are you
doing in there? You will make us late.'

'Coming!' Lucy flung open the door to Dominic.
'There! I am ready. How do I look?' And she twirled
round in front of him.

'Beautiful, but then you don't need me to tell you that, does she, Emma?'

Emma, thus appealed to, managed a weak smile of assent, but any words she might have uttered stuck in her throat. Her head was whirling with new problems. Why had she allowed herself to be persuaded into something which could only add to her tribulations? Dominic was standing there now, handsome in his black satin evening coat and knee breeches, smiling at her, as if she deserved his trust. She did not.

'Come now, Lucy, the carriage is at the door. I hope you have told Emma she need not wait up for you.'

'Yes, of course. Goodnight, darling Emma. We will talk about it tomorrow.'

'Talk about what?' he demanded, as he guided her down the stairs.

'Oh, tonight's ball,' she said airily. 'Emma will want to know all about it.'

Emma went to her own room and sat on a seat in the window. The night was fine and the sky peppered with bright stars. There were a few people about; a hackney trundled down the street; a cat climbed the railings opposite pursued by a dog which failed to negotiate the obstacle and stood barking in frustration. The night-watchman stopped beneath the window and touched his hat as the Besthorpe carriage drew out and turned down the road. Emma watched it go, torn apart by conflicting emotions.

She would have given almost anything to have been beside Dominic at that moment, riding to a glittering function they could enjoy together, but that was a hopeless dream; he was utterly beyond her reach and the sooner she stopped torturing herself the sooner she could begin to think clearly. She would do better to decide what was to be done about Lucy.

Was her friend truly in love and was Fergus O'Connor an honourable man? Did his lack of wealth or a title debar him as a husband? Papa had not been wealthy and yet he had made her mother very happy. Should money be weighed in the balance? She supposed it must if you had always been used to it.

Dominic's father had been at a low ebb when he died, but that made no difference to the way Lucy had been brought up. She took her luxurious lifestyle for granted and could have no idea what true poverty meant. Not that Dominic would allow her to sink to that, not even in his anger, but would relying on Dominic's generosity make for a happy marriage?

To give him his due, Captain O'Connor had understood that, which was why he had suggested finding employment which would enable him to make his way up in the world. It was, she conceded, the only course if both were determined to marry. That being so, it behoved her to do what she could to help. Gretna Green was out of the question.

There was no opportunity to speak to Dominic in the next few days, days in which Lucy grew more and more impatient and Emma's courage had time to dwindle almost to nothing. Dominic was out of the house a great deal and when he was not, there were callers come to offer him their congratulations on his engagement, or there were guests for dinner, or Lucy wanted Emma to accompany her to the shops or the library. It was on one such occasion Emma delivered Lucy's note to the Captain.

He read it carefully and then looked up past Emma to

where Lucy was watching a little way off, her blue eyes troubled. She managed a watery smile. He tore his gaze from her back to Emma. 'Do you think you can pull this off?'

'I shall try. But you do understand, you must stay away from Lucy, otherwise…'

'Yes, I understand. But if we should contrive to attend the same functions, I shall not be prohibited from being agreeable, shall I?'

'In public, no, of course not. But I beg you, no more private assignations. I need your promise on that.'

He sighed heavily. 'Very well. I give you my word, just so long as I do not hear Lucy has been affianced to someone else. Then, I am, afraid, I shall come running and no power on earth will stop me.'

And with that she had to be content.

That evening, for once, Dominic had no engagements and Emma found him alone in the library. He was reading a newspaper and smoking a cigar, which he hastily put out when she knocked on the open door and asked him if he could spare her a few moments.

'Yes, of course.' He rose at once, noticing her heightened colour, the brightness of her eyes, the slight trembling of her hands, and wondered if now, at last, he was going to hear the truth. He wasn't sure if he wanted to hear it. 'Come in and sit down.'

She sat down, spreading the skirt of the mauve sarcenet which she had re-trimmed with lilac ribbon, and clasped her hands in her lap. 'My lord…' Then she stopped.

He waited expectantly. In spite of the fact that he was engaged elsewhere, in spite of the fact he was almost sure she was not who she said she was, he loved her, had acknowledged it on the night of the ball and there was nothing he could do to alter that.

She had a way of looking at him when she was speaking to him which made him feel as though he were drowning in the green depths of her eyes. He swallowed every word and ended up panting for breath, convinced she could never do a dishonest act nor knowingly hurt another living being. Nor could he forget what it was like to hold her in his arms, to have her head on his shoulder and the scent of her soft hair in his nostrils.

Paradoxically, she made him furiously angry. Sometimes he wanted to take her by the shoulders and shake the truth out of her. Sometimes, on the odd occasions when they were alone in the same room, he had an almost overwhelming urge to kiss her, not as cousin to cousin, but as a lover might, to see her shocked face and to laugh at his own stupidity. How could one person, a little brown mouse, as Sophie persisted in calling her, cause such havoc?

She wasn't a brown mouse either; she had proved that over and over again. He had known it as soon as he had seen her in the sari and since then she had blossomed, with the face and figure of a goddess and a delightful personality, which grew in confidence with every day that passed. She was also intelligent and well read, able to hold her own in any discourse.

She knew how to give a put-down too, as he had discovered when Lord Billings, having been turned down by Lucy, switched his attention to her and, thinking her no more than a poor relation, had intimated that she should be glad of the honour he was doing her by making an offer.

Dominic, who had not been approached by his lordship for his permission, had been watching through the crack of the open drawing-room door and seen her pick up the hand his lordship had been bold enough to lay upon her arm and drop it, then carefully brush her sleeve as if he had contaminated it.

'My lord,' she had said, 'if I ever stand in need of a family of three half-grown children, I will remember your kind condescension.' Without waiting for a reply she had swept from the room. He just had time to move away from the door and appear to be sauntering down the hall to the library.

It was certainly not the behaviour of a lady's maid. Nothing she did reminded him of a servant. It was true she still helped Lucy to dress and kept her clothes tidy, but she did it with such quiet dignity, that no one watching her would think she was doing other than performing an act of kindness for a somewhat untidy young cousin.

Oh, she was an enigma, there was no doubt of it. He ought to have called her bluff from the very beginning, confronted her with his suspicions, asked her outright what deep game she was playing, but it was too late now. He had been hoist on his own petard, allowed himself to become ensnared. His love for her, so reluctantly acknowledged, grew with every passing day until he did not know how he was going to face the rest of his life without her.

He had tried to put her from his mind, had done his best to avoid her, knowing he would almost certainly weaken if he spent any time in her company. But it had been useless. Far from diminishing his love for her, absence had strengthened it. A dozen times a day, he decided he would have to be open about it and tell her, tell the world; a dozen times a day he realised he could not honourably break his engagement to Sophie.

Should he find Emma another post? Surely, among all

his friends, there was one who would treat her kindly? But would they love her, treat her as one of the family, as the lady she undoubtedly was? What reason could he give for sending a cousin from his door and putting her to servitude elsewhere? Oh, why had he told that silly untruth?

'Cousin Dominic,' he said, giving her a wry smile. 'Don't forget, we are kin.'

Oh, it was going to be so very, very difficult and calling him by his given name would only make it worse. 'My lord, I am surprised you are still purveying that deception.'

'It is only a little whisker, my dear, nothing to be in a quake over. I have heard far worse than that, and in this house too.'

She did not rise to the bait; indeed, he doubted if she had even noticed the hint. 'But what can you possibly gain by it? I am certainly not an asset to your household.'

'I shall be the judge of that, not the tattlemongers,' he said. 'So, if you are come here to hand in your notice on their account, you may rest assured it will not be accepted.'

'Tattlemongers,' she repeated, diverted from her task. 'I had no idea the gossip was so unpleasant.'

'It is nothing that I cannot handle. I am as good at giving a put-down as my illustrious father was and my Aunt Agatha. Now there is someone who would give them all a rightabout. But there, she hardly ever leaves her home in Yorkshire, so her talent will not be put to the test.'

'My lord…' Was he deliberately being obtuse? 'I am not come on my own behalf.'

'Ah, I thought not. What bumblebath has she fallen into now?'

'If you mean Lucy, then she has not fallen into anything that I know of. It is not Lucy who needs your help.'

'Then you? My dear Emma, you have only to say and I will do whatever I can. I told you that before, didn't I?'

'Oh, please do not go on so!' she cried in exasperation. 'Why won't you let me get on with what I want to say?'

He looked annoyed for a moment, then his brow cleared and he laughed. She was right; he had been rattling on to no purpose. It was almost as if he did not want to hear her confession, afraid that it could only mean she was in some dreadful illegal plot and his only recourse would be to hand her over to the law. 'Do go on, I shall not interrupt again.'

'I want to ask you if you could find work for a naval officer on half-pay. His name is Fergus O'Connor, Captain Fergus O'Connor. You see, he has fallen in love and until he has something to offer the lady, he cannot ask her to marry him.'

For one split second he thought his heart had stopped, but then it resumed its even beat. So that was what those tears had been about the night of Lucy's ball. A man! He almost laughed aloud. Her deception, over which he had agonised for many a sleepless night, had been no more than a quandary over a love affair. Perhaps it had happened after that incident with the horses in the park; it had not taken him long to discover who the gentleman was and that he was to be Emma's escort at Lucy's ball. Perhaps it had begun before that, before she ever came to England and she had left Miss Emma Mountforest's employ to follow the Captain to England.

His sudden inclination to laugh at himself was just as suddenly turned to grief. It hurt. But then, he told himself, he had no business to mind; he had no claim on her. Why should she not fall in love? But if this Captain O'Connor should turn out to be a scoundrel, then he would personally wring his neck.

He looked across at Emma, sitting demurely with her hands in her lap and wanted to seize them in his own and pull her to him, to tell her not to throw herself away on a sailor, to wait...for what? The nebulous thought which entered his head was pushed quickly away before it could gain more substance. There was no future in it.

'What have you—has he—in mind?'

'Something, my lord, which will make him very rich and take him away from here for at least six months.'

He sat forward, startled. 'Away? For six months?'

'Yes. Or a year. I thought, perhaps, India.'

'You do not wish him to stay in London?'

'No. He must prove himself.'

He would never have believed she could be so calculating. He sat still for a moment, almost speechless with disappointment. That was followed with a kind of relief that she could not be in love with the man or she, being a woman, could never have suggested parting from him. Perhaps all she was doing was trying to rid herself of a tiresome and persistent swain, one who had followed her half across the globe. It was a much more comfortable conjecture and allowed him to think well of her again.

'I suppose I could arrange for him to sail with the *Silken Maid* on her next voyage. She is a due back very shortly.'

'Oh, that would be the very thing!'

'What would you do in the meantime? Six months can be a very long time when you are young.'

She suddenly realised he had jumped to the wrong conclusion and was about to correct it, but then changed her mind. What did it matter if he thought she was the one Captain O'Connor had fixed his attention on? After all, that was exactly what Lucy had suggested. It had been achieved without having to lie to him. The lies about her name and her previous employment in India were more than enough. She would tell no more.

She smiled. 'Lucy tells me your wedding is not to be for another six months. You are young too; does it seem like a long time to you?'

He was about to chide her for her impertinence, then changed his mind. She had always had a great deal of spunk; it was one of her endearing qualities. 'No, for I have much to do before then, arrangements to make, alterations to the house, business affairs…' He stopped and laughed suddenly. 'Oh, *touché*, my dear. You do have a way of turning the tables, don't you?'

She smiled, though her heart was breaking. He was so easy to be with, so ready to see humour in a situation, so in tune with her, she felt they belonged together, like two halves of a whole. Why, oh, why had fate sent her here if it was only to make her miserable?

'I will do this thing for you,' he went on when it became obvious she was not going to comment. 'But I require something from you in return.'

Emma held her breath, wondering what she could do for him; he had everything a man could need and want. 'My lord?'

'You will stay here, with Lucy and me, until the Captain returns. I have a feeling Lucy is going to need you.'

His last sentence startled her. Did he know? Had she inadvertently given the game away?

'Well?' he queried.

'If you think your sister needs me, then I will stay.' Her voice was carefully controlled.

'Of course she does. I have told you how busy I am going to be and no doubt Miss Mountforest will be equally occupied; your services will be more important than ever.'

'On the grounds that a poor chaperon is better than no chaperon at all,' she replied with a light laugh which did not reach her eyes.

'You are learning all the time. Why, I'll wager in six months' time, no one will ever remember criticising me for employing you. Instead they will say how fortunate I am to have found you.' There was a strange huskiness in his voice which made her look up at him sharply. He was looking at her as if seeing her for the first time and yet, paradoxically, it was a look of affinity, as if they might be worlds apart and yet would always be close.

'Thank you, my lord.' She stood up and quietly left the room to go in search of Lucy, leaving him gazing after her, a look on his face it was just as well she could not see.

Lucy was not at all pleased to know that Dominic proposed sending her beloved to India; it was not what she had intended at all. 'I shall never see him again,' she wailed.

'Nonsense, he'll be back in no time and, if I know your brother, he will have been given every opportunity to make a small fortune. If the Captain loves you, he will come back, and before your brother's wedding too.' She smiled reassuringly. 'The time will pass before you know it and there will be plenty to keep you occupied.

His lordship has asked me to stay until then. We shall amuse ourselves.'

It was said more to convince herself than Lucy. Six months was only a fleeting moment in time, it could also be an age. She did not know how she was going to endure it, but for Lucy's sake, if no other, she would. Besides, where else could she go? The reasons she had for not giving in her notice the day after she arrived were just as valid now as they had been then.

Her head, unlike her heart, told her that fate had sent her to Bedford Row so that she could find out more about Viscount Mountforest and perhaps discover the weak link in his story about the death of that young man so many years ago. Her father had never disclosed the victim's name.

So she went about her daily tasks, none of them very arduous, and allowed the days to pass one by one without thinking of the future, doing her best to look after her charge and amuse her when she had a fit of the dismals because she had not seen Fergus for weeks, even though he had not yet left for India. Most of all she learned how to avoid being alone with Dominic.

This was not as difficult as she had feared. In fact, she sometimes wondered if he wasn't also trying to avoid her. If they passed in a corridor or on the stairs, he always seemed to be in a great hurry to go somewhere or meet someone and had no time to stop and talk. If he was dining at home, which was infrequently, they sat at the same table and though he was always polite and included her in the conversation, it was always impersonal: tales of Parliament, Royalty and the latest *on dit*. His leisure hours were spent with his bride-to-be.

Sophie was often at Bedford Row, discussing plans

for its refurbishment with an architect friend of hers, talking colours, materials and furniture to anyone who would listen. Emma hated what she was planning to do to the house and so did Lucy. It was her childhood home where she had been happy with her mama and papa and she objected to anything which might change it. She was always at loggerheads with Sophie over it and Dominic was obliged to smooth ruffled feathers and keep the peace.

'I shall be glad when the Season is over, and we can go back to Cavenham,' Lucy told Emma. They were riding in the open carriage in Hyde Park, using their parasols to shield them from the warm July sun, bowing this way and that to acquaintances they passed. 'If she says once more that French furniture is superior to English I think I shall throw something, preferably that monstrosity of a mirror she had put over the drawing-room mantel. Cherubs, indeed!'

Emma laughed, as the barouche slowed to negotiate two stationary vehicles which blocked the carriage way, their occupants deep in gossip. 'And you do not hesitate to let her know your feelings on the subject. You would do better, Lucy dear, to employ more tact. After all, she will soon be your sister-in-law.'

'I cannot understand Dominic allowing her such a free rein,' Lucy went on. 'He is not usually so indifferent. I have seen him in a towering rage over much less. Why, when Mama wanted to modernise the library which is old and fusty, just as it was in our grandfather's time and could really do with improvement, he refused even to consider it. But now it is almost as if he no longer cares.'

'Then perhaps you should drop a hint to Sophie that

she should concentrate on the library next,' Emma said, with a hint of mischief.

Lucy's laughter pealed out, making one or two ladies in the vicinity turn in their carriages to see whence it came. 'Oh, Emma! I do believe you would like to see Sophie out of favour.'

Emma did not answer.

'I shall be glad when I am married and out of it,' Lucy went on. 'The atmosphere in the house is so disturbing. And no one cares what I think any more.'

'Is that why you are so anxious to marry Captain O'Connor, simply to escape from an atmosphere you find uncongenial? You would be marrying for all the wrong reasons.'

'In my opinion, that is exactly what Dominic is doing.'

Emma sighed. She might have managed to avoid meeting and talking to Dominic, but she could not avoid hearing about him. Next to Fergus, he dominated Lucy's existence. He was the big brother who had spoiled her all her life and who now seemed to have little time for her. Poor little Lucy was jealous. But then, so was she! 'How can that be? I would have said they were well suited.'

'That's just it, they are well suited. They look well together; he is handsome and she is beautiful; he has a title and she has a fortune. What could be more suitable?'

'How cynical you are, Lucy. That does not mean that they do not love each other.'

Emma was ambivalent over these conversations about Dominic. Hearing and speaking his name was enough to set her limbs shaking and rekindle the flame he had lit in her heart; she could not help wanting to talk about

him, to learn more and more, to get inside the character
of the man. It was a kind of self-torture.

'Love is not something the matchmakers consider a
requirement,' Lucy said.

'Are you saying your brother's is an arranged marriage? They have those in India, of course, but I did not
think it happened in England.'

'No, not arranged, simply encouraged.'

'By whom?'

'By both sets of parents, of course.'

'How did they meet? Your brother and Miss
Mountforest, I mean.'

'Bertie Cosgrove introduced them. The Cosgroves and
the Mountforests have been friends for ages. I believe
Bertie's father was the Viscount's boyhood friend. From
what I have heard, they were as close as brothers.'

Emma found herself holding her breath. Was she in
possession of a piece of the puzzle? 'I thought Mr
Cosgrove was your brother's friend?'

'So he is, from their days as students, though they had
been acquaintances before that because Bertie's farm is
only seven miles from Cavenham House and the two
boys, living so close, were bound to meet on occasion.
Bertie brought Sophie over to Cavenham when she visited the Cosgroves some years ago. They were out riding, he said, and she had expressed an interest in the
house. I think Bertie has rued the day ever since.'

'Why?'

'Because he wanted her himself. I am surprised you
have not noticed the odd way he looks at her. Poor fellow—unlike Dominic, he does not have a title. In fact,
if it were not for the farm and the horses he breeds, he
would not have a feather to fly with.'

'Does Sophie know how Mr Cosgrove feels about her.'

'I am sure she does. But, of course, he is not at all *suitable*.' Her heavy emphasis on the last word, easily conveyed what she thought about that. 'It doesn't stop her flirting with him to make Dominic jealous.'

'Now, that is enough,' Emma said, belatedly remembering her role as mentor. 'We must hold ourselves above unkind gossip. You never know where it may lead.'

'You did ask,' Lucy said with a grin.

Which was only too true and she wished she had not. For one tiny second there had flared deep inside her a little glimmer of something that was almost like hope. It died almost at once when she realised that whatever the rights and wrongs of it, the announcement had been made and nothing short of the death of one of the partners could prevent the marriage taking place. An honourable man, and Dominic was one, simply did not renege on a promise to marry.

'I think it is time to turn for home,' she said, tapping the driver on the shoulder with her parasol to tell him to turn the carriage about.

Ten minutes later, they entered the front door to find the hallway blocked by a mountain of luggage and two footmen engaged in taking it upstairs, supervised by a maid Emma had never seen before. Lucy knew her, though.

'Good Lord!' she said, stopping in the act of removing her bonnet. 'Aunt Agatha has arrived. Whatever she is doing here? She never leaves Yorkshire.'

'There you are wrong, Lucilla,' said a voice from the open drawing-room door. 'It seems that you cannot even manage a simple come-out without me.' The lady was

undoubtedly addressing Lucy, but her gaze was with
equal certainty raking Emma from head to toe.

She was a plump, well-corseted woman dressed in a
deep plum and green striped spencer over a panniered
gown in green bombazine. Outmoded it might have been
but she carried it with aplomb, as if it were the rest of
the world which was out of tune. Her hair, under its
black lace cap, was still raven dark which Emma attrib-
uted to a bottle, and her face was surprisingly unlined.

Her eyes, small and dark, were sharply intelligent.
Emma was sure they missed nothing. They were certainly appraising her simple jaconet gown and matching
pelisse, her cottager hat, this time trimmed with silk dai-
sies beneath the brim, and the frilled cotton parasol she
still had in her hand. But her expression gave nothing
away.

'Hallo, Aunt.' Lucy ran forward to plant a kiss on
each of the lady's cheeks. 'We were not expecting you.'

'Evidently not, for no one was at home when I arrived.'

'I am sorry, Aunt. If you had only sent word…'

'I did, but the letter must have gone astray. Can't even
trust the mail these days. No matter, I am here now.'
She turned from Lucy to look at Emma. 'You, I assume,
are the companion I have heard about?'

'Oh, forgive me,' Lucy said. 'Aunt, may I present
Miss Emma Woodhill? Emma, this is Mrs Standon, my
Aunt Agatha.'

'Good afternoon, ma'am.' Emma bobbed a curtsy,
wondering just what the good lady had heard about her.
How could news of her have reached Yorkshire?

'I have had my baggage taken up to my usual room
and ordered tea and cakes,' she said, turning back to

Lucy. 'Go and take off your bonnet and gloves and join me. We must have a long talk.'

'Yes, Aunt.' Lucy managed to turn and grin at Emma before starting up the stairs. Emma, anxious to be free of that penetrating stare, was glad to follow. She felt sure the lady had seen right through her and had come to relieve her of her duties as chaperon.

'Both of you,' she called after them, which only served to confirm Emma's supposition. She had an unpleasant feeling she was in for a grilling beside which Dominic's gentle probing would seem innocuous.

Within fifteen minutes of sitting down to tea, the good lady had learned everything there was to learn about what had been happening in town, not only the latest *on dit*, but about the announcement of Dominic's engagement, which she already knew was imminent, and Sophie's plans for their wedding, about every outing Lucy had been on, the balls she had attended, who else was there and whom she had danced with, right down to the reason why the room she called hers had been painted and refurnished.

'Don't like it above half,' she said, pouring tea as if she were the hostess and not Lucy, who had not recovered from the shock of seeing her. As far as that young lady was concerned, it was the end of any pleasure she might have in the remainder of the Season. 'That lilac and pink striped wallpaper is hideous, it makes me feel dizzy looking at it.'

Lucy gave Emma a conspiratorial wink. 'It was Sophie's doing, Aunt. She is going to refurbish the whole house in the French style.'

'French, is it? Why, it is scarce a year since we defeated them. Now what must we do but ape them. It is downright unpatriotic. And so I shall tell Dominic when he deigns to put in an appearance.'

As if on cue, the young man himself appeared in the doorway and saved Lucy having to reply.

# Chapter Seven

Having been informed by the butler, as soon as he came through the front door, that his aunt had arrived, Dominic did not exhibit the surprise that Lucy had. He greeted Mrs Standon warmly, kissing her hand and enquiring about her journey.

'It was tedious in the extreme, hot and uncomfortable and the roads so parched, everything, horses, carriages, my clothes, were covered in dust,' she said. 'I would never have come, if it had not been absolutely necessary.'

'Why did you find it necessary?' he asked, taking a cup of tea from her and sitting back in his chair, his long, pantaloon-sheathed legs stretched out, apparently at ease. 'Could you not have written instead? I would have been pleased to effect any commission you might have in town.'

'Fustian! I needed to see for myself. It seems to me I haven't arrived a moment too soon. Lucy has had her ball and as far as I can determine, nothing came of it at all. You should have made sure beforehand that the eligibles were all there, given them a push in the right direction, if they were dilatory. Offers of marriage don't just happen, you know, they must be made to happen.'

'I did have an offer,' Lucy put in before her brother could answer. 'More than one. I turned them down. I decided I did not wish to be married until…' She caught sight of Emma's pursed lips and added, 'Until I found someone who loved me as I loved him.'

Emma became acutely aware of Dominic's gaze on her and wondered if he had guessed the truth about Captain O'Connor. She looked down to study the pattern on her teacup, unable to meet his eyes.

'You decided!' Aunt Agatha exclaimed. 'You decided! My goodness, I would never have dared to be so opinionated when I was your age. Dominic, you have spoiled her beyond redemption.'

Reluctantly he drew his gaze away from Emma. 'I would not force her into a partnership with someone she took in aversion,' he said, thinking of his own unhappy fate. 'To be miserable for the remainder of one's life because one has made the wrong choice in a husband is not something I would wish on anyone, certainly not my own sister.'

'I said nothing of making a wrong choice, did I? On the contrary, that is precisely why young people should be guided in this, as in all other things. They do not have the experience to weigh up the advantages against the disadvantages and reach a proper conclusion. Now, tell me about these offers. If Lucy has rejected someone suitable, all is not lost. It is often wise to say no at first; it shows a proper restraint. If the young man is serious, he will not be put off by a first refusal.'

'I am not such a tease, Aunt Agatha,' Lucy said, looking at Emma for support. 'When I said no, I meant it.'

'Then you have put your brother to a great deal of

expense for nothing. You might just as well have come to Yorkshire a year ago, as I suggested.'

'I am not a pinch-commons, Aunt,' Dominic said. 'I do not begrudge Lucy her Season, whatever the outcome. And I would have thought her wanting in spirit if she had accepted Lord Billings.'

'Billings! You mean George Billings, widowed last year, with three motherless children?'

'Yes.'

'Good God, Dominic, how could you have allowed him in the same room as your sister, let alone expect her to consider a proposal from him?'

'I knew she would refuse him. It was simply a courtesy.'

'And I'll wager when word got out, it brought every rakeshame in town flocking to follow suit. Do you want the world to think you have no discernment at all and will allow anyone to address your sister? That is not the way to go on. No wonder the poor child is confused.'

'I am not in the least confused, Aunt,' Lucy said.

'Then you should be.'

At which point, Emma was forced to scrabble in her reticule for a handkerchief to hide her laughter.

Mrs Standon lifted her quizzing glass from where it hung on her ample bosom and peered at Emma. 'A trifle young for a duenna, are you not?'

'Twenty-two, ma'am.' Emma was finding it very difficult to keep a straight face, especially as Dominic was grinning at her behind his aunt's back, almost daring her to stick up for herself.

'Hmm. From India, I understand.'

'Yes, ma'am.' Emma had deduced that Dominic had written to his aunt about her and answered readily, but it appeared from his expression of surprise that he had

not. He opened his mouth to say something and shut it
again.

It was Aunt Agatha's turn to smile. 'Society has few
secrets from me, you may depend upon it. Just because
I do not come often to town, does not mean I am clois-
tered like a nun. You are from India and you are connected in some way with the Mountforests…'

'Miss Woodhill was maid and companion to Miss
Emma Mountforest,' Dominic put in. 'She furnished me
with a very good reference.'

'A piece of paper, no more. Did you check on it?'

Emma looked from Mrs Standon to Dominic and
waited anxiously for his answer.

'I didn't need to. Goodness, Aunt, I am engaged to
Sophie Mountforest…

'And what would she know about it? I would question
if she ever knew of the existence of a Miss Emma
Mountforest before this. Mountforest has not mentioned
his brother in over twenty-five years, not since he was
banished to India over that dreadful business with the
Earl of Grantham's son. I doubt it even crossed his mind
that Edward might have progeny, much less confide in
his daughter.'

'Oh, I smell a scandal,' Lucy said. 'Do tell, Aunt.'

Emma held her breath, waiting for more revelations.
She dare not look at Dominic.

'Arthur Boreham was the Earl of Grantham's only
son, a rakeshame if ever there was one,' Mrs Standon
told them. 'He was shot during a youthful prank. Edward
Mountforest was blamed and fled the country. It was a
nine-day wonder, nothing more.'

Nothing more than a nine-day wonder, Emma thought
bitterly, and yet it had branded her father a murderer,

exiled forever from the land of his birth. Did no one care but her and Teddy?

'Emma, did you not say Miss Mountforest had a brother?' Lucy asked.

'Yes, she did.'

'Then he is surely Viscount Mountforest's heir. Isn't that right, Dominic?'

'I suppose he is,' he said slowly, as all the ramifications of that buzzed round in his brain and made him feel dizzy.

'That is if the estate is entailed,' his aunt put in. 'Do you know if it is?'

'No, I don't,' he said. 'His lordship could have had it broken. I never heard an heir mentioned.'

'If an heir were suddenly to appear, it would make a difference to Sophie's dowry,' Mrs Standon went on, almost as if she were thinking aloud. 'Though it could be one of those estates which can be passed down the distaff side of the family.'

'This is pure conjecture,' he said. 'I cannot believe that there is an heir or his lordship would surely know of it.'

Emma longed to shout, 'Oh, yes, there is!', but she held her tongue. Now was not the time to reveal it; it must not be done until they had all the facts about that shooting and their father's name had been cleared. She did not want Teddy to be branded with the ignominy of that. He must be welcomed for the upstanding young man he was. They had been waiting for something to happen to help them uncover the truth and now, perhaps, with the arrival of Mrs Standon, it had, but oh, what would that do to Dominic?

'Do you think Sophie knows?' Lucy turned to

Dominic, eyes shining. 'Has she been keeping something from you?'

He did not want to think about that. 'Of course not,' he said.

'Did you not mention to her that Miss Woodhill knew Miss Mountforest in India?' his aunt asked him.

It was the first time Emma had ever seen Dominic looking even slightly discomfited, but he recovered quickly. 'I had heard the story and came to the same conclusion as you did, that Sophie knew nothing of it. I did not want to upset her by quizzing her about it. After all, it is something that happened long ago and nothing to do with Miss Woodhill…'

'Besides,' Lucy put in gleefully, 'he cannot speak to Sophie about it because he told her that Emma was a distant cousin and he had promised her dying father he would look after her.'

Mrs Standon looked slowly from one to the other, but instead of asking why, which Emma fully expected her to, she smiled. It changed her whole countenance and the rather forbidding matron revealed something of the young lady she had once been, a young lady with a twinkle in her eye and a capacity for mischief. It struck Emma that it was something Lucy had inherited, and perhaps Dominic too, which was why neither seemed to care a pin about convention.

'Is that so?' the lady said, raising one finely drawn eyebrow. 'Then do you mind telling me just what Miss Woodhill's relationship is to me?'

'I said Miss Woodhill's father was my father's cousin,' Dominic said, relieved to see the amusement in his aunt's eyes, though that could be deceptive. There could be an explosion at any time.

'Which makes him my cousin too, seeing I am your

father's sister. Do you expect me to consent to this tar-radiddle?'

'I had no idea you would be coming to town, Aunt. And I did not think it would do any harm.'

'Hmph, we shall see what harm it will do.' She subjected Emma to another long look, which made her squirm in her seat. 'Do you not think people will consider it parsimonious in you to indulge your sister with all the latest mode in her dress and keep your cousin in *that*.' She pointed at Emma's made-over mauve sarcenet with distaste.

'I think she looks charming,' he said, giving Emma another grin. 'Now, do you think we might talk of something else? We are embarrassing Miss Woodhill.'

'If you wish, I will withdraw,' Emma said, half-rising.

'Sit down, Emma,' Dominic said. 'My aunt's bark is a great deal worse than her bite, and she would no more think of talking of you in your absence than I would.'

If Mrs Standon noticed Dominic's use of Emma's Christian name, she made no comment. Instead she said, 'I see I must make amends. From now on, I shall take both girls in hand. Tomorrow, we go shopping and after that, we shall go over your invitations and decide which to accept, and perhaps arrange a few entertainments of our own. Never let it be said that the Besthorpes do not know how to treat relations who have fallen on hard times…'

'But, ma'am,' Emma said. 'I beg you not to go to the trouble and expense. It was only a little whisker, I have no wish to compound it…'

'Fustian! If you are going to the trouble of telling a lie, then you should make sure it is a whopper. That way, no one dare refute it.'

Dominic burst into laughter, closely followed by

Lucy. Emma looked from one to the other and then at their aunt, who was calmly sipping a second cup of tea, with a satisfied gleam in her eye. Emma knew with a certainty that set her knees knocking that Mrs Standon knew a great deal more than she was saying and that she was playing a game with them all.

Lucy was highly delighted that Emma was to share the remainder of the Season with her and entered into the spirit of what she chose to call Aunt Agatha's jest with wholehearted enthusiasm. Emma was not allowed to protest or refuse as they went to fashionable dressmakers, hat shops and shoe shops. They bought spencers and pelisses, ribbons and lace, stockings and fans until Emma's wardrobe rivalled Lucy's. All of which were spread out for Dominic's approval at the end of each expedition.

Emma was dreadfully concerned about the expense and even more worried when Aunt Agatha began planning soirées, musical evenings and picnics with the express purpose of finding a husband not only for Lucy but for Emma herself. She could see no way out of the coil she was in.

Perhaps marriage was the answer. Dominic whom she loved was out of her reach, so perhaps she should stop rebuffing every young man Aunt Agatha contrived to introduce her to and pay more attention to their good qualities, to weigh up the advantages and disadvantages as the good lady suggested.

But how could she say, when a young man brought himself to the point of proposing, 'Oh, but my name is not Woodhill, it is Mountforest?' Was a marriage under an assumed name legal? The question was purely hypothetical; no one measured up to the one she really wanted.

The same was true for Lucy. She had set her heart on Captain O'Connor and though nothing was said, she steadfastly refused to consider anyone else, much to her aunt's annoyance. Fergus had not yet left London because the *Silken Maid* had not returned from her last voyage. Emma knew the pair were secretly corresponding because the letters always came enclosed in an outer wrapper addressed to Miss Emma Woodhill, a deception which truly appalled her. In vain did she plead with Lucy to confide in her brother.

'He is not an ogre, Lucy, he loves you. I am sure if he is angry, it will not be for long.'

'You have never seen him really angry,' Lucy said. 'He will forbid all contact. And what harm can it do? As soon as Dominic's ship comes in, Fergus will be gone and I shall only have his letters to remind me of him. You could not be so cruel as to tell Dominic of them.'

The brig was overdue and Dominic went every day to the docks in the hope of seeing it there, safely anchored, but every day he was disappointed. He had heard tales of storms and heavy seas round the Cape but told himself that the vessel was sturdy and watertight and Greenaway was an able and experienced captain, so what did a few weeks matter? It was not only the loss of the cargo which concerned him, though that would cause him no little monetary embarrassment, but the information he hoped the Captain was bringing with him.

It had begun with his curiosity about Emma Woodhill but that had faded with the knowledge that she was only waiting for Captain O'Connor to prove himself. If he

had had any doubts about that, they had faded when
regular letters arrived for her from the Captain. Until the
*Silken Maid* returned and was sent on another voyage,
Fergus O'Connor remained in town.

Now it was more a question of Miss Mountforest's
brother he needed to have confirmed, though it was
hardly possible Emma had been mistaken over his existence. Ought he to mention it to the Viscount? If he
did, it would look as if he were worried about the dowry
which he certainly was not and, knowing his lordship's
uncertain temper, he did not relish the prospect of being
roared at, especially if there was no foundation for his
concern.

Sophie had never uttered a word about a cousin, not
even when he had gently probed, and he was beginning
to wonder if she existed at all. But that led to all manner
of other questions. Who was the young lady he was entertaining under his roof and what did she know of the
exiled Edward Mountforest? Was she a confidence trick-
ster, in which case she was a consummate actress and
he was the greatest gull of all time.

He had given her a home and employment, which had
moved her smoothly from a servant to being one of the
family. Had she engineered that? But how? She had not
asked him to pretend she was a cousin; he alone was
responsible for that. He was sure she could never bam-
boozle his aunt Agatha. Come to that, just what was
Aunt Agatha's game?

The wind was rising and it was beginning to rain;
what had been little ripples on the Thames were now
large waves, surging against the dockside, making the
ships swing at their moorings. The tide had turned, the
*Silken Maid* would not dock today and he was no nearer
having his questions answered. He went in search of a

hackney to convey him home. He had taken a box at the theatre for that evening having arranged for the Besthorpe family to meet Sophie and her parents there.

He would continue to go to the docks every day until the Season ended and it was time to return to the country. Most of the *haute monde* had already gone with the lavish entertainments and matchmaking being almost over for another year. Unless something happened in the next two weeks he would be taking Lucy back to Cavenham, still unattached, but she was very young; there would be other years. If he could afford it. It all hinged on the return of the *Silken Maid*.

He arrived home with little time to spare and went straight up to his dressing-room where his valet was waiting. His evening clothes—frilled shirt, black pantaloon-trousers and black tailcoat, white brocade waistcoat and black cravat—were laid out on the bed, and his fob, quizzing glass and rings lay on the chest, together with a lace-edged handkerchief.

'My lord, we must make haste,' Simmonds said, helping him off with his frockcoat. 'Mrs Standon and the young ladies are ready and waiting in the drawing-room.'

Twenty minutes later he joined them, immaculately clad, and ushered them out to the waiting carriage. His unease over the *Silken Maid* was set aside as they rattled through the streets and he endeavoured to apologise for his tardiness.

Emma hadn't wanted to come, but as usual Mrs Standon and Lucy between them had outmanoeuvred her. She could not possibly be tired, they said, she had done nothing strenuous all day; she had admitted she had never been to a play before and it was the last outing of the Season; her gown had been especially commissioned for the occasion and paid for by Dominic, who would be dreadfully disappointed if he could not show her off in it.

It was easier to consent than fight them, though she was left wondering, as she did every single day, why Mrs Standon should take such an interest in her. She felt like a fly caught in a spider's web, whose struggles to free itself were bound to be in vain.

She had helped Lucy to dress in ivory crêpe, added an amethyst necklace, part of the family collection of jewels, which Emma supposed would soon be gracing Sophie's slender neck, dressed her hair and then turned to her own toilette.

Her gown of the palest blue *mousseline de soie*, was caught beneath the bust with a cluster of tiny silk forget-me-nots, tied with a green satin ribbon whose long ends drifted down the gathers of the skirt. The low round neckline and the bands of the little puffed sleeves were threaded with tiny blue beads. It was the creation of one of London's foremost mantua makers and the most beautiful garment she had ever worn.

It was complemented by a fine gauze shawl in tones of blue, green and silver, blending into each other like the colours of a sparkling sea. A matching scarf was tied about her hair with its ends floating over one ear. She would not admit, even to herself, that she longed for Dominic's look of approval, a sign that he saw her as a woman in her own right and not an adjunct of his sister.

However, he was so late arriving home and so anxious not to keep Sophie waiting that he hardly noticed her. 'Which is no more than you deserve for your vanity,' she scolded herself. Later, when they met Sophie, who was dazzling in amber lace which was sewn all over with amber and jet beads in a pattern which emphasised her willowy build and shimmered as she moved, Emma realised she had been outclassed. She called herself all kinds of a fool and set about enjoying the entertainment.

It was when the lights went up for the intermission and people began to move about, visiting neighbouring boxes and exchanging the latest gossip, that Dominic turned to Emma with a smile which reminded her of the tiger rug she had on the floor of her room. Its teeth were bared, though it was not so much a snarl as a smile, as if it knew something its hunters did not. When she mentioned this to her father he had laughed and hugged her to him. 'Who knows what secrets lie in a tiger's head?' he had said. She felt suddenly exposed, as if Lord Besthorpe had deduced everything. Or perhaps someone had told him her secret.

'You look very fine tonight, Emma.' He had been sitting beside her with Sophie on his other side, but Sophie had moved away to speak to her father who was seated at the back of the box. Emma had been uncomfortably aware of the Viscount, almost breathing down her neck, all evening.

'Thank you, my lord, but the credit is yours. I am afraid your aunt has had the account sent to you.'

'On my instructions, my dear. She was quite right, you know, it was not the thing to neglect your wardrobe when you are one of the family, so to speak.'

He had spoken very quietly and her answer was also in an undertone. 'It was not in the least necessary. I should have remained no more than Lucy's maid. To have raised me up as you have was, perhaps, not fair to me.'

He was startled. 'Why not?'

'I must drop back to what I was when you have finished with me and that will come very hard.'

'You make it sound as if I shall cast you off like an old shoe.'

'But you will, won't you? You have no choice.'

'Never say I have no choice, Miss Woodhill. I have always had a choice. I am man enough to do as I please. And suffer the consequences of my actions.'

'I think not, sir. You are bound by convention and etiquette and honour as every man worthy of the name of gentleman is.'

'True,' he said, with a sigh which made her turn and look at him in surprise. 'I wish the female of the species were equally bound. In their book, truthfulness is often replaced by artfulness and etiquette an excuse for duplicity.'

Her breath caught in her throat. More than ever he reminded her of the tiger, smooth, supple, but oh, so very dangerous. 'That is not fair, my lord. You cannot paint all womankind with the same brush.' She had to turn the conversation to another subject or be left wallowing helplessly. 'But I collect you are referring to the play. The heroine is, indeed, a schemer, but perhaps she is the one with no choice.'

'We shall see,' he said, enigmatically, as the orchestra began tuning up for the second half and everyone resumed their seats, including Sophie, who sat down beside Dominic and slipped her arm under his. Emma, who could not bear to see them thus, turned her head to concentrate on the stage.

Two weeks later, the whole household except for the housekeeper and a nucleus of servants, who always remained at Bedford Row, prepared to leave town for Cavenham. This involved a great exodus of baggage, trunks, personal effects, the best crockery and silver, all the bills and correspondence pertaining to the running of a great house, jewellery boxes, hatboxes, saddles and tackle, even the riding horses, which had been sent ahead the day before with Martin and another groom, whose task it was to arrange for the change of horses at each stage.

Emma assumed her services would be dispensed with now that Lucy's Season was over and she had mixed feelings about it. Her own bags and trunk were packed with the clothes she had brought with her; those which had been purchased for her since Mrs Standon arrived, remained in the closet; she could not, in honesty, take them with her.

In one way she would be glad to escape from the retribution which she was sure would not be long in coming if she remained in the household; the other side of the coin was that she had nowhere to go. She had spent a sleepless night worrying about it and wondering if she would be given any wages before she went. She could hardly expect to be paid considering the luxurious way she had been living as part of the family, but without currency she would be hard put to pay for a night's board and lodging.

Neither had she made any progress towards discovering the truth about her father's exile; Mrs Standon had never mentioned it again, but once she did, once it all came out into the open again, she would be damned in the eyes of Society for biting the hand that fed, which was how everyone would look at it. Worse than Society's condemnation, would be losing Dominic's good opinion of her.

But was it lost already? Was the smiling tiger about to pounce? He had been about the house all day, super-

vising the packing and stowing of the luggage on to the
large covered cart which was to accompany the coach.

She was carrying one of Lucy's hatboxes down the
stairs to be added to the pile of trunks and boxes stacked
in the hall, when she met his lordship coming out of the
library, closely followed by a manservant carrying a box
of books.

She put the hatbox down and stepped towards him.
'My lord, may I speak to you?'

'Why, naturally, you may. Come into the library.' He
nodded to the servant to continue with his load, and
ushered her into the room, shutting the door behind
them.

'Sit down, Emma.'

'I would rather stand, my lord.' She paused long
enough for him to see that she was struggling for words
and to notice that she was, once again, wearing that hideous brown bombazine. 'I do not know quite what to
say. You have been so very kind to me but when I said
you were also unfair, I meant it. You see, now you are
repairing to the country, I have nowhere to go and must
find lodgings until I secure another position…'

'Why?' he demanded.

'Why?' she asked, puzzled. 'I can't stay here when
you and Lucy have gone to the country, can I?'

'I cannot for the life of me think why you should want
to.'

'I don't. My lord, this is very difficult. You said fifty
pounds a year to be paid every month and though I have
had more than that in kindnesses, kindnesses do not pay
rent. I have been with you three months and a quarter
of fifty pounds is…'

'I am perfectly able to calculate it,' he said, with some
asperity. 'And if you are complaining about not being

paid, then I can only say it was an oversight and will be put right immediately.' He took a key from a bunch on the slender chain tucked into his waistcoat pocket and unlocked a drawer. 'What I do not understand is why you should choose to abandon Lucy in this fashion, without a word of warning. She will be heartbroken.'

'Abandon her, my lord? I don't understand. Am I not to be dismissed? I assumed that as the Season was over…'

He laughed suddenly. 'Oh, my dear Emma, what a ninny you are! As if we could dream of parting with you. Lucy needs you as much as ever; conventions apply almost as much in the country as in the town and, as you so correctly pointed out to me, I am bound by them. You are coming with us and you will stay until Captain O'Connor returns from India.'

He paused and searched her face for signs of guilt, discomfort, shame even, but all he saw were two green eyes, brimming over with tears. He took a step towards her to comfort her but, knowing what would happen, he checked himself and allowed his hands to fall to his sides. 'Unless there is some pressing reason why you should not?'

'No, my lord.' She blinked rapidly, but one tear escaped and rolled down her cheek. At Cavenham House she would be very close to Teddy and she longed to see him again. It was three months since she had last seen him; though they had corresponded, it was not the same as talking to him face to face. Was he also having trouble over his identity? She smiled and he was left dazzled by it. 'I will be happy to accompany Lucy to Cavenham, my lord.'

'Good. And do you think you could forget this "my

lord'' nonsense? Nothing has changed, you know. Cousins we remain.'

'I must go and finish Lucy's packing,' she said and rushed from the room, leaving him twirling the little key in his fingers, lost in thought. He smiled and counted out fifty sovereigns into a small bag which he slipped into his pocket, before relocking the drawer. Later he would give it to her. Lucy had pin money, why shouldn't she?

They left very early the following morning, with Emma sitting beside Lucy, facing Dominic and Mrs Standon, who was to stay at Cavenham House for a few weeks before continuing her journey by Mail to her home in Harrogate. Their progress was slow because the coach went at the speed of the baggage cart which followed them.

'Leaving it behind to go at its own pace would invite highway robbery,' Dominic explained, as they settled in their seats and he gave the order to proceed. 'The roads are full of soldiers and sailors home from the war with no means of livelihood, who have turned to crime.'

'How sad for them,' Emma said. 'To fight for one's king and country, to risk death and injury and then be thrown aside when victory comes. Can nothing be done for them?'

'Your soft heart does you credit,' he said, not daring to look into her eyes for fear his sharp-eyed aunt would read the truth in his glance, a truth Emma herself seemed completely unaware of. But then, she was no doubt pining for Captain O'Connor. 'We do what we can, but there are so many.'

The journey was exquisite torture for Emma who had never been so long in his lordship's company, and certainly not at such close proximity, with knee almost touching knee, and every jolt threatening to catapult her into his lap. Whenever she looked up she found herself gazing into brown eyes that seemed to be quizzing her, probing, delving into the very depths of her guilt. She was sure her eyes and the warm flush that suffused her cheeks gave her away. She turned to gaze out of the window as they left London behind and set out north-eastwards towards Chigwell.

Their steady pace gave Emma the opportunity to see the countryside which was all very new to her, and for some time there was silence, broken only by the steady clopping of the horses' hooves, the rattle of harness and the creak of the springs. Now and again she heard the gruff voice of their driver as he called to the horses. Before long light snores told them Mrs Standon was catching up on lost sleep.

'Oh, this is so very boring,' Lucy said. 'Emma, why are you so quiet?'

'I was thinking.'

'What about?'

'India, and how different the countryside is here. I think it is the scale of everything, I suppose.'

'Do tell us about India, Emma,' Dominic said, noticing her wistful look. 'I believe you are homesick for it sometimes.'

'If I am homesick, it is for the people I left behind, my father, my friends, the servants, who were also friends…'

'And Miss Mountforest?' he suggested.

She was startled for a moment, then said, 'Yes, Miss Mountforest too.'

'You were close?'

'Yes.'

'And yet she never spoke of English relations?'

'No.' She managed a smile, though it was an effort. 'But you have said that Miss Sophie Mountforest has never mentioned having kin in India. If the brothers were estranged, it is hardly surprising, is it?'

'Have you noticed a family likeness between your Miss Mountforest and Sophie?' Lucy asked.

'I cannot say I have. But the Viscount is very like P—' She stopped suddenly when she realised what she had been about to say. 'I mean there is something about him that reminds me of Major Mountforest. It is the eyes, and the forehead, I think. The mouth is very different.'

'Tell us about Major Mountforest,' Dominic said. 'I assume from the title he was an army man.'

'He was with the Indian army and was a very brave and honourable man. I never heard him utter a bad word about anyone, not even his enemies. He would fight them because he was a soldier and that was what he had been trained to do, but he also understood the culture of the Moslems, the Hindus, the Sikhs and Buddhists which make up the country, which is not a single country at all but many different ones, with different traditions, different climates. Europeans have taken over vast tracts of it, but they have hardly touched the real India.'

She paused; it was difficult to speak of her father in that, impersonal way and she had to be very careful not to say 'Papa', but the opportunity to put the record straight was too good to miss. 'Major Mountforest realised that. He was always respectful to the natives and did his best not to upset them by trampling over their most treasured beliefs, as some have done. He cared for people, whatever their colour and creed. The servants would have died for him. I believe one of them did.'

'Go on.'

He was looking at her intently but she forced herself to meet his gaze, though her heart was pounding. Now she had started, she must not lose her nerve. 'His name was Chinkara. It means gazelle in Hindi.' She smiled, remembering the little Indian with affection, and went on to talk of Chinkara and what she had learned of that last dreadful battle in the hills of Nepal. Once she began the words flowed easily and she was soon talking about Sita, and Calcutta, with its cosmopolitan population, the fort and the temples, the narrow alleyways, the surrounding plains and *jheels*, shallow marshy lakes.

From there, gently encouraged by Dominic who seemed genuinely interested, she went on to speak of the mountains where they went to stay during the oppressive heat of the summer. She talked of forests and ravines, of tigers and wildflowers, of elephants and festivals. She forgot Aunt Agatha, gently snoring, and Lucy, listening to every word; she was talking to him and him alone, sharing something of herself with him. They hardly noticed the stops to change the horses every dozen or so miles, which scarcely took three minutes.

'One day I shall go there,' he said. 'It seems wrong to benefit from trade with a country one has never visited.' It was as if she had been sent to open his eyes, to make him see more clearly. He wanted to reach out and take her hand, to tell her to take heart; that he would protect her, even that he would take her back to India. Nothing seemed impossible at that moment, as the coach trundled on its way through the cool green countryside of England.

'If Sophie agrees,' Lucy put in, and broke the spell. 'I collect she hates all things Indian.' Then she added with a grin of mischief, 'Except diamonds and rubies and silks and muslins, of course.'

Realising that he had been leaning towards Emma, as if hanging on every word, he sat back in his seat, smiling and trying to come back from the dream-like state in which he had been indulging. 'No, Lucy, that is unfair. It is simply that she does not understand.'

'Talking of trade,' Emma said, in an effort to prevent an argument. 'When do you expect the *Silken Maid* to dock? I had thought it was expected two or three weeks ago.'

'It is a little overdue, but it is too early to be concerned,' he said. 'It is a long voyage and it may have met rough weather. I am sorry that Captain O'Connor's voyage has been delayed. You must be feeling very impatient.'

Emma risked a quick look at Lucy, but before she could reply, Mrs Standon woke up with a start and straightened her bonnet which had fallen over her eyes. 'Where are we?' she demanded, looking out of the window.

'Just coming into Bishop's Stortford, Aunt,' Dominic said. 'We will stop here for refreshment.'

'Thank goodness for that. It is hours since breakfast and I am as hungry as a hunter.'

The coach drew up in the yard of an inn and, while the horses were changed again, they went inside for a meal, after which they resumed their journey. This time Aunt Agatha remained awake and kept up a constant flow of chatter. The earlier intimacy disappeared and Emma spoke no more of India or her father.

Had she been able to convey a true picture of her papa, his goodness and compassion, his strict code of honour which would never allow him to betray anyone, not least his own brother? When the truth came out, would Dominic, Marquis of Cavenham, be inclined now to believe it? And if he did not, did she care?

Oh, she cared, she cared so much it hurt.

They reached Cavenham House, which was situated between Bury St Edmunds and Newmarket, just as dusk was falling. It was approached through an avenue of elms, whose canopy made the road very dark. Emma sat forward, looking out of the window as the carriage emerged from the trees and bowled along a gravelled driveway.

With the sun low on the horizon throwing long shadows, Emma saw a large mansion set in lightly wooded parkland. Its façade of ivy-clad grey stone, three storeys high, was pricked by rows of long windows, reflecting the light of the setting sun. In the centre a deep portico shaded the front door and at each end was a round tower. She let out a little gasp of delighted surprise.

'It is magnificent.',

Dominic smiled, unaccountably pleased by her reaction. 'The front is relatively new. It was built by my grandfather. The rest of the house is older, some of it very old indeed. I will take you on a tour of it tomorrow, if you like.'

'I should like it very much,' she said.

It was as if they had decided, almost as if it had been mutually agreed, to set aside the feelings they had for each other, to pretend they did not exist, and put their relationship on a safer footing. Respect and affection must replace the intense passion which had engulfed them if they were to live under the same roof.

Until he was convinced Fergus O'Connor was the right husband for her and she was safely married, he was

determined that they would. If he could not have her for
himself, which he patently could not, he would appoint
himself her guardian.

The next morning Mrs Standon elected to stay in bed
to recover from the journey. As soon as breakfast was
over, Lucy dashed off to the stables to make sure her
mare had come to no harm on the journey from London,
so Emma, in a cerise cambric round gown, found herself
touring the house with only Dominic for company. He
was dressed for the country in nankeen coat and supple
leather breeches tucked into long, tan riding boots.

In spite of its outward grandeur, it soon became apparent to Emma that the whole place was in want of a
coat of paint, new carpets and curtains. The rooms which
were in daily use were warm, inviting and comfortably
furnished, but elsewhere, the cold was striking, even
though it was the height of summer, and the furniture so
sparse it was almost non-existent. Here and there, in
more distant parts of the building which were never
used, there were damp patches on some of the walls and
green mould on the carpets.

'Grandpapa was a gambler,' Dominic said, putting a
hand beneath her elbow to steady her where some of the
floorboards were loose. 'He lost a great deal of money
and everything went downhill. Papa was never able to
recoup. He did his best with economies but they were
never enough and when Mama died, he lost heart and
gave up. I inherited a crumbling pile and land that had
been so long neglected, it was infertile.'

'But Lucy told me you were coming about.' He had
not removed his hand and she was acutely aware of it.
His touch set her pulses racing and made her sound
breathless.

'Yes I am, thanks to profitable trading, but so much has to be put back into buying more cargoes, it is a slow process. My priority was to put some heart into the land, so the house had to wait, but now I think I can make a start.'

It would be a mammoth task, Emma realised, but the old house was so well-proportioned, with large, high rooms and a magnificent carved staircase which went up from an imposing entrance hall and curved round to a long gallery, that it would be a joyful one. She envied Sophie for being able to share the enterprise with Dominic. But then she envied Sophie for a great many other things too. It was becoming more and more diffi-cult to keep the little green god at bay.

Dominic moved away from her to allow her to pre-cede him through a door which, to her surprise, brought them back to the front hall. 'Well, what do you think?'

'I think it is lovely. More than that, it has an atmo-sphere…'

He laughed. 'Ghosts?'

'No, I didn't mean that, but if there are ghosts, they must be benign. I can sense a certain sadness, but there is great happiness too. I think this is a happy house. Does that sound foolish?'

'No,' he said softly. 'I have always felt it. No matter how pinched in the pocket we are, or how many econ-omies we have to make, I am determined to keep this house.'

'Thank you for showing it to me.'

'There is more, of course, outbuildings, stables, land, farms, but I will let Lucy show you those. I am sure she is impatient to take you out riding.'

She chuckled suddenly. 'Must I ride side saddle?'

'No, here you may do as you please. I want you to feel at home.'

'Thank you, my lord.'

'Dominic,' he corrected her.

'Cousin Dominic,' she said, laughing. 'I don't know what it is, perhaps it is the ambience of the house, but I do feel at home and privileged to be here.'

He bowed before her smiling. 'Now, alas, I must go and see my steward.'

'And I should like to write to my brother to tell him I am here. He is not so very far away, so perhaps, I shall be able to visit him…with your permission, of course.'

'You have only to ask and I will arrange transport for you. Or you could ride, though it is seven miles…'

'I should like to ride. Thank you, my…Cousin Dominic.'

'No need to write then. We will ride over this afternoon. I want to see Bertie about a horse. I will have Brutus saddled for you at two o'clock. Is that convenient?'

'Quite convenient, thank you. I will be ready.'

'I will see you then, Cousin Emma.' He sketched a bow and then bounded off down the front steps in search of his steward, feeling unaccountably pleased with life, which he put down to being back in his beloved Cavenham.

## Chapter Eight

Emma had expected Lucy to accompany them on their ride to Cosgrove Manor and was disappointed when they gathered for nuncheon at noon to be told that Lucy had been riding most of the morning and had exhausted her mare. She did not think Dominic would consider escorting her without a third person being present.

'I planned to walk to the village to pay a visit to Mrs Payne this afternoon,' Lucy explained to Emma. 'She was our nurse and our father's before that. She is very old now and living in retirement. I always go and see her when I come back from being away. She likes to hear all the news. I had thought you might accompany me.'

Emma hesitated only a second before saying, 'Yes, of course. We can go to Cosgrove Manor another day.'

'I'm afraid I do have to see Bertie today and I am sure you cannot wait to see your brother again,' Dominic put in, glad that his aunt had remained in her room, because he was uncomfortably aware she would not approve of the arrangement he was about to propose. 'We will go anyway. You can have a comfortable cose while I talk to Bertie.' He had no particular business with his friend, but the opportunity for a long ride in Emma's company was something he did not intend to forgo.

Thus it was that Emma, riding astride on Brutus, and Dominic on Cavenham Prince set out that afternoon for Newmarket, walking their horses along the leafy lanes between green hedgerows. The sun shone, the birds sang and so did Emma's heart. To be riding beside the man she loved on such a day was sheer ecstasy. She smiled to herself as she rode, her capable ungloved hands easy on the reins.

That he was pledged to someone else she intended to try and forget for these few precious hours. Tomorrow, Sophie could have him back, to make happy or unhappy, but today, he was hers. There was no need for words, words only tripped them up, made them say things they did not mean; words were the stuff of lies and she had had enough of those.

'You are looking pleased with life,' he said, seeing the smile. It wasn't just the smile he noticed. She was dressed in a dark green riding habit which, though far from new, was well made and emphasised her slim waist. The tall hat, with its sweeping feathers, framed a face that was perfectly proportioned. The straight nose was complemented by a firm little chin and both were softened by the peach bloom of her cheeks, no longer tanned, and the wisps of auburn hair which lay on her forehead beneath the hat's brim.

'Yes, I am. It is such a perfect day and riding has always been my greatest pleasure. Teddy and I used to ride a great deal.'

'Tell me about it.'

She smiled, her memory conjuring up the happy days before her father's death. 'We would go out on the plains around Calcutta, almost as soon as it was light enough to see, and ride for hours. Sometimes we wouldn't come across another living soul; sometimes only a bullock cart or two or an elephant with its *mahout*—that's its keeper—and some Indian dignitary, or even a princess, riding in the *howdah* on its back. Occasionally we met an army patrol coming back to the cantonment or a group of hunters bringing home their trophies: boar, tahr, which is a kind of mountain goat, hog deer, leopards, tigers.'

'Did you hunt yourself?'

'No, I never cared for it. Papa killed a tiger once, but that was because it was a man-eater and had been terrorising some villages on the outskirts of the jungle. It was a magnificent beast, but I was sad it had to die. Papa had it made into a rug. I still have it.'

Not one word, he noticed, about Miss Mountforest, about her life as maid and companion. He was tempted to ask about it, to enquire how she managed to have so much time free of her duties, but decided it would spoil the day for them both.

'I really must go there some day. Not for the hunting, but simply to see the countryside and the way the people live.'

'You would find it very interesting and enlightening, I think,' she said. 'There is unbelievable wealth as well as great poverty, not only in the towns, but in the interior, which has hardly been explored. There are maharajahs and nizams who live in the most magnificent palaces, rich as Croesus. The maharanees and princesses have so much gold and jewellery they are weighed down by it and yet, just beyond the palace gates, in the bazaars and little villages, the people have nothing.'

'Do they not resent that, these poor people? I imagine they often rise up against their rulers.'

'Hardly ever, because they believe their place in the scheme of things is preordained and nothing can be done about it in their present existence. If they lead good and virtuous lives, they will rise to a higher level in the next life.'

'So a maid could never become a princess, or a stable boy a prince?'

She laughed. 'It is not so very different from society here, is it? The strict hierarchy of the nobility is maintained; isn't that what convention and etiquette and come-outs and primogeniture are all about? To preserve the lineage and the wealth of the great families.'

'You do not approve?'

'I did not say that. I was merely making an observation, but I cannot commend a system that gives everything to the eldest son and leaves nothing for his brothers and sisters, who might, in any case, be more deserving.'

'The eldest son, the heir, is duty-bound to look after his siblings, Emma. Lucy will never want for anything while I have a shilling of my own. As soon as I inherited, I made sure she had a portion no one could touch and as good a dowry as I could manage.'

'Oh, my lord—Dominic—I was not talking of you. Oh, how thoughtless of me! I know you are the most generous of men. Look how you have taken me into your home and I have given nothing in return but trouble.'

She was so obviously distressed, he reined in and turned towards her, reaching out and laying his hand on her arm. 'I am not offended, Emma, and you are no trouble to me at all. In fact, I should miss you very much if you were not here.'

She pulled up and faced him, her lovely eyes registering surprise. 'Oh, Dominic…'

He should not have said that but he could not retract

it. He *would* miss her if she left; he had become accustomed to her presence, to her quiet dignity, her sharp wit, her humour, her sense of justice, even the exasperating air of mystery which surrounded her. 'We should all miss you,' he said, removing his hand from her arm and returning it to the reins. 'Who would keep Lucy in order, if you were not here?'

She pulled herself together to speak lightly. 'It is not so very long ago I was accused of leading her astray,' she said, with a slow smile which enchanted him. 'Lucy is not a silly schoolgirl, you know, she is a young lady with character and a very strong will, but she loves you and respects you. She knows what is right and proper without me telling her. She does not really need me. You are to be married and no doubt Lucy will marry before long. And I…' she gulped quickly. '…I must move on.'

'What about Captain O'Connor?'

She had forgotten all about the Captain and it showed in the startled glance she gave him. 'What about him?'

'I am afraid the *Silken Maid* is considerably overdue and until it returns I cannot fulfil my undertaking to give him an opportunity to advance himself. But perhaps three months is long enough for you to make up your mind about him.' He paused, watching her closely and was rewarded with the sight of the colour flaring in her cheeks. 'Or perhaps it was not you he had fixed his attention on, but Lucy.'

'Whatever do you mean?'

'I am not a fool, Emma. Besides, I spoke to the Captain before we left London and he made no bones about which young lady he was dangling after.'

'Then it was very unfair of you to pretend…'

'I pretend! That is the outside of enough, coming from you. You led me to believe it was you…'

'No, I did not. You assumed what it pleased you to assume.'

He found himself laughing. 'I know. I realised it as soon as I spoke to the Captain and went over in my head everything you had said. You are very clever, you know.'

'Am I?'

'Yes, you always contrive to evade issues you do not wish to speak of and yet you are very open when it pleases you. One day, you will trip over your own feet, you know.'

'Then I must watch my step, mustn't I?'

'I would rather you confided in me.'

'What about?' She managed to sound calm, but her hands were shaking. Some of her nerves must have been communicated to Brutus for he side-stepped restlessly. She turned her attention to settling him into walking forward again.

'I don't know,' he said, coming up alongside her. 'I wish I did. You are an enigma, a puzzle, and I am intrigued.'

'You flatter me, my lord.'

'Where will you go, if I was so foolish as to allow you to leave?'

'I expect I shall set up home with my brother. We might even return to India.' It was the first time such a notion had entered her head, but now it was there, she wondered if it might not be for the best. The farther away she was from the man she wanted but could not have, the better. In Calcutta, where she had never known him, she might learn to live at peace with herself. What would Teddy think of the idea?

'Is there anyone out there, someone you are fond of, someone you might marry?'

She risked a glance at him and saw him looking at her so intently, she felt almost naked, her every thought and emotion laid bare. 'No, there is no one.'

'I thought perhaps it might be Miss Mountforest's brother. You speak so highly of the father and yet the brother is never mentioned, almost as if you are afraid to say his name.' He paused, waiting for her to comment, but she remained silent, concentrating on the back of her horse's head. 'Am I right?'

'No, you are not, my lord, and I cannot think why you should have come to such a conclusion.'

'It came to me when you were talking about primogeniture and brothers and sisters perhaps being more deserving than the eldest son. If it was not me you were talking of, then it must have been Viscount Mountforest and his brother.' He turned down a bridleway which led onto the heath and she followed. 'Knowing Major Mountforest as well as you did, you would naturally see his banishment from his point of view. You might think his son was being deprived of his birthright...'

'I do indeed, but Major Mountforest's son is not of marriageable age, Dominic. You are glaringly abroad if you think that.'

'Did you know I was betrothed to Sophie Mountforest when you first came to Bedford Row?'

'No, I did not.'

'But had you heard the story of Major Mountforest's exile?'

'A little of it.' Words again, words piling up one upon another, making barriers and much as she would have liked to say the words which would tear them down, she could not. New structures would replace the old, as soon as she had uttered them. Teddy's determination, and her

own, too, to clear their father's name would be one.
Another was Sophie.

'Now, could we please not talk of it,' she said, suddenly brisk. 'I was enjoying the ride.'

'As you wish. We will talk of Suffolk and Cavenham
and farming and horses, anything that takes your fancy.
I would hate to spoil your enjoyment.'

'Let us not talk at all,' she said, seeing the heath
stretched out before her, acres of open land, dotted with
heather and gorse and a few sparse trees. In the distance
was a group of buildings and horses grazing in a pad-
dock which she assumed was their destination. 'Let's
gallop.' Suiting action to words, she spurred her mount
forward and was soon surging ahead of him. Her hat fell
down her back on its ribbons and her hair streamed out
behind her as the horse carried her forward.

For a moment he reined in to watch her. Slight though
she was, she was a superb horsewoman—better than a
great many men of his acquaintance—and obviously
quite fearless; she had jumped a ditch with consummate
ease and was flying on, and still he sat watching. His
heart was beating so fast and hard he could hardly
breathe; he wanted her, wanted to hold her in his arms,
to feel her body close against his, to squeeze her into
submitting to his kisses. Desire, strong and undeniable,
surged within him.

He thought he heard her laughter, carrying on the
wind back to where he sat. 'Come on!'

He went after her then, digging his heels into Prince's
flanks, crouching over his neck, urging him to greater
effort. Slowly he gained on her, but she must have heard
him behind her, for she increased her speed. By God!
She was going to outrun him. He could not believe it.

He went after her in real earnest, but by the time he

caught up with her, they were within sight of Bertie's house and his efforts had deflated his desire. He almost hated her for frustrating him and yet, in the back of his mind, was a grudging admission that she had saved him from making a fool of himself.

'I hope you have not ruined that horse,' he said as they dismounted in the stable yard. 'I never saw such a display of hellfire riding from a woman in my life!'

'Of course I have not ruined him.' She stroked Brutus's neck. 'He loved it as much as I did. I would never hurt a horse or any other living thing.'

'Has Emma been giving you a hard time, sir?' Teddy had come round the corner of one of the buildings which lined the yard. He was smiling broadly. 'She can ride with the best of them, but she is so light, the horse is hardly aware of her on his back. It does give her a great advantage.'

Emma turned and ran to her brother, flinging herself into his arms and hugging him. 'Oh, Teddy, it is so good to see you again.' She stood back to appraise him. In the short time they had been apart he seemed to have grown from a boy to a man; he was not only taller, but broader and more muscular, the golden tan of his Indian days had become a rugged, almost weather-beaten brown; he wore tough leather breeches and a cloth jacket. 'My little brother has grown into a fine-looking man.'

'Where is Mr Cosgrove?' Dominic interrupted.

'I believe he is in the house, sir. Shall I fetch him?'

'No, I'll find my way. You enjoy your time with your sister.' Then, to Emma, 'Be ready to return in an hour. We must be back before nightfall.' He moved away, calling over his shoulder, 'I'd appreciate it if you could give Prince and Brutus a rub, Woodhill.'

'Yes, my lord.' He grinned at Emma, grabbing Prince's reins to lead him into an empty stall. 'You do the bay and I'll do the black. We can talk while we work.'

She followed him, leading Brutus. 'Your new life seems to suit you.'

'It will do until we uncover the truth,' he said, unsaddling Prince and picking up a curry-comb. 'You're quite the lady, aren't you? I thought you were going to be a lady's maid.'

'So I am, only Dominic—Lord Besthorpe—told everyone I was their cousin.'

'Whatever for?'

She unsaddled Brutus and rubbed him down with firm, sure strokes and tried to explain but he obviously did not understand; the ways of Society had been difficult enough for her to comprehend, a boy such as he was found them impossible.

'Seems to me the Marquis has taken a shine to you,' he said. 'I said so before, remember?'

'Don't be a goose.' Her answer was a little too sharp. 'He is engaged to marry Sophie Mountforest—our cousin.' She laughed suddenly in case she gave away her feelings. There was no need for him to know of her unhappiness on that score. 'I'll wager that surprises you.'

'No, it does not. She is staying here. The head groom told me Mr Cosgrove's mother invited her to stay to be near Cavenham House. Doesn't want to let his lordship out of her sight.'

'Did you know she was our cousin?'

'I guessed. Top-lofty, ain't she? Came round to the stables yesterday and ordered me to saddle up a horse for her as if she owned them and me too. I very nearly told her the truth then and there.'

'Why didn't you?'

'We have to have proof of Father's innocence first. I do not want the Viscount to wriggle out of his responsibilities.'

'Have you met him?'

'Not yet.'

'I have. He's very like Papa, except his mouth. It is thin and mean. He has a way of pressing his lips together when he is vexed that makes me think he will not give way without a fight.'

'Neither will I.'

'It will not be easy, Teddy. I have heard the popular version of the story and everyone believes Papa was to blame.'

He looked sharply at her. 'You don't, do you?'

'No, of course not, but it is going to be difficult to prove anything.'

'You seem to have learned more than I have. I do believe it was fate that sent to you the Besthorpes and we should take advantage of it.'

'Oh, Teddy, I could not, truly I could not. They have been so kind to me and...'

He looked at her sharply. 'And what?'

'Oh, Teddy I am so tired of all the deception, the lies. Besides, I am sure the Marquis knows, he keeps quizzing me, trying to make me confess.'

'You haven't let the cat out of the bag, have you?'

'No, but Mrs Morton was at Lucy's ball.'

'Mrs Morton?'

'You remember, John's mother. She was looking at me through her quizzing glass as if she were trying to place me.'

'Oh, her!' He dismissed the lady without a second's thought. 'She only saw you for a day in Calcutta, I doubt she would make the connection. And if she had said anything to Lord Besthorpe, he would surely have faced you with it before now.'

'Yes, I expect you are right.' But remembering that tense conversation she had had with Dominic after seeing Mrs Morton, she wasn't sure at all. He seemed to have a facility for finding things out and saying nothing until he chose the moment. Look how he had waited to tell her he knew all about Captain O'Connor and Lucy, just when she had forgotten misleading him.

'James Mountforest is a murderer, hiding behind the goodness of his own brother,' he said. 'I am not such a paragon as Father was. I think he deserves to hang.'

His vehemence frightened her. 'Oh, Teddy, they would never do that, not after so long, even if we could prove it. And it may avail us nothing. I heard the Marquis's aunt say Lord Mountforest may have been able to break the entail so that Sophie can inherit.'

'What do I care for that? Did you suppose that all I want is to be the next Viscount? No, Emma, it is more than that, it is a question of honour. I owe it to Papa.'

'I was afraid you would say something like that.'

He dropped his brush to take her by the shoulders and gently shake her. 'What is the matter with you, Emma? Have you gone soft on me?'

'No, of course not, but we must also think ahead, to what might happen as a result. We must plan what we will do.'

'The outcome will be a disgraced Viscount who must acknowledge us as his kin. I am sure there ought to be a legacy of some kind to Papa, which he never collected. I'll warrant James Mountforest has been using it. If there is not, he is bound to recognise us and look after us financially. I mean to have a stud farm of my own.'

'That will take lawyers and legal arguments and a great deal of money which we do not have. And, Teddy, it smacks very much of blackmail.'

'You think we should let him get away with murder?'

'Papa did.'

'Only because he married Mama and she did not want to come back to England. Why do you think he told you the story? Not to amuse you, you can be sure of it. He wanted us to clear his name and I intend to do it. I had not thought you so pudding-hearted.' He picked up the curry-comb and began work again, making the horse quiver with delight. 'Find out what you can and let me know.'

He looked up as Dominic strolled into the stable with Sophie. She was dressed in a pink spotted muslin with a high waistline, puffed sleeves and was hanging on to his arm with both hands, looking up at him with her mouth slightly open. It was a stance which said, 'He's mine. Don't anyone try taking him from me.'

'He's ready, my lord,' Teddy said, surprisingly coolly considering they had just been discussing the Marquis and he might have overheard. 'He's a rare beast. You are fortunate to have such a one. I am surprised Mr Cosgrove has not tried to have him off you.'

Dominic laughed. 'Oh, he has, but Cavenham Prince is not for sale. I hear you had a fine success at the races last month?'

'Yes, my lord, we did tolerably well.'

'From what I hear, it was more than tolerably well. Mr Cosgrove made a killing. I hope you made something out of it yourself.'

'Indeed, I did. I make no secret of the fact that I would like a stud of my own and anything I make goes towards that.'

Sophie uttered something that sounded very much like a snort. 'Just because you can ride doesn't make you capable of running a stables, boy.'

'You cannot blame him for having ambition, my dear,' Dominic said, mildly reproving. 'I admire him for it.'

'I think I shall tell Bertie he is nursing a viper in his bosom, learning all he can from him in order to stab him in the back.'

'Mr Cosgrove is already aware of my intention...' Teddy paused and then added, almost insolently, 'Miss Mountforest.'

Emma, worried that her brother would go too far, stepped forward. 'Is it time to return, my lord? The horses are ready.' She gave Teddy a meaningful look and he set about resaddling both mounts.

'Why don't you stay for supper?' Sophie said to Dominic. 'I am quite sure Miss Woodhill can find her own way back.'

'I would not dream of asking her,' he said. 'It will soon be dark and the heath is dangerous at night.'

'Then send the bratling with her. I want you to stay with me.'

'No, Sophie, I cannot. My aunt and Lucy are expecting us. Come over and see us whenever you like.'

Emma turned to say goodbye to her brother and led Brutus out into the yard, leaving the engaged couple to their argument. Sophie had reclaimed Dominic sooner than she had anticipated and the day had been spoiled for her. She did not wait for the outcome of the altercation, but found a mounting block and was soon sitting in the saddle.

'My God!' She heard a shriek of laughter from Sophie who had come out of the stable with Dominic, who was

leading Prince. 'She is riding astride! It's disgraceful!
Dominic, I forbid you to ride with that Jezebel.'

Dominic was so startled by her outburst, it was several
seconds before he recovered enough to remonstrate with
her, but before he could say more than, 'Sophie, you
have gone too far', Teddy, a ball of rage, dashed forward
to face her.

'You will not call my sister by that dreadful name.
Apologise at once or I'll…' He was standing so close to
her, his fists clenched in anger and his nose only inches
from hers, that she stepped back in alarm.

'How dare you speak to me like that, boy! Dominic,
don't just stand there, do something.'

Dominic had quickly recovered his composure and
was anxious to defuse the situation. 'What must I do?
Cross swords with him at dawn because he defended his
sister? I would think him a poor tool if he had not.'

'Don't be silly. He's nothing but an impertinent stable
boy, how can you duel with such a one?'

'So, if he were a gentleman, you would expect me to
do so?'

'Now, you are making fun of me.'

'Not at all, but I think, my dear, you should apologise
to Miss Woodhill. It was a very unkind thing to say.'

'I will do no such thing. If she flaunts her legs like
that, then she is a demi-rep, and everyone knows what
that means.'

'Do they?' Emma asked mildly, looking down at the
toe of her riding boot, peeping out from beneath her
well-spread riding skirt.

Dominic turned to Sophie, his jaw hard and his eyes
glinting angrily. 'That's enough! You have gone too far,
Sophie. Miss Woodhill is my kin and I hold her in the
highest esteem. Do you think I would have her anywhere

near my sister if she were anything but impeccable in every way? Now, please apologise.'

Sophie knew she had overstepped the mark. 'Very well,' she said, looking up at Emma with an expression of such fury, it belied her words. 'I will say sorry to Miss Woodhill.'

'Thank you,' Emma said, though Sophie had not been speaking directly to her, but to Dominic.

'But that does not mean I will forgive the impudence of her brother. If you won't do anything about him, I shall speak to Bertie. I'll make sure he dismisses him.' With that she flounced into the house.

Emma expected his lordship to go after her, but instead he turned to Teddy. 'Don't worry, she will calm down, and Mr Cosgrove is not such a sousecrown as to give you the bag when you are making him so much money and he knows half the country's racing owners would gladly take you on.'

'Thank you, my lord.'

He leapt into the saddle. 'Come, Emma, it is time we left.'

'I am sorry that happened,' Emma said, as they rode side by side. 'My brother is sometimes a little hot-headed.'

'It is I should apologise on behalf of Miss Mountforest, Emma. I do not know what came over her.'

'It was not your fault and I thank you for defending me.'

'And why would I not?' he demanded. 'I meant what I said. You have my complete trust.'

'Oh, my lord, I...' She stopped. How could she ever tell him the truth now? How could she admit his trust had been misplaced? She could not. 'I am truly sorry for being the instrument of a quarrel between you and Miss Mountforest.'

'I beg you, think no more of it. Sophie, like your brother, is a little headstrong. She will soon come about. You'll see, she will be over to Cavenham House tomorrow or the day after, all smiles.'

And he was right. Sophie arrived next day accompanied by Mrs Cosgrove in the family barouche, driven by Bertie. They joined Dominic and Lucy for tea, but Emma kept to her room.

It was the first of many visits. Sometimes Sophie came in the barouche with her hostess, sometimes in a phaeton with Bertie, sometimes she rode over, accompanied by a groom. She always made herself completely at home, as if she were already the mistress of Cavenham House.

She issued orders and instructions to the servants, gave Lucy advice about her wardrobe which incensed her, and fetched in an architect and designer to look over the old house with a view to modernising it. In no time at all she had alienated all the servants, who grumbled bitterly among themselves, though, loyal to their master, not one of them complained to Dominic.

Observing the proprieties, she did not stay overnight at Cavenham House, but if Bertie were there to accompany her back home, she would frequently stay for dinner. On these occasions, Emma pleaded a headache and her meal was sent up to her on a tray, but she could not do that every time and sometimes she had no choice but to go down to dinner, which they ate at five o'clock.

On these occasions, she spoke very little, answering when someone asked her a question, sometimes venturing a remark to Lucy or Mrs Standon, whom she had come to like for her forthright, no-nonsense approach to everything, but generally she tried to merge into the background, unnoticed. She was so successful in this that Sophie hardly saw her.

She certainly did not see her the afternoon Emma came upon her and Bertie in the conservatory locked in each other's arms, kissing each other with a passion that appalled her. How could they do it?

She crept silently away, but she could not stop thinking about it. Why did Sophie need anyone else when she had Dominic, who was so good and generous and loving to her? Did he know what was going on? Ought he to be told? Should she tell someone else, Lucy or Mrs Standon? In the end, she decided to do nothing; it would hurt Dominic dreadfully and she could not bear that.

Dominic, sensitive to her every mood, could not help observing how quiet and subdued she was and assumed it was Sophie's insults which had upset her. He wished with all his heart he had not allowed Sophie to come to the stables to see him off that afternoon. He could not understand her outburst. It was almost as if she were jealous, but that was silly; he had never given her the slightest justification for it. And she could not read what was in his heart, could she?

She had acted abominably; it was Emma who had behaved like a lady, remaining calm throughout. Dear Emma! How he hated to see her so unhappy. He would have liked to talk to her about it but whenever he approached nowadays, she shied away like a frightened deer.

In some ways she had changed. She was no longer the bright outspoken defender of her beliefs, no longer unafraid. It was as if the heart and spirit had been drained out of her. Had he done that to her? Had he frightened her with talk of the Mountforests, reminding her of a deception which was totally unimportant to him now? All that mattered was her happiness. Perhaps he should tell her that, but if he did, how could he also refrain from revealing the love he felt for her?

She had mentioned returning to India, though he didn't see how that was possible because she had no money. Should he give her enough to see her safely there and settled down? She would never accept it from him and besides, he was in financial difficulties himself. He felt tempted to sell Besthorpe House, everything he had, leave England and take her to India himself, make a life there just as Edward Mountforest had done.

That was an impossible dream. He could not abandon his heritage and his responsibilities, Lucy and Sophie. It would be such a dishonourable thing to do, no happiness could come from it. He was trapped.

'I never thought Dominic would be hen-pecked,' Lucy said one afternoon when she and Emma were out riding together. It was a lovely sunny day in late autumn; the leaves on the trees in the avenue were turning gold, red and russet, and beginning to carpet the ground. Having spent a good hour cantering across the stubble fields, they were walking their horses companionably side by side back to the house. 'He looks so Friday-faced, and it is not like him at all.'

Emma, too, had noticed it, even though nowadays she spent more and more of her time in her own room, riding or visiting with Lucy. It was not out of fear, but simply to protect Dominic from another embarrassing scene with Sophie and because she could not look at him without thinking of Sophie in Mr Cosgrove's arms. She was afraid her resolve not to say anything would melt away.

'I think he is worried about the *Silken Maid*, Lucy. It

is long overdue. If it is lost, the consequences could be very serious.'

'Oh, I didn't know, he didn't say, but then he always makes light of his troubles. I suppose that means we will have to make economies.' She smiled. 'Sophie will not like that one bit. She hates him trading, but she is ready enough to enjoy the proceeds. Look at the fuss she made over that diamond ring. The money that cost would feed the whole family for a year, I'll wager.'

'Lucy, you must not say things like that. Sophie is soon to be your sister-in-law.'

'I do not need reminding of it.' She laughed suddenly. 'There is one good thing to come of the loss of the brig. Fergus cannot be sent to India, after all.'

'Perhaps not, but that doesn't mean you can start seeing each other again. Dominic knows the truth. He told me he had spoken to Captain O'Connor and he had told him it was you he loved and wanted to marry.'

Lucy looked startled. 'Why did Fergus do that? He knew we agreed to let Dominic think it was you.'

'Dominic can be very forceful when he chooses. I expect he did not leave the poor man much choice.'

'No, but it is of no consequence now. I shall go to him very soon. I will not stay in this house a day after Dominic marries Sophie. She will make my life a misery. If it were not for leaving you, I would have gone before.'

'Oh, Lucy, I do hope you will not do anything so foolhardy. Whatever would your brother say? He has enough to worry about without you adding to his burdens.'

'Do you think I haven't thought of that? I am not so unfeeling, but Sophie makes me very angry with her ''do

this'' and ''do that'' and one day I shall tell her so. And
then I shall go to Fergus.'

'No, you must not. For Dominic's sake, you must try
and keep the peace. Nor must you see Captain O'Connor
again until Dominic has given him leave to speak to you.
You must promise me that.'

'Oh, Emma, I do wish it was you Dominic was marrying. I would be content to wait, if it were.' She smiled
mischievously. 'At least, a little while.'

She did not wish it any more than Emma herself, and
now added to her concern for Dominic was an added
worry over Lucy, who had evaded giving her the undertaking she asked for and would be bound to do something very foolish if she were left to her own devices.
Lucy and Teddy were of a kind in that respect.

Though he said nothing to anyone, Dominic was troubled. There were many things he found disturbing about
his betrothed, traits he had not noticed before: a streak
of cruelty, selfishness and a disregard for the feelings of
those whose place it was to serve her. Surely a man in
love should never find fault with his beloved, but more
and more he found himself remonstrating with her, or
biting his tongue in an effort to avoid conflict. Was this
what his married life would be like?

Why had he never seen these imperfections in her
before? Why was it difficult to recall the charming, beautiful girl he had imagined himself in love with? He
prayed her contrariness was only a passing phase, nerves
over the wedding preparations, which didn't seem to be
going smoothly; she was continually grumbling about
dressmakers and lamenting about his carriage in which
they were to ride from the church. 'Shabby,' she called

it. 'I do think you should buy a new one. I do not want to begin married life paying calls in that old thing.'

He was also worried about the ship and its cargo; he had so much money tied up in it and if it was lost, everyone would have to make economies. He certainly could not afford a new carriage, nor the expensive alterations to the house that Sophie was planning. He dreaded having to tell her, but to let her go on thinking he was not serious about economies would be unkind and come as an even greater shock when she did learn the truth.

Sophie's reaction to his carefully rehearsed explanation the following day was to fume with anger and disappointment. She had ridden over from the Cosgroves on one of Bertie's horses and was dressed in a black silk riding habit with a white frilled shirt. Her black beaver hat was swathed in a length of white gauze, the ends of which floated down her back. She stood facing him in the drawing room, tapping her boot with her whip. 'India!' she shouted. 'I am sick of hearing about it. Now you have had your fingers burned, perhaps you will concentrate on behaving like a peer of the realm and not a shopkeeper.'

'But, my dear, you do not seem to understand. Much of my wealth was tied up in that cargo. If she is lost, I lose a great deal. The goods must be paid for and the crew's dependants compensated.'

'Why should you pay compensation? The crew knew what they were risking when they signed on. And as for paying for goods you have not received, that is ridiculous.'

'I am bound to honour my commitments, Sophie, and that means those things which are not so important must wait a little while.'

'Meaning I must live in this tumbledown mausoleum and do without a new carriage. You will be telling me next we shall have to live in a cottage.'

'Would you mind that so very much if we were together?'

'Now you are being silly. You are a Marquis and I am the daughter of a Viscount, how could we live in a cottage?'

He sighed. 'Then I must do what I can to come about.'

'You should never have meddled in something you know nothing about. Papa said you would come to grief over it and he was right.'

'Is that so? And what does he know of trading with India?'

'Nothing, that is just my point. Neither do you.'

'But I have learned a great deal in the last year.'

She gave a cracked laugh. 'It is a pity you did not learn that ships can be wrecked and cargo lost.'

'It is a risk everyone takes.'

'Not everyone,' she snapped. 'Gentlemen don't indulge in trade. A nabob, that's what you are making of yourself.' She paused and gave a hollow laugh. 'Except that nabobs are usually rich.'

'Why are you so against all things Indian? After all, you have family connections in India.'

'Who told you that?' she asked sharply. 'Oh, it would be the little brown mouse. I might have known she would be a tattlemonger.'

'Miss Woodhill was companion to a Miss Emma Mountforest, whose father was a Major in the Indian army. She came to me with a very good reference from Miss Mountforest.'

'I know that, Bertie told me. Unlike you, he thought

I ought to know. You have been keeping things from me, Dominic.'

'No, I was not aware you knew the story and did not want to upset you.'

'Of course I know the story. Edward Mountforest was a murderer and was exiled to India to save the family name, otherwise he would have been hanged. Papa said he was heartbroken over it and never speaks of it. As far as he is concerned his brother is dead.'

'I believe he is now. But if your papa never talks of his brother, how do you know about it?'

'I heard a rumour, oh, it was ages ago when I was a little girl, and asked Papa about it. He told me his brother Edward had killed Lord Arthur Boreham over an argument with a gun. He had arrived on the scene too late to prevent it. He said Grandpapa had a devil of a time persuading Lord Boreham's parents to drop the charges. They only agreed if Edward never set foot in England again.'

She laughed harshly. 'The scandal nearly killed my grandpapa. So, you see, any reference from that family is utterly worthless and anyone who associates with them deserves to be tarred with the same brush and that includes your precious Miss Woodhill.'

'That is grossly unfair, Sophie. I wish you had not said it.'

'Well, I have. I knew she had come to cause trouble and I was right. You are always cross these days, and finding fault and it is all because of her. I'll wager she has been turning your head with nonsense about how wonderful India is and how rich everyone is. You would never have risked a second voyage if she had not enticed you. It is her fault you cannot buy a new carriage.'

It was such an absurd notion he burst out laughing. 'Oh, Sophie, I do believe you are jealous!'

'Me? Jealous of the little brown mouse? You flatter yourself, sir. I think I would do well to reconsider my decision to marry you, if all you can do is laugh at my sensibilities.'

'You must do as you think fit,' he said, becoming serious again as he suddenly realised he did not much care if she called off the wedding.

She looked at him in astonishment. 'You don't mean that, do you?'

'If you think we should not suit after all, then I would not insist on holding you.'

He looked at her petulant face and wished she would take him at his word. The hope was stillborn; she knew she had gone too far.

'Oh, Dominic!' she cried, moving over to take his arm and look up into his face, the tears she found so easy to shed standing on her lashes. 'Why are we quarrelling? I am sure I never wanted to be at odds with you. We should be looking forward to our wedding. Why, it is only a few weeks away and the preparations are almost complete. I did not mean to say I would call off the wedding, truly I did not.'

'Then let us forget all about it.' He forced himself to smile and pat her hand.

Her tears disappeared like magic. 'And you will buy a new carriage?'

He sighed. 'Sophie, did you not listen to a word I said? With the *Silken Maid* lost, and I fear she is, there can be no new carriage. And no refurbishment of the house either.'

'Oh, there is no talking to you when you are on your high ropes,' she cried. 'I am going out.' Then she dashed

from the room. He did not go after her; there was no
point. He returned to the paperwork he had on his desk.

Lucy and Mrs Standon had decided to take the barouche out to pay calls that afternoon and Emma, left to
herself, went to the stables intending to ride Brutus. He
was not in his usual stall and she assumed Martin had
taken him out for exercise which he did if she was not
riding him. Instead of returning to the house, she sat on
a bale of hay to wait for his return, intending to help
groom him. She had an apple in her pocket. He knew
she always brought one and would sidle up to her, nudg-
ing her until she produced it.

She loved being in the stables, working with the
horses. It was so peaceful and the animals repaid her
care of them with affection, whinnying when they saw
her. Even the most spirited was gentle with her. It was
her escape when life in the house became too difficult.

She had been there only a few minutes when she
heard the sound of a horse being ridden very fast into
the yard. It was not like Martin to approach at a gallop
and she went to the door. Sophie was dismounting from
a lathered Brutus whose flanks bore clear evidence of
the whip. Emma cried out with horror, as Sophie pulled
off her hat and marched off towards the house. She disappeared through a side door as Emma emerged and ran
over to the stallion who stood blowing uncomfortably
and bleeding from the many weals on his back.

'Oh, you poor thing!' she said, putting her arms round
his neck. She turned to Martin who had appeared from
one of the other boxes. 'How could anyone hurt a dumb
animal like that?'

'I thought you had saddled him yourself and taken

him out, Miss Woodhill,' he said. 'I was busy at the back. One of the mares is foaling.'

'But, Martin, you don't think I did this? He was gone when I came for him.'

'Course I don't,' he said. 'I'm not blind.'

'You saw?'

'Yes.' His voice was grim.

'Why take Brutus when Mr Cosgrove's horse is in the stall? And why dismount and leave him without making any effort to see he is looked after?'

Martin did not answer, it was not his place to do so, though he shared her sentiments exactly. He unsaddled the horse and fetched out salve and liniment. 'Let's see what we can do for him. His lordship won't like this, not at all he won't.'

Sophie stormed into the library where Dominic was working. 'I have just come from the stable yard,' she said without preamble. 'I was going to ask for my horse to be saddled, so that I could ride back, but there wasn't a groom in sight.'

'I thought you were staying for dinner, Sophie,' he said, slightly put out that she had interrupted him when he was juggling his accounts to see if there was any way he could manage a new carriage.

'I changed my mind. You were so cross...'

'I was not cross, Sophie, unhappy perhaps, that I could not please you. If you are determined to return to Cosgrove Manor, then I will see that your horse is saddled. Martin will escort you, I am afraid I have too much to do here to accompany you.'

'Never mind that now. That bay stallion of yours is standing in the yard all alone. He's been ridden too hard.'

'Emma rides him most afternoons,' he said mildly.
'She knows what she is doing.'

'Give me leave to doubt it. I think you should go and
see for yourself what happens when you let a bruiser
like that make free with your horses.'

'Why, what has happened?'

'Go and look. I could hardly believe my eyes.'

Mystified, he put down his pen and went out to the
stables, where he found Martin trying to bathe the stallion's wounds and Emma, hanging on its neck with tears
coursing silently down her cheeks.

'What happened? Who did this?'

Neither answered him. Brutus edged away from the
hand that was ministering to him and Emma soothed him
with gentle words so that he stood still again.

'I demand an answer,' Dominic said. 'Martin, the
horses are your responsibility. If you have been negli-
gent…'

'This ain't negligence, my lord,' Martin said grimly.
'It were done on purpose.'

'By whom?'

'Tain't for me to say, my lord.'

'Emma?' he queried, turning to her.

Before Emma could say a word, Martin rose to her
defence. 'Don't you go blaming Miss Woodhill, my lord.
She didn't take the horse out today. As if she'd do a
thing like that!' He pointed at the bloodied flank of the
animal.

'Then who did?'

Martin and Emma both remained silent. Dominic
turned to Sophie and noticed for the first time that she
was still carrying her crop and that it was smeared with
blood.

It was obvious who had done it, but he was shocked

to think that Sophie could go to such lengths. He had let her have her own way over so many things, allowed her to act the mistress of the house before the wedding ring was even on her finger, but thrashing a horse, a beautiful, obedient animal which had never given him a moment's unease was beyond anything he could have believed of her.

He did not doubt she had done it, though he was at a loss to know why, and blaming someone else was the last straw. He was tied to a woman who was vicious and vengeful, but there was nothing he could do to free himself.

'Take him into the back stall and do what you can for him,' he instructed Martin. 'I'll be there to help directly.'

Martin turned to obey and Emma released her hold of the horse and stood watching him limp away, the tears still wet on her lashes. Dominic took a step towards her, then stopped. There was little he could he say to mitigate the hurt she must be feeling and Sophie was watching him. 'I am sorry, Emma.'

'You are sorry!' Sophie shrieked. 'What are you apologising to her for? You should be begging my pardon, not hers.'

He turned to her. 'I do beg your pardon, I forgot you had asked for your horse to be saddled.' He turned towards a groom who was crossing the yard with a forkful of hay. 'Ben, saddle Miss Mountforest's horse and escort her back to Cosgrove Manor.' And as the startled man looked round at him, 'Look lively, man.'

Ben hurried to obey. Sophie gave Emma a look of such venom, it made her recoil. 'Do not think you will get away with this,' she said, almost spitting the words. Then, to Dominic, 'I shall expect to see you at Newmarket tomorrow and look forward to hearing that

you have dismissed this…this apology for a lady's
maid.'

If it wasn't for the effect it might have on Dominic,
Emma would have laughed, might even have told her
that she was no lady's maid. Instead she turned away
and walked slowly back into the house.

# *Chapter Nine*

Emma was alone in the small salon, trying to read, when Dominic joined her half an hour later. She put the book down and looked up at him. He appeared exhausted, his shirt was crumpled and stained, his face was grey and his eyes lacked their usual shine.

'How is Brutus?' she asked. 'Will he recover?'

'The scars will heal,' he said, sinking onto the sofa beside her. 'But he will not be happy about having anyone on his back again for a long time.'

'I can't tell you how sorry I am.'

'Goodness! You didn't think I blamed you, did you? I know who did it and I know why.' He sounded grim.

'Why, Dominic? He is a strong horse to be sure, but he is easily controlled. There was no need to whip him.'

'It was not the horse she wanted to whip.'

'Me? What have I done to make her hate me so? If she is angry with me, why take it out on a dumb animal?'

'Who knows why people do the things they do?' His voice was infinitely weary, infinitely sad.

'I am so sorry, Dominic,' she repeated. 'You have

enough troubles without me causing more. I think it will be better if I leave as soon as it is convenient.'

'It is not convenient,' he said sharply. 'Do you think I am not master in my own house? I say who comes and who goes.'

'But I can't bear to be the cause of dissension between you and Miss Mountforest. If I am not here to upset her...'

'It is nothing to do with you, Emma, it is me she is angry with. I am afraid I was obliged to tell her about the loss of the *Silken Maid*.'

'Is it really lost? Is there no hope?'

'I fear not. I am afraid it means economies.' He picked up her hand from where it lay in her lap and held it fast. 'I had to tell her, I couldn't let her go on making plans for renovating the house and buying new carriages. I simply could not afford it.' He surprised himself with this disclosure because he usually kept his problems to himself, but she was easy to talk to, listening sympathetically and looking at him with those expressive green eyes, as if his problems were also hers. 'I am afraid she did not understand.'

'Has she no dowry?'

'Yes, but I could never use that.'

She didn't ask him why, but she knew if Teddy had his way Sophie would not be treated so generously. The bad side of her, the side which wanted revenge, took a perverse delight in thinking of that, but the good side, the side which would put Dominic's happiness above her own, deplored it. 'I am sure you will come about,' she said softly.

'Emma, I...' His voice was husky with suppressed emotion and he could not go on. Whatever his feelings, he neither could nor dared put them into words.

When she looked up into his face and saw the look of tenderness in his eyes her heart almost stopped. But it could not be; she was seeing what she wanted to see, not the reality. She shivered and looked away.

'Lucy and your aunt will be home soon,' she said flatly, too emotionally exhausted to continue the conversation. 'It is time I changed for dinner.'

He smiled slowly and released her hand.

Although Sophie was not present at the dinner table, her presence was felt by everyone, a sort of spectre at the feast. There was no conversation and though Mrs Standon made one or two attempts to break the brooding silence, she soon gave up, and concentrated on the food on her plate. The servants padded around, offering dishes, but no one took very much.

As soon as the meal was over, Dominic excused himself from joining the ladies in the drawing-room, saying he had a great deal of work to do, and returned to the library.

'What is the matter with everyone?' Lucy said, after they had settled round a comfortable log fire. 'The atmosphere in this house is so gloomy, it's enough to give anyone the dismals.' She picked up her embroidery but made no attempt to work on it. 'It is all Sophie's doing.'

Her aunt who had been reading now lifted her head to look at Lucy over the top of her spectacles. 'Why so?'

'She ruined Brutus and tried to blame Emma. Oh, I know Emma would never say so, but I saw that horse and I talked to Martin. As if anyone would believe that Emma could mistreat any animal, let alone a horse!'

'Why would Sophie do that?'

'Because she had to have someone to blame, didn't she? She knew she had hurt Brutus very badly and

Dominic would be angry about it and she would rather he were angry with Emma than with her.'

Agatha turned to Emma who was trying to hide her fiery face behind the pages of a *Ladies Magazine*. 'Was he angry with you, Emma?'

'No, ma'am, but I beg you not to mention it. It was all a misunderstanding and done with now.'

'I don't know why Dominic doesn't break off the engagement,' Lucy went on. 'He is surely not so blind he can't see what life with her will be like.'

'Lucy, he can't break it off, even if he wanted to, you know that,' Mrs Standon said. 'He is an honourable man and honourable men do not break off engagements, no matter what the provocation. It is as good as being married already.'

'Then I wish she would tire of him, but it is unlikely because she wants to be a marchioness too badly. If she did not, she would have married Bertie Cosgrove ages ago. Except he hasn't enough money.'

'Lucy!' Emma was shocked; could Lucy possibly have seen what she had seen? 'You must not say such a thing.'

'It is true. Viscount Mountforest and Bertie's father were like that…' She linked her two little fingers together to demonstrate. 'And Bertie and Sophie have known each other all their lives. Sir William Cosgrove was very plump in the pocket in his younger days, but he lost almost everything, which means Bertie is not at all a good catch.'

'How did he lose everything?' Emma asked.

'I don't know. Do you know, Aunt Agatha?'

'I believe it was all to do with that scandal over Arthur Boreham's killing,' Mrs Standon said. 'Some say Sir William had a hand in it, but whether he did or no, it certainly affected him badly. He took to drink and gambling and ruined himself. I admire Bertie for the way he has come about since his father's death and looked after his mother.'

Emma's elation when she realised that Sir William had probably been present on that fatal day, slowly drained away. Dead witnesses were no good and she doubted if there had been any more. She let out her breath slowly and looked at her two companions to see if they had noticed her agitation, but Mrs Standon had picked up her novel again and Lucy was stabbing at her embroidery.

She stood up. 'If you will excuse me, I think I will go to my room and write to my brother. He is good with horses and their ailments, he might be able to do something for Brutus.'

She needed to talk to Teddy, not only about what she had learned, but about her need to leave Cavenham House; asking him over to look at Brutus would provide the opportunity. Besides, he very well might be able to help the horse.

On her way past the library she noticed the door was open. Dominic was sitting at his desk surrounded by papers, many of which also littered the floor. He had his elbows on his desk and his head in his hands. He must have heard her light footsteps or the quick intake of her breath because he looked up and attempted to smile. His face was haggard.

'Come in, Emma.'

She advanced into the room, overcome with sympathy and a longing to say something to comfort him. 'Is there anything I can do for you, Dominic?'

He rose, walked round the desk and took both her hands in his own, holding her at arm's length to look at her. She was wearing a plain merino wool gown in a soft green which enhanced the colour of her eyes, gentle eyes so full of sympathy and understanding. 'Nothing except to be your usual compassionate self and pray this nightmare ends for me.'

'I will do that with all my heart,' she said, wishing fervently that she could do what she most longed to do, which was to put her arms round him and hold him close to comfort him, but she knew doing that would make matters infinitely worse.

He moved nearer and, one by one, lifted her hands and put them to his lips, watching her changing expressions. His own dread, tenderness, hope and despair, were all mirrored in those lovely eyes. 'Bless you, Emma.'

'I thought I would write to my brother,' she said, endeavouring to sound calm and practical, even though her insides were in tumult. 'He has always been good with sick and injured horses and perhaps he can do something for Brutus.'

'Oh, Emma, how thoughtful you are! If Brutus were my only problem… But thank you, all the same.'

'Do not give up hope, the *Silken Maid* may yet come safely home,' she said gently. 'I believe Captain Greenaway is an excellent seaman.'

'Then, pray for that too, though I fear it will take a miracle.'

'Miracles have been known to happen.'

'Then I must have faith.' He smiled wryly and bent his head, gently putting his lips to hers. For one wild moment, she responded, putting her arms about his neck, her hands into his hair, drawing him closer so that the kiss, which had been so featherlight, deepened into an expression of a passion so urgent, so undeniable, she was engulfed by it, lost in wonder and desire.

'Oh, Emma,' he murmured. 'How I wish I had met you long ago...'

His voice was enough to bring her to her senses. She pulled herself away, breathing hard and shaking uncontrollably. 'Please do not go on, my lord. Please, please don't say anything. You must let me go.'

'I don't think I can.' He reached for her hands again, stroking them with the side of his thumb, watching her face. His touch sent shivers of desire coursing through her. It was her own fault, she scolded herself, he had not meant to kiss her like that, she had instigated it out of her own selfish need and she had set an avalanche in motion. She had to stop it, had to return to sanity.

'I must go and write my letter,' she said, turning from him and running from the room.

He started after her but by the time he reached the door, she was already halfway up the stairs. 'I have to ride over to Cosgrove Manor tomorrow,' he called after her. 'I will take your letter and ask Mr Cosgrove if he can spare your brother.' She gave no indication if she had heard him and he returned to his desk, though not to work. The figures he had been studying danced before his eyes and made no sense.

Once in the safety of her room, Emma flung herself on her bed and sobbed. The time had come to leave; it was impossible to stay. She loved Dominic with all her heart, loved him enough to turn her back on him. They had no future together; he was bound in honour to marry Sophie and staying near him would not help either of them to do what was right.

She had told Teddy they must think ahead, but try as she might, she could not do so because it meant planning a life without the man she loved. The future seemed too bleak to contemplate. It was a long time before she felt calm enough to fetch out pen and paper and write her letter.

In spite of a sleepless night, Dominic rose early, dressed in buckskin breeches and riding coat and went to see Brutus. He spent some time in the bay's stall, talking to Martin, and it was mid-morning before he returned to the house. He went straight to the salver on the hall table, but the longed-for message telling him the *Silken Maid* had docked had not arrived. There was nothing there but Emma's letter to her brother.

He picked it up and put it to his nose to sniff the scent of her which lingered there, a faint smile on his face as he remembered her kisses, so sweet, so compelling. It was when he put it down, his attention was taken by the way she had written the name Woodhill. The initial *W* finished with a curl which ran over the next letter. It seemed familiar to him and he stood puzzling for some moments, wondering where he had seen the name written before, then he turned and hurried into the library.

He went to his desk, pulled out a drawer and shuffled through the contents until he found the reference Emma had furnished him with. Opening it out, he laid it on the desk beside the letter addressed to E. Woodhill Esq. Miss Mountforest had written Emma's name in exactly the same way, with the curl on the *W*. And there were other similarities. He was sure Emma had written both letters, which could only mean she had forged the reference.

His first reaction was anger, his second amusement. After all, it was not uncommon for servants to fake references and he should not have been so gullible. But he could have sworn Emma would not do such a thing. He paced the floor with the letter in his hand, tapping it on his chin thoughtfully, remembering things she had done and things she had said, particularly about Major Mountforest.

She had spoken of him with such affection, such intimacy, that it was difficult now to recall when she had been talking of her father and when the Major; it was almost as if they were the same person.

Neither was her demeanour like that of a servant, not even in the beginning when she had been so green about the ways of English society; he had thought then that she was a gentlewoman fallen on hard times. A servant would never have dared to give Lord Billings the right about that she had!

Woodhill and Mountforest, strangely apposite names and both called Emma! Could it be that Emma Woodhill was really Emma Mountforest?

He dashed from the room with both letters in his hand and strode down the hall to the drawing-room, intending to confront her with it and demand an explanation. However, Emma was out visiting Mrs Payne with Lucy and the only person he saw was his aunt, immersed in a book of Lord Byron's poetry.

She looked up at him and smiled. 'You look agitated, Dominic. Is something wrong?'

'Look at these.' He dropped the letters into her lap. 'See the way the name is written on the outside of this one, and here, in Miss Mountforest's letter, when she says she has found Miss Woodhill a competent and trustworthy companion? It is the same. I am sure Miss Woodhill and Miss Mountforest are one and the same.'

Her eyes twinkled. 'Of course they are. What I cannot understand is why you have taken so long to wake up to it.'

'You knew?'

She chuckled at his look of astonishment, set aside her book and straightened her cap which, like her bonnets, never seemed to sit securely on her head. 'Of course.'

'How?' He dropped into the chair opposite her.

'Emily Morton wrote to me because she was afraid something smoky was going on. She was at your ball, you remember, and saw Emma there and recognised her. Emma was once engaged to marry her son but he died of fever before he had been in India a year; Mrs Morton met her when she went to visit his grave.'

'Why didn't you say?'

'It amused me not to. It was evident you had no idea and I wanted to see how long it would be before you tumbled to it. I was also curious to know why Emma had undertaken the deception. And how far she would go to maintain it.'

He picked up the letters. 'I have been well and truly gulled and you find it amusing!'

'Oh, come, boy, you are not such a gowk as all that. You knew there was something strange about her from the first and you chose to shut your eyes to it.' She paused and looked closely into his face. 'I wonder why.'

She was looking at him with a smile of satisfaction which made him suddenly very annoyed. 'I felt sorry for her, she had nothing but what she could cram into a carpet bag and a small trunk and yet she had such presence…' He paused. 'And Lucy liked her.'

'Oh, it is your sister's fault, is it? I am ashamed of you, Dominic, putting the blame on a seventeen-year-old hardly out of the schoolroom. I wonder Lucy has a shred of reputation left.'

'It wasn't as bad as that, Aunt. You know how the gossips like to make mountains out of molehills.'

'Yes, I do, which is why I decided I had to come to London to see for myself, in spite of my creaking bones.'

Dominic could think of no one of his aunt's age whose joints creaked less. He smiled wryly. 'And you made matters worse by taking her under your wing like some motherly fowl with a baby chick, heaping clothes upon her and taking her out and about in Society.'

'After you had told the world she was your kin, would you have me deny her and call you a liar?'

'No, certainly not.'

'Besides—' she chuckled suddenly '—when you marry Sophie, Emma *will* be your cousin—by marriage.'

'Sophie. Oh, God, what shall I tell Sophie?'

'That depends on what she knows already and what Emma has in mind.'

'I do not understand.'

'You remember that conversation we had about Viscount Mountforest's brother and whether Sophie knew of him?'

'Yes, and I have since found out she does know.'

'Which means of course she probably knows she has a cousin—two cousins, in fact.'

'Teddy!' he exclaimed. 'He's working in Bertie's stables. Do you think he has come to claim his inheritance?'

'Very probably.' She paused, watching the changing expressions on his face: confusion, anger, curiosity. 'I never did give much credence to that Banbury tale they told after Arthur Boreham was shot. It didn't make sense.'

Curiosity won. 'Why not?'

'Because of the different characters of the young men. Edward was a gentleman in every sense of the word, he was definitely not quarrelsome. And I know many and many a time he stood buff for James's mischief. As for James, he had a quick temper and, from all accounts, drank too much, even as a young man. He has not changed.

'But he was the heir, the future Viscount Mountforest, and he was engaged to be married to Lady Dorothea Brinkley, who, as you know perfectly well, is the daughter of the Earl of Lincoln. The old Viscount set great store by that match. Unfortunately, the only outcome was Sophie, no son and heir.'

'Do you think that is why Emma has taken against Sophie—she sees her as a threat?'

Mrs Standon smiled. 'In more ways than one, I'll wager.'

'So, you think Emma is out to make trouble?'

'What do you think?'

'No. I cannot believe that. She had no idea of my connection with the Mountforests when she came to us, I know because I asked her.' It did not occur to him that if she had lied about her identity she could have lied about that too.

'Perhaps, but she does love her brother and you have only to hear her speak of Major Mountforest to know she adored her father. What would you do in her place?'

'I'd fight tooth and nail to have his name cleared.'

'Then, nephew, you have a problem on your hands. And do not tell me it is nothing to do with you, because I am not blind. I can see the way the wind is blowing, even if you cannot.'

Dominic put his head in his hands. 'Why didn't she tell me? I gave her every opportunity to confide in me…'

'Are you talking of Emma or Sophie?'

'Emma, of course.' Sophie was the last person on his

mind at that moment. 'How could she deceive me like that?'

'She could only have gulled you if you wanted to be gulled. You knew she was not who she said she was, didn't you? And yet you would not confront her with it and send her away. You even made it more difficult for yourself by telling everyone she was your cousin. I say again, I wonder why?'

He did not answer but got up and, for a minute or two, she watched him pacing the floor. 'Nothing has changed, you know,' she said. 'I'm not the only one to have doubts about that killing, but all the witnesses are dead, and Mountforest will not recognise the boy.'

'You think I should tell Emma that?'

'I doubt you need to, she is not a fool. But I do think you need to speak to her about it.'

'I asked Captain Greenaway to make some enquiries for me in Calcutta…' He shrugged. 'It makes no difference now since you have told me what I wanted to know. What is more worrying is that I believe the brig is lost and the good Captain with it. I feel that very keenly…'

'Has it ruined you?'

'Not quite, but I shall have to sell more land and cancel the improvements Sophie has put in hand. She won't like it above half, but it cannot be helped. And I'll have to let Bertie have Cavenham Prince. I'm going over to see him about it now.' He tapped Emma's letter. 'I told Emma I would deliver this.'

'Then do that. The ride will give you time to think about what you are going to do.'

'Do I have a choice?' he asked miserably.

'Oh, yes, you have a choice.' She smiled knowingly. 'The question is, will you make the right one?'

He put the letter in the pocket of his riding coat and went out to the stableyard, collecting his hat and gloves from the table in the hall as he went. His actions were automatic, his mind was elsewhere, as he mounted Prince and set off at a trot, which soon slowed to a walk, as if he were in no hurry to reach his destination.

Emma had pulled the wool over his eyes, given him a false reference, made of him the biggest gullcatcher in Christendom and yet, try as he might to fuel the flames of his anger, he could not condemn her. He had loved her from the first, which was why he had condoned what she had done, had even said she was his cousin to silence the tattlemongers, and he loved her still. Nothing she had done could change that. Supposing he told her so? What would happen then?

He would also have to tell Sophie. And what would Sophie do? The thought that she might free him lifted his spirits for a moment, but then he realised that he would be condemned in the eyes of the world, and rightly so, as a man who jilted his betrothed. Not only jilted her, but turned to her cousin instead, the sister of the true Mountforest heir, because that story would all come out too.

They would say he had his eye on the main chance, an impoverished peer looking for a fortune. He could not do it. He laughed harshly. Aunt Agatha was wrong; he had no choice, except that between misery and dishonour which was no choice at all.

Deep in his reverie, he did not hear someone shouting his name until it had been repeated several times, each time more loudly and urgently. He turned and saw Martin galloping up behind him, waving frantically. 'My lord!'

He stopped and waited for the groom to reach him.

'My lord, the *Silken Maid* has been sighted.' He handed Dominic a letter. 'This came by messenger just after you had gone. Mrs Standon said to catch you with it.'

Dominic took the letter and quickly scanned its contents, then he turned and galloped home as fast as Prince could take him, having first given Emma's letter to Martin to deliver. In less than an hour he was on his way to London. He did not see Lucy and Emma returning from their outing.

That afternoon, Emma sat disconsolately looking out of the drawing-room window, watching the wind swirling the fallen leaves into heaps. This was her first autumn in England and, in spite of a warm log fire, there was already a damp chill in the air which made her shiver. She missed her home in Calcutta, missed her Indian servants, who were so much more to her than servants, missed the rich colours and noise of the bazaars, even the smells, the rotting vegetation, the dust, the heady scent of the yellow kikar blossom, the jasmine and frangipani. None of that would have mattered if she could be with Dominic. But she could not and there was an end to it; she was suffering this heartache to no purpose.

They had come to England on a wild goose chase. It was not necessary to clear their father's name because whatever was thought of him nearly thirty years before had no relevance to the present. To everyone who had known him since, he had been an honourable and courageous man, devoted to his family. What better reputation to take to the grave? Making the Viscount squirm, as Teddy put it, would not bring Papa back to life.

So many other people would be hurt, not least

Dominic, Lucy and Mrs Standon, because no one would believe those good, kind people were ignorant of who she was and what her intentions were. When mud was thrown it stuck, even on those who were merely bystanders.

If she and Teddy went ahead with what they had planned, they would set in motion a whirlwind which, like the wind swirling the leaves in the drive, would scoop everyone up and tear them apart. Revenge would not be sweet, it would be as bitter as gall. Could she make Teddy understand that?

She had said nothing of her thoughts in her letter; she had simply explained there was a horse needing help and she wanted to talk to him. She assumed Dominic had taken it as he said he would; it was no longer on the salver in the hall where she had left it.

Even if Mr Cosgrove allowed Teddy to leave for Cavenham at once, she could hardly expect him for some time. The waiting was affecting her nerves; she was jumpy as a frightened deer and could not concentrate on sewing or reading.

She looked across the room to where Lucy, in a blue merino afternoon gown, was playing Patience, a new card game recently introduced. Mrs Standon, cap askew as ever, was sitting at the table writing in a notebook.

To the outward eye it appeared a normal family scene, but the atmosphere was vibrating with tension, as if they were all waiting for something to happen. She supposed some of it was down to the news that the *Silken Maid* had survived, but no one knew in what condition, and Dominic had rushed off to London.

But it was more than that. Mrs Standon had looked at her once or twice as if she meant to speak to her and then changed her mind, and Lucy was on edge, possibly because now the brig was in, Fergus might be sent to India, after all.

'Oh, this will never come out!' Lucy exclaimed, scooping up the cards. 'Whoever invented this game must enjoy tormenting people.'

'My dear, that is why it is called Patience,' her aunt reproved her. 'Try again.'

Patience, Emma thought, wishing Teddy would hurry up and come. She could not leave without seeing him first and the waiting was almost unbearable. Would he want to come too? She did not think that would serve; he was in a situation he enjoyed with the chance to make a name for himself, it would be a pity to uproot him. She must try and convince him she knew where she was going and what she was going to do. But what was she going to do?

Whatever she did, it were better done soon; the longer she delayed the harder it would become to put Cavenham House and everything she had come to love behind her.

'Please excuse me,' she said and, without waiting for Mrs Standon's consent, hurried from the room.

She dashed into her bedroom and began filling her portmanteau with underwear, stockings and gloves from the drawers of the chest which stood beneath the window, then pulled out her tin trunk and lifted the lid.

Her sari lay in tissue in the bottom of it. She took it out and ran the silk through her fingers, remembering the night of the ball, hearing the music, feeling Dominic's arms about her as they waltzed, remembering the taste of his lips when he kissed her. Memories were all she would have, memories that were sweet as honey and bitter as aloe.

Brushing tears from her eyes with the back of her

hand, she folded the sari back into the trunk and opened her wardrobe, looking with dismay at the rows and rows of garments hanging there. Dominic had paid for those; she had no right to them.

She sorted through them, pulling out the mauve sarcenet, the brown bombazine, the green riding habit and one or two other gowns brought from India. She folded them carefully and put them in the trunk on top of the sari, then turned to the tigerskin rug which lay across the carpet at the foot of the bed.

The glass eyes of the dead tiger stared balefully back at her. Every morning she had padded across its lovely striped skin in her bare feet to go to her washstand and every morning it had reminded her of the father she had loved and respected. She knelt beside it and put her arms around its glorious head, hugging it to her as if embracing her father. 'Oh, Papa, what am I to do?'

She had been sitting there for several minutes, stroking its head when her attention was caught by a row of stitches under one of its ears, one or two of which had been broken. There was something there, something hard which was not part of the stuffing. It did not take much poking to reveal a velvet pouch. She fetched a pair of scissors from her sewing bag and gently enlarged the hole.

A minute later the contents of the pouch had been upturned in her lap and she found herself gazing in astonishment at a fortune in precious gems, diamonds, rubies and other lesser stones, which winked up at her. She sat looking at them, mesmerised by their sparkle, unable to move or think.

Slowly she put out a hand, wondering if her eyes were playing her false and she was imagining them. They felt hard and unyielding under her fingers, no figment of her imagination. They were real. She was sure they were valuable. Papa had provided for them after all, and handsomely too—to think she had nearly sold the skin!

If the gems were valuable enough to make her and Teddy independent, then her life was about to change dramatically. She had already decided she could no longer stay at Cavenham House; now that decision had been reinforced and miraculously a way forward had been found. It was as if fate had taken a hand.

She was about to put the jewels back in the pouch when she realised there was a piece of paper folded inside it, which had not come out when she tipped it up. Opening it out, she found herself staring at her father's handwriting.

'My dearest children,' he had written. 'If you have these gems, then it means that I am dead and Chinkara has fulfilled his promise to tell you of them.' She stopped for a moment, recalling the little Indian who had served her father all his life. He had died with his master and so could not have revealed the hiding place, an eventuality her father seemed not to have considered.

She scrubbed at her eyes with a handkerchief and resumed reading. 'They were honestly acquired years ago, before the Regulating Act banned Company soldiers from private trading. Sell them and spend the money wisely. They are all I have to bequeath you in the material sense, but I hope I leave you with a greater inheritance: a sense of pride and honour, compassion and forgiveness. Do what is right and be happy, my children.'

Emma could not read the signature for the tears which blinded her. Carefully she folded the paper and put it back in the pouch along with the jewels and put the pouch in the pocket of her skirt. Then she stood up and made her way back downstairs, wondering how she was going to break the news to Lucy and Mrs Standon.

She had barely reached the ground floor when a footman hurried towards her. 'Mister Woodhill has arrived, miss. He told me to tell you he would be in the stables.'

She thanked him and went on past the door of the drawing-room where she supposed Lucy and Mrs Standon were still sitting, and out of the side door to the stables, where she found Teddy in Brutus's stall with Martin, administering to the animal.

He looked up. 'Hallo, Em. This is a bad business, don't you think?'

'What? Oh, yes. Teddy, I must talk to you.' Even the poor horse's plight had been driven from her mind by her discovery.

'In a minute, when I've finished here.'

She watched, hopping from one foot to the other like an excited child, while he finished tending the horse.

'He should do well enough now,' he said to Martin, wiping his hands on a piece of cloth. 'Give him that mix in his drinking water, it will keep him calm while the wounds heal. You'll need to be very careful when you try to mount him. He'll not like it.'

'No, I'm sure he won't, but being able to ride him again was more than his lordship expected. He will want to add his thanks to mine, I am sure.' He smiled and shook the young man's hand. 'Now, I'll leave you to talk to your sister.'

Emma waited until he had left, then grabbed Teddy's hand and drew him down beside her on a bale of straw. She did not speak, but simply spread out her skirt and tipped the contents of the little bag into her lap.

'Good God, Emma! Where did they come from?'

'I found them in Papa's tiger less than half an hour ago. He put them there.'

He picked some of the jewels up and weighed them in his hand. 'It's a fortune!'

'Yes, and they're ours. This was with it.' She handed him the letter.

Teddy read it quickly and was reduced to tears. Unable to hold back her own, Emma held him close, just as she had done when he had been a small child and had fallen and hurt himself, and they wept together. 'We're rich!' He laughed, through his tears. 'Papa didn't forget us. We're rich. We need not be servants, at a master's beck and call.'

She wiped the tears from her cheeks with a handkerchief and smiled at him. 'No, but first we have to turn them into hard currency. And London is the place to go if we want a good price. Then we must decide what we are going to do.'

'I know what I want to do. I want to buy a stud farm and breed race horses. But first, there is the matter of the Viscount…'

'Oh, Teddy,' she said. 'I do think we should reconsider…'

He turned to her in surprise. 'Reconsider what?'

'What we said. Vengeance is not for us. It can achieve nothing…'

'But our father was wronged. Have you forgotten that?'

'No, I have not forgotten, but we cannot prove anything. The only other witness was Mr Cosgrove's father and he is long dead. There is no one alive who remembers what happened except our uncle and he will not admit he was at fault.'

Teddy was obviously reluctant to let go. He glowered

at Emma. 'I know what it is. You are thinking of your precious Lord Besthorpe, not Papa at all.'

'No, I was thinking that the desire for revenge is a destructive emotion. It diminishes the soul. Papa's was a good life with much love in it. You must not spoil that by doing something which would shame him. I think that's what he meant in his letter when he spoke of forgiveness.'

'I will not shame him,' Teddy insisted. 'But I want Viscount Mountforest to know that while I live he will never be free of what he did.'

'I think he knows that already,' she said.

He was not fully convinced, but he had been very moved by their father's letter. Balanced as he was between childhood and manhood, his anger on his father's behalf was weighed against his sister's more gentle nature. She sighed with relief when his scowl turned to a smile.

'Well, I am not hiding behind a false name any more. I am my father's son and I am not ashamed of it. From now on, I am Edward Mountforest and our uncle may please himself what he does about it.'

'Good,' she said. 'But we can't do anything until we have sold the stones. I can leave straight away. I had been planning to go anyway.'

'Why?' he asked, momentarily diverted from the prospect of wealth.

'It's a long story and doesn't matter now,' she said.

'I'll not let you go alone. I'm coming too.'

She could not dissuade him and in truth she would be glad of his company. So they agreed that he would ride back to Newmarket to return the horse Mr Cosgrove had lent him and tell him he was leaving, then he would take the stage in Newmarket the following morning which

called in at the Jolly Brewers in Cavenham on its way
to the capital and Emma would board it there.

Emma's task was to look after the jewels, explain to
Lucy and Mrs Standon that she had to return to London
on family business and make sure she was at the inn at
eight o'clock the following morning.

Telling Lucy and Mrs Standon she was going was, as
she expected, not easy.

'Why?' Lucy demanded. 'I thought you were happy
here. You said you would stay until…' She stopped and
looked from Emma to her aunt, who knew nothing of
Captain O'Connor. 'You must stay for Dominic's wedding. Why, it is less than a month away.'

'I'm sorry, Lucy, but my business cannot wait.'

'What business? You never spoke of family affairs
before.'

'Lucy, do not quiz Emma like that,' Mrs Standon put
in. 'It is not polite, you know.' She turned to Emma. 'I
am sorry, my dear. We shall miss you. How will you
manage? Have you any money?'

'I will have. I have discovered there is a legacy…'

'Then I am very glad for you. When do you go?'

'On the morning stage.'

'So soon!' Lucy cried. 'Oh, Emma I wish you would
not.'

Although Lucy spent the remainder of the evening
trying to change Emma's mind, Emma remained adamant. Now the die had been cast, she must find the
strength to turn her back on what had been in many ways
a happy period of her life; though her heart was heavy
at leaving Dominic, she knew it was for the best and
was determined to try and look forward to the future.

She found herself wondering if she and Teddy would

ever have embarked on the voyage to England if they had known about the jewels in the tiger. But she could not regret it. She had learned to love England, even in winter, and she had also learned to love a man. It was a love that was doomed from the start, but she was the richer for it. When she was back in India, hot and sticky, she would remember this year and the man who possessed her heart and she would be thankful for the experience.

Her conviction that she was right was confirmed when Mrs Standon came to her room that night, as she was undressing.

'I never get up before half past nine of a morning and do not intend to start now,' she said, sitting on the end of Emma's bed. 'So I shall say goodbye to you tonight. I shall miss you, you know.'

'And I shall miss you. I have been very happy here.'

'And a little miserable too, I'll wager…'

'What do you mean?'

'I am not blind, my dear. I have seen the looks, the blushes, the secret tears. Dominic is not free, nor likely to be. You are very wise to leave, though I wish it could have been otherwise.'

'I did not think anyone knew.'

'I am not so old I do not remember what it is like to be in love. I loved your father and I lost him.'

'My father?' she queried.

'Yes, your father. Edward Mountforest.' She smiled at Emma's look of astonishment. 'Did you think I did not know who you were?'

'When did you realise it?'

'I knew from the beginning. Emily Morton is a good friend of mine. She wrote to me.'

'Oh, will you ever forgive me for deceiving you?'

'Of course, child.'

'When did you meet my father?'

'The Mountforests, the Cosgroves and the Besthorpes, all came from East Anglia; we grew up knowing each other and if it had not been for James Mountforest and that business over Arthur Boreham we would have been married...'

'Do you know what happened?' Emma put in eagerly. 'Were you there?'

'I did not witness what happened, but your father told me about it afterwards. I believe I was the only one he did tell.'

'Please tell me the true story, Mrs Standon. It would help so much to know what really took place.'

'Edward idolised James when they were children,' Mrs Standon began, her voice taking on the soft quality of remembrance. 'James was of a somewhat wild disposition and always in scrapes for one thing or another. Edward, being the younger, followed where he led and often took the blame when their escapades were uncovered. He did not seem to mind, perhaps because his mother usually interceded on his behalf and the punishment was never very severe.

'James would give him presents or money for keeping silent. I remember he gave him a shotgun once and it transpired that Edward was a good shot, which I suppose was why he decided on the army as a career. When his mother died, he lost his champion and life was never as pleasant for him again.

'James went to Cambridge University and when he came back a suitable aristocratic wife was found for him, the daughter of the Earl of Lincoln, no less. It was a very prestigious match. It was about that time that

Edward and I realised our attachment to each other was more than childhood friendship...' She paused to push a wisp of grey hair back under her cap. 'Ah well, no use going over spilt milk...'

'Then what?' Emma gently prompted.

'One day Edward and James, Arthur Boreham and William Cosgrove spent a day at Newmarket races, where James won a great deal of money. They went off to celebrate and everyone became more than a little bosky. It was then that a bet was made over who was the better marksman...'

'That would have been Papa, wouldn't it?' Emma put in.

'Yes, but Edward told me he never had the gun in his hand. They set up a target and loaded two pistols. James shot first and then Arthur Boreham, but before anyone else could take a turn, they began quarrelling over which shot had hit the centre because both seemed to have gone through the same hole.'

'That was good shooting.'

'Either that or one of the shots was so far off the mark, it didn't register, which was what James maintained had happened to Arthur's. The dispute became very heated and James, who had reloaded for a second attempt, aimed the gun at Arthur. I am sure he would never have fired it, but Edward was afraid he would and tried to knock his brother's arm to deflect the shot. James was furious and pushed him to the ground. The trouble was he had already cocked the gun and it went off. Arthur fell.

'They fetched a doctor and tried to save him but he died a couple of hours later in a bedroom of the local inn. There was a terrible scandal. Arthur was the only son and heir of an earl and his parents were inflamed and out for blood. In their eyes it was not an accident but murder and because they had an enormous amount of influence, it looked as if the culprit would stand trial.'

'But that was James, not Papa.'

'True. Edward told me they had a very uncomfortable interview with their father. James said that if Edward had not tried to take the gun from him it would not have gone off. Edward told his father that when the pistol was fired, he was sprawled on the ground, but old Lord Mountforest would not listen.

'He said whoever was to blame, he did not intend that the family name should be besmirched and James's advantageous marriage put in jeopardy. Edward was told it was his duty to protect his brother and take the blame. His father bought him a commission and arranged for him to go to India.'

'I know the rest,' Emma said. 'He was sent an allowance only so long as he stayed away. Mr Chapman, his banker, told me that but he did not say why.'

'It was a gross injustice.'

'Could you not have said anything?'

'I tried, but I had not witnessed what had happened and I was told I was biased towards Edward and naturally he would try and make himself look innocent in my eyes.'

'But you did believe Papa was telling the truth?'

'Of course I did. William Cosgrove confirmed it to me just before he died, but that was only five years ago, much too late to do anything about it.' She smiled. 'So you see, there is still no proof.'

'It must have been dreadful for you as well as Papa.'

'One gets over broken love affairs, my dear. After Edward was sent away, I married the man my parents chose for me and moved to Yorkshire. We did well

enough.' She paused, watching Emma's pensive face.
'And so did your papa by all accounts.'

'Yes, he loved my mother. She died when I was
eight.'

'Now you must rebuild your life as we had to do. It
will not be easy, but you are strong enough to do it.'

'Thank you for telling me,' Emma murmured, deeply
moved by the story.

'You had a right to know. But, Emma, I do hope you
can dissuade your brother from doing anything so foolish as to try and make a noddicock of Viscount
Mountforest.'

'We have already decided that would be wrong. The
only thing I regret is that Teddy will never inherit the
title.'

'Never is a long time, Emma, and his lordship is still
hale and hearty. Anything can happen before the time
comes for him to wind up his accounts.'

'I wish…'

'No good wishing, child, no good having regrets.'

Emma glanced down at the floor and saw the muti-
lated tiger which she had not yet put in her trunk. 'Mrs
Standon, would you like the tiger rug? I would like you
to have it to remind you of me…' she paused. '…and
of my father. It needs repairing, but I can easily do that
before I go.'

'Oh, child, how very generous of you! I should like
to have it very much.'


And so it was that the tigerskin was left at Cavenham
House when Emma left the following day.

As soon as Emma had disappeared down the drive,
Mrs Standon ordered out the coach and set off to see
James Mountforest. If she had married Edward as she

wanted to, Teddy might have been her child and there would have been no question about who was the heir when it became apparent that James would never have a son. James Mountforest owed her a favour for her years of silence.

# Chapter Ten

Dominic arrived home feeling a great deal more cheerful; the brig was safely in dock after a voyage which Captain Greenaway described as hell. There had been one storm after another with waves as high as houses, he told him. They had been blown so far south the sea froze on the rigging as it washed over the ship. The men had had no hot food for days because they dare not light the fire in the galley and in the end there was nothing to cook anyway. They had lost the mainmast and the sails were shredded.

'As if that wasn't enough,' he had said, 'when the storms abated we became becalmed in a fog so thick and silent, I swear we could hear the fish swimming below us. It gave us an opportunity to do what repairs we could and mend the sails, but our biggest problem was food and water. God knows how we survived. When the fog cleared and we were able to pinpoint our position, we set new sails on the remaining mast and thus limped home.'

'And thank God for your deliverance.'

He had stayed long enough to see the cargo being unloaded and to speak to the crew, promising them a bonus for their good work, and then hurried home. It was Emma he longed to see, to thank her for her prayers, to watch her slow smile...

He knew he should not have been thinking of her, that his mind should have been on the good news he was now able to convey to Sophie, that the brig and its cargo had come safely to port and she could have the alterations to the house, the new carriage, all the fripperies she wanted.

Instead his mind was intent on finding Emma and telling her the good news, telling her also that he knew her real identity, that he did not blame her for her deception, but that he wished she had told him everything from the first. His euphoria evaporated when he hurried into the house and discovered Lucy alone, sitting disconsolately in the morning-room looking out across the terrace, her hands idle in her lap.

'Where is Emma?' he asked, after the briefest of greetings.

'Gone.'

'Gone? Gone where?'

Lucy shrugged. 'She said she had family business to conduct in London. She left this morning.'

Emma had gone to the capital and he had come from there; they might even have passed on the road. The irony of it struck him like a blow. 'What business?'

'That's what I asked her but Aunt Aggie said I was not to quiz her, so I didn't.'

'Where in London? Has she found a new post?'

'I don't know. She said there had been a legacy, but I think that was just a hum. It's my belief she was too unhappy to stay.'

He lifted his tails and sat down on the window-seat beside her, suddenly deflated. 'Unhappy? Why so?'

She twisted round to look at him. 'I should not have thought it necessary to tell you.'

'Surely not because of that business over Brutus?'

'No. Oh, Dominic, are you blind? Don't you know she loves you and you are breaking her heart marrying someone else?'

'Did she tell you this?'

'Of course not, but I could tell.' She sighed. 'When you are in love yourself, you understand the signs.'

'Is that so?' he asked, amused.

'Yes, it is. You know, too many people are made unhappy because of the strict rules of society. There is too much store set on titles and wealth and suitability and not enough on the character of the people concerned. Love is not made to order, you know.'

'I know,' he said softly.

'Now the *Silken Maid* is in, I suppose, she will turn about and go back for more cargo?'

'When the repairs are completed, but they may take some time. But what has that to do with Emma?'

'Nothing. I was thinking of Fergus—Captain O'Connor.'

'Oh, I see. You have not changed your mind about him then?'

'No, nor will I.'

'Can you not be patient just a little longer?'

'I am trying, but without Emma it will be so difficult. She was so good at diverting me and now I have no one.'

'There is Aunt Agatha. Where is she, by the way?'

'She went out in the carriage ages ago, I don't know where. But I think she means to return to Yorkshire as soon as you are married. Then there will only be Sophie.'

'Sophie,' he said, and stood up. 'Has she been over?'

'No, not since the trouble over Brutus.' She paused. 'Dominic, you do not believe Emma did that to Brutus, do you?'

'No, of course not.' He smiled wearily. 'But, Lucy, you cannot call off a wedding because of a horse.'

'No, more's the pity.'

He turned from her before she could read the telltale signs in his face too. 'I must go over and tell her the good news. I suppose she is still staying with the Cosgroves.'

He left her, musing on the way people fell in love without rhyme or reason. Lucy was right—too many people were made unhappy because of social convention and she should not be made to suffer because of it. It was too late for him, but he could do something about Fergus O'Connor. If he could not be happy himself, he could make sure his sister was.

He fetched Cavenham Prince from the stable and set out for Newmarket, glad that he would not now have to part with him.

It was a misty afternoon and he wore a long cape over his riding coat with his hat pulled well down over his brow. The weather did not bother him; he was content with whatever was sent, the spring with its daffodils and burgeoning shoots, the summer's haymaking and harvest, autumn with its rosy hips and falling leaves, even winter when the fires in the house were ablaze with logs and outside the frost made patterns on the window panes. It was all to be seen and enjoyed at Cavenham, but how much better it would be with the woman he loved beside him.

He sighed. Dwelling on what might have been only made him more miserable and he must stop himself do-

ing it. But he hoped Emma was not running into more
trouble. She might not find a position as congenial as
the one she had with Lucy and she had gone without a
reference. Why hadn't she waited until he came back?
Was she afraid he might persuade her to stay? She was,
he decided, infinitely wiser than he was. A clean cut was
much better than a ragged wound which would never
heal properly. As for the scar, that would always be
there, hidden in his heart. Dear Emma, he thought, be
happy.

By the time he rode into the Cosgrove stableyard it
was growing dusk. There was no one about so he dismounted and looped Prince's reins over a rail, noticing
that a lamp burned in the office beside the stables and
Bertie was undoubtedly at work there. He would tell him
the good news about the *Silken Maid* before going into
the house to see Sophie.

They did not hear him coming, did not even hear the
gentle tap at the door, so engrossed were they with each
other. He had been standing in the doorway for several
seconds looking down on them before Sophie caught
sight of him over Bertie's shoulder. Her eyes opened
wide and then she laughed in an embarrassed fashion
and pushed her lover off her. 'Bertie, we have company.'

Bertie scrambled to his feet. Sophie stood up and
smoothed down the skirt of her gown. Dominic turned
on his heel and went outside, where he stood beside
Cavenham Prince and looked up at the swirling clouds,
waiting for his anger to abate. Anger and desperate misery.

He heard Bertie come out of the building behind him
but he did not turn round. 'I suppose you want to call
me out?'

'No.' He was perfectly calm now. 'You have done me

a favour. I shall, of course, go away for a time. When I come back I hope Sophie will have decided we should not suit, after all. That is the way it is done, is it not?'

There could be no wedding. He would have to take the blame, of course, be branded a mountebank and shunned by society, but that was preferable to going through with a marriage that would make them both miserable.

'Is that all you've got to say?' Sophie's voice came to him from the doorway. 'Don't you want to know why?'

'The why does not trouble me,' he said, without turning round. 'Only my own blindness.'

And picking up the reins he vaulted onto Prince's back and galloped out of the yard.

Emma soon discovered it was not easy to sell gems if you had no documents to prove they belonged to you, particularly if they were outstandingly fine ones. Honest jewellers refused to deal with her and she knew dishonest ones would fleece her. With a bag full of precious stones and very little money between them, they had been obliged to look for lodgings which were respectable without being expensive and they had taken two bedrooms and a sitting room in a lodging house off Oxford Street.

Having dined frugally off pork chops, potatoes and cabbage, they were sitting round the small coal fire which smoked abominably, discussing their next move. What they needed was a go-between, someone whom they could trust and who was trusted by the diamond merchants. She knew no one except Dominic and she could not ask him to act for them. She had made a clean break and for her own peace of mind, she must stick to it.

There was Captain Greenaway, of course, and he was in town while the *Silken Maid* was being repaired. He was used to selling his cargo, including jewels; he might help them. The disadvantage of approaching him was that he might tell Dominic he had seen them.

'What if he does?' Teddy said. 'We have nothing to hide.'

'No, of course not,' she said, unable to explain the hurt it would cause her to see the Marquis again. 'So, you think we should approach the Captain?'

'We don't know anyone else, do we? We could start off by showing him just one stone and see what he says.'

Thus it was the following morning they hired a hackney carriage to seek out Captain Greenaway in the dry dock where the *Silken Maid* was undergoing extensive repairs.

Emma, dressed in her old brown burnous with its hood up against the bitingly cold wind which came up over the river, went with some trepidation in case she should come face to face with Dominic. It was something she both longed for and dreaded, knowing that a confrontation with him would make all her feelings for him flare up again when she had been trying so hard to keep them under control.

She need not have worried; Dominic was not there and neither was Captain Greenaway. He was lodging at Fladong's in Oxford Street, they were told by one of the crew who was still on board. They climbed back into the carriage and directed the driver to take them to the hotel.

Here the Captain greeted them like long-lost relatives,

clasping their hands, saying how glad he was to see them again. He ordered food and drink for them, for it was noon by then, and led them to a quiet table in the corner of the parlour.

'Sit down. Sit down.' he commanded. 'Tell me what I can do for you and, if it is in my power, it shall be done.'

He was so jovial and so friendly Emma abandoned the idea of showing him just one jewel in favour of telling him the whole story, some of which he had already gleaned.

'An extraordinary tale,' he said, when it was told and Emma had shown him the gems. 'In the head of the tiger, you say? Safe there as anywhere, I suppose. And you really had no idea?'

'None at all.' Emma smiled. 'I remember Papa saying something once about who knows what secrets are concealed in the head of the tiger, but I thought he was speaking generally. I would never have dreamed of looking for anything there.'

'And neither would thieves,' the Captain said. 'A secure hiding place if ever there was one.'

'Now, of course, we must dispose of them. We thought you might be kind enough to help us. We would pay you a percentage, of course.'

'I will be glad to sell the stones for you and no need to offer me an inducement, but you must put the proceeds straight into a bank. I suggest Child's. They will also advise you about investment and income and matters of that nature, which I am not qualified to do, being nothing but an old sea dog.'

Emma thanked him and handed over the pouch and he promised to come to them at their lodgings as soon as he had disposed of its contents and escort them to the bank. 'Better to have as many strong men around you as you can,' he said, with a gruff laugh. 'There are thieves and footpads everywhere and it will be a fortune you are carrying.'

And so it was. Though the bulk of the money was to be set aside to buy the farm and horses Teddy wanted, they did not resist the temptation to renew their wardrobes and move to better accommodation while they looked for a place to buy. It crossed Emma's mind that if the Captain were to tell Dominic he had seen them and where they lodged, they would have moved on. Then she laughed at herself. His wedding day was only two weeks away; it was very conceited of her to think he would be interested in her whereabouts.

She did not want to think of the wedding and forced herself to put the last year behind her, to try and forget it had ever happened, just as if they had come straight from India to this new home in Jermyn Street. Whenever thoughts of Dominic invaded her mind, she pushed them firmly away. Whatever had been between them, unspoken as it had been, must be allowed to shrivel and die. And with it a small part of her shrivelled and died too. She did not feel quite whole but not one word of it did she utter to Teddy.

She became her brother's housekeeper and fulfilled her role as cheerfully as she could, while Teddy went about the business of acquiring a property and bloodstock, which was more difficult than he had supposed. His requirements were so particular that it was difficult to find something which was exactly right in size and location as well as at the right price. 'It has to be close to Newmarket,' he said. 'It is the centre of the racing world now.' He laughed suddenly. 'And I want Viscount

Mountforest to know we are there, close by him. He won't like that by half!'

By the time the new year of 1817 arrived with firework displays and first footing, Emma was beginning to wonder if what Teddy was looking for existed at all. For his sake she shared his disappointment, but the thought of living within a few miles of Cavenham was something she could not contemplate with equilibrium.

'Teddy, have you ever given a thought to returning to India?' she asked him one day in early January when the snow lay in brown slush at the sides of the roads where it had been thrown by the vehicle wheels and horse hooves and the smoke from a thousand fires drifted on the cold air creating a dense, freezing fog. She was sitting with her knees almost in the grate and a warm shawl about her shoulders, but still she shivered.

Teddy had been scanning a catalogue from Tattersall's, but he looked up surprised at her suggestion. 'What would we do there? Besides, we came to England to…'

'To clear Papa's name, I know that, but we have done that to our own satisfaction, thanks to Mrs Standon. And as for vengeance, we decided not to pursue that path, didn't we?'

'Yes, but we were also going to find you a husband.'

'I have decided not to think of that either. I shall not marry. Let us go back to India, Teddy. There is a new game being taken up by the Indian Army called polo. It is a team game played on horseback. From what I have read of it, it needs special ponies, very wiry and strong and fast. I'm told it is going to be all the rage before long. If you could breed the ponies, you could make a name for yourself. What do you think?'

He looked thoughtful. 'I heard about that too, but do you really want to go back?'

'Yes,' she lied. No need for him to know what she really wanted was to live at Cavenham, to be loved by Dominic, to be his wife and live happily with him forever. Such was the stuff of her dreams, but that was all it was, unattainable, hopeless dreaming. 'It is home, isn't it? We have friends there…'

He was not convinced, but he knew Emma was unhappy and when his sister was sad, so was he. If she found life intolerable in England, then he would leave for her sake. 'Very well. We'll go,' he said. 'When?'

'Just as soon as we can wind up our affairs here. It shouldn't take long; there is only the lease of this house to dispose of, the passage to book and our baggage to pack.'

Once the decision had been made, Emma felt easier. She had to turn her back on Dominic and look for a new life, as far away from him as possible. Half the circumference of the globe might just do it, might just ease the ache which was ever present in her heart and mind.

Then, on the very morning Teddy set off to arrange their passage, something happened which threw Emma's fragile peace of mind into confusion once again.

The wind had risen in the night and lifted the blanket of fog, which had shrouded the city for more than two weeks. The sun had broken through and the day was bright but very cold and Emma, who had been confined indoors for several days, was longing for a little fresh air. Wrapped up in a fur-lined green velvet cloak with her hands in a fur muff, she set off for a brisk walk. Her short sojourn among the elite of Society was behind her and the impropriety of walking out alone did not cross her mind.

She had no particular destination, but was enjoying the busy street scene, the carriages of the rich bowling past, the carts of the market gardeners, the street hawkers selling anything from hot peas to bootlaces, storing it all in her memory to be brought out in future years when she was in nostalgic mood and the hurt had faded. It would fade, she told herself sternly, if she were determined enough.

She looked up to cross the busy road and was startled to see a familiar figure dressed in a long grey cloak and a grey velvet bonnet, hurrying along ahead of her. She was carrying a small portmanteau. Curious, Emma followed and watched as she turned into the yard of the Golden Cross coaching inn.

It was Lucy, wasn't it? Had she been persuaded to return to Yorkshire with Mrs Standon? But they could have made that journey from Huntingdon, which was not so far from Cavenham and on the Great North Road; there was no need to return to the capital. If they had, Lucy certainly would not have been expected, or allowed, to make her own way to the stage. There was something very strange going on.

Heart beating very fast, anticipating she knew not what, Emma followed her. It would be pleasant to talk to Lucy and hear all the latest news of Cavenham, but supposing Dominic was also there—could she face him? He must have discovered her deception by now, if not from Mrs Standon, then from Captain Greenaway. It must have made him very angry. She hesitated, then pulled herself together.

She no longer had anything to hide. Her days of deception were done and if he were there, she would simply have to defend herself. But he would not be there. He was newly married. Why would he be sitting in a London coaching inn when he had a house, carriage and horses of his own? If the girl she had seen was really Lucy, Emma was ready to wager Dominic knew nothing of it. Taking a deep breath, she made her way into the yard.

A coach was due in and the ostlers and grooms were busy bringing out four fresh horses ready for a quick change. There were several passengers waiting to board and the yard was littered with travellers' boxes and baskets. There was no sign of Lucy, nor Mrs Standon. Had she been mistaken and it was not Lucy, but someone very like her?

Stepping between the luggage and avoiding the busy grooms and restive horses, she went into the inn. The first room she came to was crowded with passengers, eating and drinking between stages, but no Lucy. Half-sorry, half-relieved, she turned to go.

'There's room in the back parlour, miss,' a white-aproned waiter told her, jerking his head towards a passage which led to the rear of the premises. 'More congenial for ladies.'

Emma thanked him and went to look. Lucy was seated at a small table and was in the act of removing her gloves and cloak and ordering from a waiter who stood over her. She was alone and obviously nervous.

'Lucy!'

The girl looked up at the sound of her name and her whole face lit with pleasure. Ignoring the waiter, she rose and crossed the floor to fling herself into Emma's arms.

'Oh, Emma, I never thought to see you again. You don't know how much I've missed you. How are you?

Are you well? Have you concluded your family business? Have you found another situation? Come and sit down and tell me all about it.' She took Emma by the hand and dragged her back to the table.

Emma gave a laugh of genuine pleasure, something she had done little of recently. 'So many questions and not a word about what you are doing here.' She looked about her. 'And alone too. Have you no escort?'

'I shall have bye and bye. I am waiting for Fergus.'

'Captain O'Connor. Oh dear, Lucy, I have a feeling you have got yourself in a bumblebath. You are not planning to elope, are you?'

'Yes, why not?' Lucy's blue eyes looked at her defiantly. 'Life at Cavenham is insupportable. Aunt Agatha is going back to Yorkshire and Dominic wants me to go with her. And he is determined to send Fergus to India. It has taken a long while to repair the *Silken Maid*, but it is almost done now and it will set sail in the next day or so and Fergus with it.'

'But that was all arranged long ago, you knew that.'

'Yes, but if he had gone when it was first suggested, he would have been back before now and Dominic would have had to keep his promise to let us marry. Now everything is at sixes and sevens and there's no talking to him. He is like a wounded animal; he snarls and growls and won't let anyone near him. He has even fallen out with Bertie Cosgrove. Oh, Emma, he is so unhappy.'

Emma could not suppress the question which came immediately to mind. 'But what about Sophie?'

'She postponed the wedding, though whether she is punishing him and means to change her mind when he has come to heel or whether she truly intends to jilt him,

I do not know. She went home to Mountforest Hall. We haven't seen her for weeks.'

Emma's heart gave a little skip of pure joy but then settled as she thought of how that would affect Dominic. He would be hurt and humiliated; there would be gossip and he would be reviled whether it was his fault or not. She longed to go to him, but she knew that would only make matters worse.

'But if your brother is so unhappy, Lucy, should you have left him? Your going will make him even more miserable and the scandal of an elopement on top of everything else will be very damaging to you both. I beg you to reconsider.'

'No, it is too late, everything is arranged. I persuaded Dominic to let me come to London with him. I said I wanted to do some shopping before I left for Yorkshire, where there are no shops worth speaking of.'

'And you have taken the opportunity to meet Fergus. Oh, Lucy, it is a dreadful thing you are doing. Please don't do it.'

'I might not have done if you had not left.'

'Oh, Lucy, that is not fair! I could not stay, you know that. My brother needs me. He is only young and about to set up in business.' She paused, knowing she had to take a hand, though what exactly she could do she did not know. 'Enough of me. We were talking about you. Go home and have a little more patience.'

'Patience! I am done with being patient.' Lucy could be as stubborn as her brother when she chose. 'Anyway, Dominic is more concerned with the relaunch of the *Silken Maid* and the commissioning of a new brig than with me. He has put everything into a second vessel. I do believe he means to have a whole fleet. If you ask me, that is why Sophie is angry with him; she does not approve of his trading.'

'Then if you will not go back to Bedford Row, come home with me. We will talk about it and see what can be done.' She had no idea what she could do, but she was playing for time; anything was better than allowing Lucy to go ahead with this plan. If she could not persuade her, then perhaps it would be best to approach Captain O'Connor and trust to his good sense.

Before Lucy could answer the Captain himself appeared in the doorway. Lucy saw him almost at the same time as Emma and rushed to fling herself into his arms. Emma watched as he hugged her to him and then held her away from him so that he could look into her upturned face.

There was no doubt in Emma's mind that they truly loved each other, and she wished Dominic could see them thus; he would not hold out against them. Surely he was not so wrapped up in his own affairs that he could not see how unhappy his sister was? And how determined.

Lucy, hanging on to Fergus's arm, brought him over to Emma. If he was surprised to see her, he gave no sign of it as he bowed before her, smiling. 'Still taking good care of my darling, Miss Woodhill?'

'Yes. I have to admit I have been trying to persuade her to abandon this plan to elope.'

He turned from Emma to Lucy. 'And is that what you want to do, sweetheart?'

'Emma has been telling me it is very unkind of me to add to Dominic's burdens,' she said. 'I know she is right, but I do so want to marry you, dearest Fergus.'

He smiled down at her. 'And I you, sweetheart, but I want you to be very, very sure.'

'Of course I am sure.'

'Then let us go to my home,' Emma said. 'It is barely
five minutes' walk away and we can talk comfortably
there.'

Although Lucy was a little reluctant, Fergus was quick
to agree and they set off for Jermyn Street. It surprised
and delighted Lucy, when she found herself being ushered into a large comfortable house and discovered that
Emma was mistress of it.

'Our family fortunes have taken a turn for the better
and we have been able to lease this house,' Emma said,
as a maidservant took their gloves and cloaks. She motioned them towards the comfortable sofas which flanked
the blazing fire. Fergus and Lucy sat side by side and
Emma took a seat opposite them.

'Then the story of the legacy was true?' Lucy said.

'Yes, though other things were not.' She paused. 'I
think before I begin to lecture you on deception, I had
better tell you the whole truth now there is no longer
any need to dissemble.' And this she proceeded to do,
succinctly and without trying to justify herself.

'You mean you are Sophie's cousin?' Lucy queried
when she had finished. 'Does Sophie know this? Does
Dominic?'

'I do not think so. Unless Mrs Standon told them.'

'Aunt Agatha knew? She knew and never said a word!
Oh, what a heap of humbug it has all been.'

'Yes, and all my fault, for which I am truly penitent.
But, you see, it makes it so much worse to think that
you are planning to add to your brother's troubles. I am
sure he will not stand in your way, once he is convinced
that you will be happy with Captain O'Connor.'

'What do you say, Lucy?' the Captain asked her.

'Shall we defer our plans until we have appealed to your brother?'

She turned towards him, a worried frown wrinkling her forehead. 'Have you changed your mind about marrying me?'

'Not at all, my love. There is nothing I want more than to have you for my wife, but I have news of my own...' He paused and took her hand. 'I have, only this morning, been offered the position of master of the brig, *Lucilla*, which sails for India in a couple of weeks.'

'*Lucilla!*' She giggled. 'Who named it that?'

'Your brother.'

'Dominic!'

'Yes. I am to have a percentage of the profits. It will make me independent and in a position to offer for you. So, you see, I am indebted to the Marquis and to repay him by running away to Gretna Green with his sister would not be at all an honourable thing to do. I had meant to tell you about it when we met at the inn, but Miss Woodhill was there and...'

'Oh, you truly cannot turn your back on your brother now,' Emma said. 'Oh, Lucy, please go home. You will break Dominic's heart if you do not.'

'Very well, but only if you come too. You will be able to persuade him when I cannot; he always listened to you. Tell him I want to marry Fergus before he goes to India. I want to go with him, to see all the places you have told me of, the palaces and temples and the bazaars and the countryside.'

The thought of seeing Dominic again, of watching his slow smile, of hearing his gentle voice, even if it was reproving her, was something Emma longed for with every breath she took. But if there was any chance that his marriage to Sophie might yet go ahead, she would be torturing herself for nothing.

Even if he did not marry Sophie, it did not mean he would turn to her. She had deceived him, told untruths, pretended to be other than what she was; it was enough to turn any man against her. Her feelings of guilt rose in her like bile and she felt the heat of it spreading up from the pit of her stomach into her face. She brushed a hand over her forehead. 'I can't do that, Lucy. I cannot go back, you must know that.'

'Then I will not go either.'

'Lucy!' Fergus exclaimed.

'I mean it.'

'Oh, Lucy, that is too cruel,' Emma said. 'Your brother does not deserve such treatment from you.'

'Then you must speak for us. I am determined on it, Emma, otherwise it is Gretna Green.'

Emma hesitated. If Lucy carried out her threat she would ruin her reputation and Dominic's too, as well as Captain O'Connor's chance to make good. She could not let that happen. She could be cool and calm, couldn't she? She could speak only of Lucy and never let him know how much she longed for him. Business-like, that is what she would be.

She would see him again. Her heart sang at the prospect, though she knew deep inside her, that her despair would be all the deeper after the encounter.

'Where is he now?'

'I left him, not an hour since,' Fergus said. 'I believe he was going home to Bedford Row.'

'And expecting to find Lucy there, no doubt,' Emma said, a little tartly.

'Yes, for we were to return to Cavenham today,' Lucy

told her, reaching out to put a hand on her arm, a smile of cajolement on her face.

'Then I suppose I must go now, before he begins to wonder what has become of you,' Emma said. 'But you must come with me, Lucy, and Captain O'Connor must return to his lodgings until everything is sorted out. We must ensure there is no hint of scandal. Is that agreed?'

'Yes,' said Fergus firmly. 'If we can bring this about without resorting to Gretna Green, then I, for one, shall be thankful. It would not have made a good start to married life, though I was prepared to do it for Lucy's sake.'

'Then if you will excuse me, I will write a note to tell my brother what has happened,' Emma said. 'Then we can leave at once.'

As soon as Emma had left the room, Lucy turned to Fergus. 'I knew it! I knew she would go. Am I not the clever one?'

'What do you mean?'

'Dominic needs her and she needs him but they are both too proud to admit it. I had to do something. And I was sure she would go for my sake when she would not dream of going for her own.'

'But you surely did not know she would be at the inn?'

'No, but one must seize one's opportunities, isn't that what you always say? As soon as she begged me to go back to Dominic, I realised how I could bring them together.' She giggled and reached up to kiss his cheek. 'Besides, if anyone can persuade my brother to let us marry and go to India together, it is Emma.'

Dominic paced the drawing room from window to door and back again. His bag was packed and the car-

riage had been ordered for noon. It was already one
o'clock and Lucy was nowhere to be found. Drat the
girl! She knew he wanted to be back at Cavenham tonight. He could not believe she had any shopping of
importance to do. After all, he had already spent a fortune on clothes and fripperies for her come-out and she
would not need anything new for Yorkshire.

He knew she did not want to go with their aunt, but
there was no help for it; he was going away himself and
she could not be left in the house with no one but servants to look after her.

When he told Sophie and Bertie he was leaving he
had meant it. He needed to come to terms with what had
happened but he could not do that at Cavenham, nor
even in London, where the tattlers would make life insupportable, both for himself and Sophie. He wanted to
spare her that.

After finding Sophie with Bertie he had galloped
home in a blind rage at her betrayal, but long before he
reached Cavenham his thoughts had turned to Emma.
Now, at last, he could declare himself, could tell her
openly of his love, ask her to wait until the fuss of the
broken engagement died down. It was the last twist of
the knife, the final irony, that she had disappeared. He
had hunted for her all over London but could find no
clue as to her whereabouts.

Why had she left in the first place? Was the story of
the sudden legacy as much a fiction as her name and
that reference from Emma Mountforest? She had deceived him, but it made no difference; he would have
fallen in love with her whatever she called herself.

On the other hand, if she had come to him in the
beginning, as Emma Mountforest, he would never have
taken her on as Lucy's companion, would he? It would

have been unthinkable. Then he would not have learned to love her for what she was, caring, mischievous, independent, proud and wholly delightful. The past year would have been completely different; he would have married Sophie.

Or would he? Bertie would probably still have cuckolded him, still made him look and feel a fool. Sophie had asked him if he wanted to know why and he had said no. Despite himself he had wondered why, not only why, but how long it had been going on. And, more to the point, whether he really cared.

Sophie had come to Cavenham the next day, trying to excuse herself. 'I just wanted to make you jealous, Dominic, dear,' she had said, pacing the library in muddy riding boots. 'It meant nothing. I was upset. You were being such a pinchcommons over a new carriage and the alterations to the house and I am not used to having to economise. It isn't as if I didn't have a good dowry; you could have paid for everything with that after we were married.'

As if he relished the idea of being an apron-squire! As if that was all there was to it! He had told her so, but she had laughed and said better men than he had been dependent on their wives and thought nothing of it. He had no cause to be top-lofty when he spent all his time and money buying and selling cargo like some common haberdasher. Then to his horror, she had said she would forgive him if he mended his ways. Not a word about her own lapse, which in his eyes was far more serious, not a hint of repentance.

He had stared at her as if seeing her for the first time. How could he have ever thought those hard grey eyes were beautiful, or that those red lips were anything but mean? He had eulogised over her fine qualities when he

had first met her and basked in the favour when she
deigned to smile at him. Callow, callow youth that he
had been!

He didn't want her forgiveness, he wanted his freedom. The only way he was going to obtain it was to go
away and let the world think what they liked. He could
leave the estate in the capable hands of his steward for
a few months, which would give Bertie and Sophie time
to marry if they wanted to and let the gossip die down.
So he had told her.

He had told her father too, in a most unpleasant interview at Mountforest Hall, whence he had gone, out
of courtesy, to explain his intention. His lordship had
just come in from a hunt and received him in the gun-
room, which was cold and unfurnished except for a table
and cupboards for the guns.

The Viscount's temper, always volatile, was at its
most fiery because he had been thrown from his horse
and the fox had escaped. He let himself go on that subject for several minutes before allowing Dominic to
speak and then had subjected him to a recital of his
grievances at the arrival of an upstart who claimed to be
heir to the Viscountcy.

Dominic had been accused of raking up old scandals,
harbouring a traitor, nurturing a viper, and other equally
florid metaphors. His lordship had worked himself up
into a froth over it, saying that his daughter was being
denied her birthright; unless she was married quickly and
her dowry handed over, it might be lost. And what did
the Marquis of Cavenham think about that?

'Then you know about Teddy, my lord?'

'Yes, thanks to that old bat, Agatha Standon.'

'Aunt Agatha? What has she to do with it?'

'Nothing, but she seems to think she has a right to

come here and threaten me just because she once set her cap at my brother.' He had smiled at Dominic's look of surprise. 'You didn't know that, I see. Well, it's neither here nor there now. All in the past.'

Dominic had been temporarily diverted from his problem with Sophie. 'What did she say?'

'She said she had a duty to protect Edward's offspring and to see he had justice.'

'You are prepared to recognise him, then?'

'Got no choice. She said she knew what had happened and she'd squeak beef if I did not. But that don't mean I'm prepared to embrace the fellow, not yet, I ain't. I'm not going to stick my spoon in the wall for an age yet. Besides, if Lady Mountforest were to wind up her accounts first, I might remarry and get me an heir. Nothing's certain.'

'No, sir, we can none of us predict the future, but I am glad you acknowledge the boy is your present heir.'

'That don't mean you are let off marrying my daughter, Besthorpe. I'm not having another scandal in the family.'

'But, my lord, we have both realised we should not suit. Sophie prefers Cosgrove to me and who am I to argue with that?'

'He's got no title.'

'No, but you have influence at court, my lord, I am sure you can get him one. For services to racing, something of that sort.'

'Hmph. Could be done, I suppose. Not a marquis though. Set her heart on being a marchioness, you know.'

'Not if it made her miserable, surely?'

'Can't see why she should be miserable. She has a

good portion and you ain't pinched in the pocket. Did well out of the Indian trade, I hear.'

'That is one of the items she has listed against me, sir.' He had smiled. 'Along with a stubborn pride and a determination to be my own master. We should fight like turkey cocks.'

'Dammit, man, are you reneging?'

'No, that is for Sophie to do, but I wish you would be so good as to persuade her that it is for the best. I am sure she already believes that; she only needs your concurrence to send me on my way.'

'It wouldn't have anything to do with another lady, would it? Someone my daughter refers to as a little brown mouse?'

'No, my lord. Miss Woodhill...'

'You mean Miss Mountforest, don't you?'

'Yes, I gave her the name she adopted out of consideration for you. Miss Mountforest has left. I do not know where she is.'

His lordship had given a cackling laugh at that. 'Hoisted on your own petard, ain't you? You've lost them both and come home by weeping cross.'

There had been no answer to that and he had taken his leave.

To prove his independence he had sunk most of the profits from the last voyage of the *Silken Maid* into a second brig which he had named *Lucilla*. It was while he was inspecting the progress of this that he had made up his mind to sail on her. A spell in India in a different climate, a different culture, with new scenery and new people might help to mitigate the hurt.

When they returned he would consent to Lucy marrying Fergus O'Connor, if she was still determined on it. As for his own affairs, there was nothing he could do, but bear up and make the best of it without the woman he loved. But it was going to be damnably difficult.

He stopped his pacing and turned towards the door as he heard footsteps in the hall. The next minute Lucy came into the room.

'Where have you been, Lucilla?' His low spirits made him speak sharply. 'You know we were to be away by noon. It is already gone one and you have not yet eaten.'

She was smiling, apparently unaffected by his scold. 'Yes, I have, but that is by the bye. We have a visitor.'

'Visitor! Lucy, you know we are in haste to be away…' He stopped suddenly, his mouth half-open, as Emma appeared in the doorway.

She stood there enveloped in a green velvet cloak with a fur lined hood which framed her face. He would have said she was an apparition, if she had not looked so rosily substantial, with her cheeks pink from the cold air and her eyes bright as emeralds. 'Emma!'

She smiled to cover her nervousness. 'Good afternoon, my lord.'

'Emma! What are you doing here?'

'I am sorry to intrude, my lord,' she said, determined to address him formally. 'I would not have done so, had not Lucy persuaded me.' She swung round as a soft click of the door told her that Lucy had left them alone together. 'Lucy, come back,' she called after her, but her friend was already out of earshot.

'Why don't you take off your cloak and sit down, Emma?' he suggested, indicating a chair by the fire. 'We cannot talk comfortably with you standing in the doorway as if you were going to take flight at any moment.'

Emma turned back to Dominic and took a deep breath, reminding herself of her resolve to be cool and businesslike. 'No, thank you, my lord. I would rather stand. And this will not take long.'

'Why are you angry with me?'

'I am not angry,' she said, realising she had taken refuge in acerbity. 'But I am surprised at you and disappointed, too.'

'Why?' He had always prided himself on his coolness under stress, his ability to hide his feelings, but now he found he could not keep the hurt from his voice. 'If anyone should be disappointed, surely it should be me? You were the one practising deceit, not me. I have been open with you, befriended you when I thought you needed a friend and you repaid me with lies...'

'I know, my lord, and I am deeply ashamed of that, but that is not why I am here now.'

'Oh, then why are you here?' Now he was the one who sounded angry when all he wanted was to take her into his arms and tell her how much he loved her, that there would never be anyone else for him and he would brave scandal, ridicule and condemnation rather than let her go.

'Because of Lucy. Because you have been so wrapped up in your own affairs, you were oblivious to what was going on under your own nose.'

'I beg your pardon?' He was astonished at her forthrightness. He should not have been; she had never been afraid to speak her mind, even as a servant.

'I am sorry to be so blunt, my lord, but did you not realise how unhappy your sister was?'

'Unhappy? I know she did not want to go to Yorkshire but she has to go somewhere...'

'Why? She has a home with you.'

'Without a female companion that is not possible, and you left her, remember?'

'Why do you keep bringing me into it? I left for very good reasons and you could have engaged another companion.'

'What! And go through all that again! Besides, Lucy would have no other.'

'I did not know that.' Emma realised she was losing the advantage, and struggled to regain it. 'But no doubt she thought it unnecessary when she wanted so much to be married.'

'And so she may. When we come back.'

'We? You are going away?' Her dismay showed in her lovely green eyes and his spirits lifted suddenly.

'Yes, with Captain O'Connor to India. You described it so vividly and with such strong affection, I thought I would go and see for myself. And it would be an advantage to know where my cargoes come from and the hazards of the voyage. I sail on *Lucilla* for Calcutta in two weeks' time.'

She was astonished. Only the night before she and Teddy had decided to return there. The European population of Calcutta was a close-knit community and everyone, sooner or later, met everyone else. They would have been bound to come across each other. Teddy, who had gone this very morning to book their passages, might very well have taken berths on *Lucilla*. Fate, she decided, had a cruel sense of irony.

She hid her hands in the folds of her cloak in case they gave away her agitation. 'Captain O'Connor said nothing of that.'

'From that I conclude that you have seen him recently?'

'Yes. I met him at the Golden Cross this morning. And Lucy, too.'

'Lucy! What was she doing there?'

'I believe she was eloping, my lord.'

'Good Lord! You must be mistaken.'

'No, I am not mistaken. You know of her attachment...'

He smiled suddenly, remembering how he had mis-
takenly thought it was Emma who had set her cap at the
Captain, and she had allowed him to think it. 'Yes, for
Captain O'Connor, but he would not elope with her. He
is to be Master of *Lucilla*. I made him the offer this very
morning.'

'So he told us, but that was not until after Lucy had
persuaded him to elope with her. She means to keep him
to his promise if you do not allow them to marry. She
has her mind fixed on going to India with him. And you
know, my lord, how stubborn she can be.'

He smiled and made her heart turn over. 'So stubborn
that you felt obliged to step into the lion's den on her
behalf.'

'It was that or see her ruined, my lord.'

'And that was your only reason for coming here today?'

'Yes, what other reason could I have?'

'None, I suppose.' He paused. 'Unless it was to beg
my pardon for deceiving me about who you were, for
running away, for making me...' He stopped suddenly.
'Never mind about that.'

'Oh, but I do mind, my lord. I never meant to hurt
anyone, please believe me. I do most humbly beg your
pardon. You see, we thought we were penniless and our
father—'

'Was Edward Mountforest.'

'You know?'

'Yes. Aunt Agatha told me.' He paused, searching her
face, trying to make her look at him, to make her see

the longing in his eyes, the love and passion he had never been able to express and hardly dare express, even now. But he could not let her go, not until he had heard from her own lips that she did not love him. 'What I do not know, is why.'

'When our father died, we thought we had been left destitute, my lord, and we knew we had kin in England…'

'You came to appeal to the Viscount, your uncle?'

'I thought we might, but Teddy was more concerned with learning the truth about our father's exile. You see, we knew he had been banished but we didn't know why. We did not believe he could ever have done anything bad enough to deserve that.'

'And Aunt Agatha told you the truth?'

'Yes.'

'So, having discovered what you wanted to know, you simply packed your bags and left without so much as by your leave.'

'Oh, my lord… Dominic, it was not like that at all.'

'What was it like?' he demanded.

'You know very well I could not stay. I had deceived you. That letter of introduction was all a hum. I had never been a lady's maid or a companion, never even worked for a living.'

'That much I deduced from the first, but it made not one jot of difference. I still fell in love with you.'

Her heart gave one huge leap and then began to beat like a distant drum, thumping away inside her chest until she thought she would burst. 'My lord, you must not say such things. You must not…'

'Must I not?' He noticed her heightened colour and the extra sparkle to her eyes; was it caused by tears or pleasure? he wondered. 'It is not the first time you have tried to tell me what I must and must not do. You, my dear deceiver, are in no position to dictate to me.'

'No, my lord, I beg your pardon. I only meant to remind you that an engaged man should not be so free with his affections.'

He took a step towards her, knowing he had a silly grin on his face, but he could not stop himself. 'Emma, I am no longer engaged. There is to be no wedding.'

'No wedding? Never?'

'Never,' he said firmly, holding out his hands to take both of hers and looking down into her upturned face. 'At least, not between Sophie Mountforest and me. We have decided we should not suit. On the other hand, there might be…'

'Might be?' The rapid beating of her heart was making breathing difficult and the words were a whisper.

'There might be if you would consent to be my wife. Oh, Emma, you would make me the happiest man on earth.'

'But…' She was stopped from going on by his mouth which sought hers and stopped her words with a kiss which left her in no doubt he meant what he said.

'Dominic, oh, Dominic, I have loved you for so long,' she said at last, looking up into his eyes, and seeing in them all she wanted to know. 'I never dared to hope. I had come into your home under false pretences; I had been a poor companion to your sister and led her into scrapes and I upset Sophie and caused poor Brutus to be hurt. Can you forgive me for all that?'

'Only if you do lifelong penance.' He laughed aloud and drew her into his arms to kiss her again. It lasted a very long time, but when at last they paused to draw breath, he said, 'That is your penance, today and every day from now on.'

'Then I'll gladly do it, my lord.' And she reached up and put her arms about his neck and drew his head down to kiss him again.

She heard the door open behind them and knew it was Lucy returning. Dear Lucy. 'Dominic,' she whispered. 'You do not expect Lucy to do penance too, do you?'

He laughed. 'Oh, I can see I am going to have no peace until I give in.' He turned to his sister. 'Very well, Lucy, you have my blessing.'

She ran and threw herself at her brother and then grabbed his hand in one of hers and Emma's in the other and danced them round and round until they were giddy.

\*   \*   \*   \*   \*

# *Historical Romance*™

## *Coming next month*

### THE VIRTUOUS CYPRIAN
### by Nicola Cornick

*A Regency delight!*

Nicholas, the Earl of Seagrove, was certain that his new tenant was none other than Susanna Kellaway—the notorious Cyprian. But if that was so, why was she shocked at his suggestion that she become his mistress?

### DOUBLE DILEMMA
### by Polly Forrester

*1910 The Edwardian Age*

Could this dashing socialite really be the same Geoffrey Redvers who was Louisa's neighbour and whom she could barely get a word out of? With her own blend of gentle persuasion Louisa was determined to solve the mystery!

## On sale from 10th August 1998

*Available from WH Smith, John Menzies and Volume One*

# 4 FREE

## books and a surprise gift!

We would like to take this opportunity to thank you for reading this Mills & Boon® book by offering you the chance to take FOUR more specially selected titles from the Historical Romance™ series absolutely FREE! We're also making this offer to introduce you to the benefits of the Reader Service™—

    ★ FREE home delivery
    ★ FREE gifts and competitions
    ★ FREE monthly newsletter
    ★ Books available before they're in the shops
    ★ Exclusive Reader Service discounts

Accepting these FREE books and gift places you under no obligation to buy, you may cancel at any time, even after receiving your free shipment. Simply complete your details below and return the entire page to the address below. ***You don't even need a stamp!***

**YES!** Please send me 4 free Historical Romance books and a surprise gift. I understand that unless you hear from me, I will receive 4 superb new titles every month for just £2.99 each, postage and packing free. I am under no obligation to purchase any books and may cancel my subscription at any time. The free books and gift will be mine to keep in any case.

H8YE

Ms/Mrs/Miss/Mr ...................................Initials ...............................
                                                                  BLOCK CAPITALS PLEASE

Surname ...............................................................................................

Address ...............................................................................................

............................................................................................................

...........................................................Postcode.................................

**Send this whole page to:**
THE READER SERVICE, FREEPOST, CROYDON, CR9 3WZ
(Eire readers please send coupon to: P.O. BOX 4546, DUBLIN 24.)

Offer not valid to current Reader Service subscribers to this series. We reserve the right to refuse an application and applicants must be aged 18 years or over. Only one application per household. Terms and prices subject to change without notice. Offer expires 31st January 1999. You may be mailed with offers from other reputable companies as a result of this application. If you would prefer not to receive such offers, please tick box. ☐

Historical Romance is being used as a trademark.

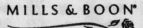